A knocking. A rin                                        1ese are
the sounds that ha                                      like the
songs of sirens, hypnotic and deadly. And we must either
give in, or resist with everything we have...and hope it's
enough.

*Listen: The Sound of* Fear offers ten stories written exclusively by trans and nonbinary authors that explore the chilling, perplexing, terrifying nature of sound.

*Kill Your Darlings.* When two shop workers in 1894 New York discover a haunted phonograph, they must race to solve the mystery of its tragic past before it's too late to save their budding romance—and their lives.

*Exhibition.* A performance artist inspired by the inhumane treatment of refugees finds her gallery transformed into an equally inhospitable environment. Trapped inside the confines of her Plexiglas box, she struggles to piece together what is happening—and how to keep herself alive.

*On the Other Side of Sound.* A ringing in the ears; a coded message from beyond explanation. It will only ruin your life if you let it.

*Her Little Joke.* When Mave Kitten is asked to investigate a creepy phenomenon, little does she know to what depths the trail will lead: Ghosts, a haunted well, ignorance, a flapping bird. What of the woman in green?

*M/other.* I am alone. I do not know exactly how long I have been alone. My husband and child are...*gone.* Aren't they?

As a storm rages outside my decaying house, I begin to hear and see things that cannot possibly be there. Or can they?

*Holy Water.* Adolescence can be hell. Adolescence in an all-girl's Catholic school as a trans teen surrounded by mean girls is a special kind of hell—especially when your school is haunted.

*Snipper-Snapper.* Cats make the best pets—loving, thoughtful, and loyal. Amour even brings home his own takeaway meals. Except for the stains, and damage to the shag pile, Mummy couldn't be happier. Everyone needs a playmate.

*The Knocking Bird.* Knock three times to keep yourself safe. Follow your love across the sea. Obsession threads through nearly every aspect of Steffi's life. But what happens when it drives her to do the unthinkable?

*Bride of Brine.* Sylvie hasn't heard the song of the siren in years. But when she's called home to help her estranged father find her brother, she's faced with an impossible choice: save him, or save herself.

*Haunt.* When Kevin inherits his family home and decides to fix it up with his partner, he quickly discovers that the past can haunt you in more than one way—and he must choose, once and for all, exactly who he is.

# LISTEN

## THE SOUND OF FEAR

R.B. THORNE, LAUREN JANE BARNETT,
E.E.W. CHRISTMAN, EULE GREY,
RIDLEY HARKER, JON JAMES,
T.S. MITCHELL, ALEX SILVER, A.R. VALE

EDITED BY ELIZABETTA MCKAY

A NineStar Press Publication

www.ninestarpress.com

# Listen: The Sound of Fear

Cover Art © 2022 Jaycee DeLorenzo

Editor: Elizabetta McKay

First Edition, September 2022

ISBN: 978-1-64890-543-8

Also available in eBook, ISBN: 978-1-64890-542-1

CONTENT WARNING (ALSO SEE INDIVIDUAL STORIES):
This book contains sexually explicit content, depictions of violence with knives, blood, gore, haunting, voluntary confinement in a small space, panic attack, historical homophobia, discussion of abortion, unwanted pregnancy, loss, body dysphoria, death of infant, mold and rot, car wreck, semi-graphic description of a dead body, ghosts, water/drowning, thunderstorm, discussion of infanticide and postpartum depression, school bullying, homophobia, lesbophobia, misgendering, ableism, implied CSA, dead cat trophies, dark, kidnapping/abduction, OCD, self-harm, morbid ideation, animal death, death, depression, codependency, obsession, injury.

# TABLE OF CONTENTS

# EDITOR'S NOTE

A special thank-you to R.B. Thorne for coming to NSP with the fantastic idea of a collection of horror/thriller stories based on the "sound of fear" theme. R.B. was also instrumental in coordinating SM blasts, interfacing with the anthology authors, helping with the story blurbs and cover concept, as well as contributing their own piece to the collection. I've had the good fortune of working with R.B. on other NSP projects—always a pleasure. And to the other authors in the anthology—kudos for your grisly, lyrical, thought-provoking contributions!

# KILL YOUR DARLINGS

## RIDLEY HARKER

WARNING: This story contains sexually explicit content, which is only suitable for mature readers, scenes of graphic violence with knives, including blood and gore, and haunting of a physical object.

"I HAVE TO fire one of you, Maxwell. Times are tough, and the owner can't be expected to pay both of your wages. We need to cut costs. I mean, what with the Panic last year—did you know that 35 percent of New York is unemployed? People just aren't buying like they used to."

I nodded along numbly. Of course I knew. I passed the lines for the soup kitchens every day on the way to work and counted myself blessed not to be among them. It had been a terrible year, 1893.

My boss, Mr. Highmore, lit a cigar and continued, "Good lad. Knew you'd understand."

I hung my head and stood. My voice cracked as I held back tears. I was not about to cry in his office. "I'll g-get my things…"

"Oh?" He let out a barking laugh. "Don't be absurd, Maxwell. It's not you that I'm firing." My heart leapt, and I sighed with relief, wiping my eyes on my sleeve. "It's McKenna."

"What?" My stomach dropped. "You can't fire Cillian!"

Mr. Highmore blinked stupidly at me. No one spoke

back to him. The manager was a large man of English descent, in full favor with the shop's owner, and as such, he was used to getting his way.

"M-McKenna has a sister and infant nephew to care for," I remarked, unable to look him in the eye. "Please, sir, you can't fire him now."

"Damned Irish, breeding like rodents." Mr. Highmore scoffed, blowing smoke in my direction. "I can't be blamed for that. No, McKenna's got to go."

"Can I have a week to think about it?"

"'Think about it?' What's there to think about? It's you or McKenna!"

"Please, sir. Just one week?"

"Surely you don't mean to sacrifice your livelihood for his! Whatever for?"

I remained silent, but resolute. I clenched and unclenched my hands at my sides.

Finally, he sighed and shook his massive head. "All right, fine. I can't lose both of you." He narrowed his eyes and jabbed his cigar at me. "You're a fool, Theodore Maxwell. A damned fool. Take your week and think hard on it."

Leaving Mr. Highmore's office with my head down wasn't that unusual. I had the apologetic stoop of the overly tall and the shuffle of one who wore thick glasses. I wasn't much to look at. Unlike Cillian McKenna.

He stood in the entryway of the Second Chance Resale Shop, sweeping out snow that the customers had tracked in. He was of shorter than average height, with rusty brown hair and the fiercest green eyes I had ever seen. When he turned and saw me, his grin became a frown of concern. He set down his broom in the corner of the entryway and picked his way through the maze of tables and racks, all brimming with secondhand items. With everyone selling their possessions to put food on the table, the Second Chance was never short on merchandise. Books, fur coats, instruments, toys—you name it, we had it.

"What's wrong, Theo?" Cillian asked in his fine Irish brogue. "Did Highmore bully you again?"

"N-no."

"He did, didn't he. Your eyes are red."

"It's just the smoke—"

"He's a bloody ogre!" Cillian clasped my shoulder, rocking me on my heels. "Well, come on, out with it. What did he say?"

"He, um..." I wracked my brain for a convenient lie. I couldn't tell him the truth. "He told me I look sharper without my glasses. He asked me not to wear them."

"Again? I thought the matter was settled when you ran into a set of china."

My cheeks colored at the memory. I'd ruined the whole set, and the crash still resounded in my head when I thought about it. It had come out of my paycheck too. Cillian sighed and stretched to throw an arm around my shoulder. I leaned down so he didn't have to stand on the tips of his toes.

"You can't let him bother you, Theo," he said.

"I know, I know."

"You're twice the man he is, glasses and all."

I blushed, my mouth twitching toward a smile.

Cillian grinned and clasped my shoulder. "There we go. Good man."

The door chimed. Cillian released me while we both put on our best customer service smiles. I needn't have bothered, however; it was my friend, Frederick Watkins. At twenty-three, Freddie was younger than me by a couple years, but we'd been neighbors in the days before my father died. He was my best customer, and today, he wanted a phonograph.

"I mean to propose to Jessica with it," he explained. "I'll play her some music, and just when she least expects it, I'll hand her the cylinder. She'll turn it on, and then my recorded voice will pop the question. When she turns around, I'll be on bended knee with this." He took a lovely golden ring from his pocket.

"That's—wait, *Jessica*? What happened to Felicity?"

"Felicity is old news," Freddie said, waving the name away. "Jessica and I have been courting for three weeks."

"I see."

"You should see her, Theo. Golden hair, the deepest blue eyes, a trim figure, and a laugh like an angel! Why, she would stir even your blood."

"My blood is just fine, thank you." I sniffed and readjusted my glasses. "Let me check if we have any phonographs in stock."

I went to the back room, where our newest merchandise awaited processing. There on the counter sat an Edison Home Model D. The wood gleamed, the steel was polished, and the black witch's hat horn was in perfect condition. It even came with a recording stylus and a wax cylinder. It was a beautiful piece of equipment, and I wondered how I'd missed it this morning. Just as I picked it up, a wave of dread went through me, and I nearly dropped the machine.

Mr. Highmore loomed in the doorway. I smelled his cigar smoke without having to turn around.

"Are you selling that?" he asked, and I nodded, unable to speak. I didn't like having my back to him. "Erase that cylinder before you do."

"What?"

"There's a crude recording on that. I want it erased before you sell it."

"Oh." What sort of recording would Mr. Highmore find crude? "Yes, of course!"

"Good lad."

I felt him recede. I took the wax cylinder off the mandrel and set about shaving off the recording. When it was finished, I brought the phonograph out to Freddie. He was deep in conversation with Cillian, who leaned against his broom with an amused glint in his eye as Freddie described the virtues of his latest girlfriend. I pursed my lips.

"Here we are." I placed the phonograph onto the table.

"It's marvelous," Freddie replied. He found a spot near the bedplate where the veneer had chipped and rubbed at it with his finger, frowning.

"That won't affect the sound," I reassured him.

"Oh, good. How much is this, by the way?" he asked, and I told him the price. He smiled again. "Wonderful. It's so hard to find a decently priced phonograph these days. If I had to buy one new, I wouldn't have been able to afford the ring!"

Freddie purchased the phonograph and then said his goodbyes, looking the very image of happiness as he walked out into the snow. I shivered as I waved him off. It was cold in the entryway, but it warmed again as soon as the door closed.

A FEW DAYS later, I was still agonizing over what to do. I'd looked over my finances, and I could scarcely afford a month without employment. The apartment alone took up much of my wages, not to mention food. What would I do if I couldn't find another job? I had no family to stay with. I would be out on the streets, lining up at the soup kitchens with the other poor souls. I passed a kitchen as I walked to work. The line went clear around the block.

I pictured Cillian standing in such a line, his hair dusted with snow. He would no doubt give up his coat to shield his sister and her infant from the worst of it. That was just the kind of man he was. In my mind, they stood at the back of the line, freezing as they waited. If that happened, would the pride be lost from those emerald eyes of his?

I shook my head. No, I had a few more days to think on it. Through the snow, I trudged on. I had no sooner entered the shop doorway when Mr. Highmore rounded upon me. Clutching my hat, I shrank back.

"I thought you sold that thing," he said, jabbing his finger at the phonograph on the table.

I stammered something about needing to see it first and made a cursory inspection. Judging from the chipped veneer, it was indeed the same phonograph. I nodded meekly.

"Then why did I find it left at the door this morning?"

"I-I'm not sure..."

Had Freddie tried to return it?

"There are no returns," Mr. Highmore said as if reading my mind. "Besides, you don't return something by leaving it at the door!"

"Is it broken?"

"Check it yourself. And have you given any thought

to—" He broke off as the door chimed, and Cillian entered the shop, his overcoat encrusted in snow. Mr. Highmore's cheeks grew pink from the cold air. "McKenna! Look at that muck you're tracking in!"

"Sorry, sir." Cillian stood halfway in the doorway, shaking out his hat and overcoat.

"You're letting out all the heat!"

"Sorry, sir."

Once Mr. Highmore's back was turned, Cillian rolled his eyes at me. I bit my lip to stifle a smile.

Mr. Highmore followed us into the back room, where we hung up our overcoats and hats. He continued, "We'd better have customers today, even in this weather."

"I'm sure we will, sir," Cillian said dutifully.

"Hmph," Mr. Highmore said with a grunt before returning to his toasty office. He shut the door behind him. We wouldn't see much of him for the rest of the day.

"Bloody nuisance is what he is," Cillian said as we returned to the sales floor. "I reckon we could handle the shop just fine between the two of us. I don't know why the owner keeps him on. He doesn't do much at all."

"He buys the merchandise."

"You could do that. You've a good eye for appraisals. You'd give out a fair price too."

I blushed at his praise. Of course he was just being nice to me.

Cillian took the broom and managed to sweep out the melting snow the three of us had tracked in. I grabbed the mop to help. Between the two of us, the floors were soon sparkling. That left me with the phonograph. I frowned at it, wondering why it had been returned and in such a careless manner. Freddie had money, but not so much as to throw away such an expensive toy.

"Does it work?" Cillian asked.

"Let's see." I took a section of Beethoven's Symphony no. 9 from our box of wax records and placed it on the mandrel. The cutting stylus was still in place, so I fished through our box of phonograph pieces for a playback one. Once that was finished, I wound the box and set the stylus. Orchestral music filled the room. "It works wonderfully."

"I wish I had one of those." Cillian sighed.

"Perhaps someday you will."

"Only if it was on sale."

"Turn that racket off!" Mr. Highmore shouted from inside his office.

We did as he commanded. Cillian pulled faces in his direction while I wished for Cillian's bravery. We left the phonograph on the front table and then set about cleaning the shop, for there was nothing else to do for a full hour before the customers arrived.

When they did show up, we sold coats, books, and board games mostly. Everyone wanted something to do should they become snowed in. Around midday, I started wondering what had happened to Freddie and his proposal. Had it gone wrong?

"Something troubling you?" Cillian asked as we closed the doors for lunch. We sat in the back room eating our sandwiches, nested among the junk.

"I'm worried about Freddie. Do you think she turned him down?"

Cillian snorted. "If she did, I think your friend will bounce back again soon enough. He's in love with being in love, that one."

"I suppose you're right."

"Do you think you'll ever marry, Theo?"

"M-me?" I blushed and nearly choked on my ham and cheese. "Heavens no. What girl would want me?"

"Plenty of girls would love a man like you," Cillian said with a wry grin. "You're kind and loyal."

"Clumsy is what I am."

"It's endearing."

"Don't be absurd," I said, my cheeks blazing. "I'm a terror to have around the house. Mother always said so."

"With all due respect to your mother, I think you're a delight to have around the shop."

Cillian continued with his sandwich while I sat in turmoil, my mouth too dry to eat. How could I possibly let such a good friend end up in the workhouse? No, not even in the workhouse, for even that was full. Damn this Panic, and damn myself for being so indecisive. I was the worst sort of person.

After lunch, a well-dressed woman came in looking for something to entertain the guests at her dinner party. Who would come to a dinner party in this weather was anyone's guess, but that was what she wanted. I showed her our board games, but she dismissed them. I showed her some small gifts she could use as party favors, but she was uninterested in those too. Finally, her eyes lit upon the phonograph, and she brightened.

"It's just the sort of thing that would liven up my party," she said. "How much is it?"

I told her the price, and after taking off a dollar for the chipped veneer, she agreed it was reasonable. Next, I showed her the box of wax records, and she ended up buying a few of those as well. Her purchases were too heavy for her to carry herself, so we arranged for her husband to come pick everything up by the end of the day. She left with a smile on her face. Cillian, meanwhile, trailed his fingers across the polished wood and sighed.

"What's wrong?" I asked.

"Oh, nothing." He straightened up and grinned at me. "I had this harebrained idea that I'd be able to purchase this for my sister. Silly, isn't it?"

"Perhaps the next one?"

"Yes, the next one," he said, though he didn't sound sure of it.

After work, I stopped by Freddie's house to see what had happened. I knocked on the door, but had no answer. After waiting for a few minutes, once it was clear the house was empty, I turned to leave. A neighbor, who lived in the very same house my parents and I had once occupied, came out to the porch. He stared at me, underdressed for the weather in just his shirtsleeves. His ill-fitting shirt sagged around his middle as though accustomed to a heavier man.

"Hello," I said, just to be polite.

He merely continued to stare at me.

I cleared my throat. "I'm looking for Frederick Watkins." More staring. "I'm a friend of his."

"Oh, I thought you were one of those reporters," he finally replied, beckoning me over to his porch.

I tramped through the snow to his front door, which was still open, and blessedly warm air hit my face. I averted my eyes to avoid looking inside the house, not wanting to see how much it had changed. "Reporters?"

"Oh, yes. Haven't you heard the news?"

"No," I said, wishing he would stop baiting me and get on with it. "Tell me what's happened."

"A murder's what's happened."

"A murder!"

"Aye, a murder," he said, nodding. He took out a pipe and began stuffing it with tobacco. "Young Mr. Watkins shot his lady friend before turning the gun on himself. The family's gone north to visit relatives and escape the media circus. Such a tragedy."

My voice shaking, I bid him thanks and went on my way home. Surely, he must have been mistaken. Freddie was a womanizer but a harmless one. A murder-suicide? Did Freddie even own a gun? No, the man must have been mistaken. That was what I told myself, but when I went to a stand and bought a newspaper, my friend's picture stared back at me from the front page.

THE NEXT DAY, I came to work ill. Freddie had haunted my dreams all night. In the nightmare, there was a bullet hole above his right ear, and every time he spoke, it oozed blood. The things he told me were horrible, but I found that, by morning, I didn't remember them, only a lingering feeling that everything was my fault. Perhaps not remembering was for the best.

"You look terrible," Cillian said, breaking away from an early customer. "Is everything all right?"

"I'll tell you later," I mumbled. I went to the back room to hang up my hat and overcoat and found Mr. Highmore waiting for me. I stared down at him, my eyes no doubt ringed by shadows. I was too tired to be timid.

"Jesus, Maxwell, what's wrong with you?"

"I didn't sleep well," I said, which was a sidestep rather than an outright lie. I didn't feel the need to tell him about Freddie.

"Well, you're late," he replied, checking his watch. "You'll have to work through lunch to make up for it."

"Yes, sir."

Mr. Highmore nodded, started to return to his office, then paused. "And didn't you sell that phonograph?"

"Yes, sir."

"Then why's it back again?"

I blinked in confusion. Sure enough, when I went back to the sales floor, I found the same phonograph waiting for me, chipped veneer and all. For a moment, I was spared thoughts of Freddie. How was it back? Mr. Highmore never allowed returns.

"It was on the stoop this morning," Cillian informed me.

"How?"

"I don't know."

"Do you think there's something wrong with it?"

"It worked just fine yesterday."

There was already a cylinder on the mandrel, so I wound it up and set the stylus. It played as beautifully as it had the day before. I turned it off before Mr. Highmore yelled at me again. It was a complete and utter mystery.

When the phonograph didn't sell that day, I resolved to take it home and find out why it had been returned. I caught Cillian eying it as I started out the door. I remembered he had wanted to purchase it.

"I'm trying to find out what's wrong with it," I told him.

"Perhaps I could help?"

"You?" My face grew hot at the thought of inviting Cillian to my apartment.

He laughed. "I am rather good with equipment."

"Y-yes, of course." I shook my head, trying to fight the blush on my cheeks. "I'd be delighted to have you over."

"Give me your address," he said, pulling on his overcoat. "I'll be right over after I check on Mary and Thomas."

"Wonderful."

I hefted the phonograph and walked home. The apartment was a dreadful mess. I hadn't dusted in weeks, and there were books scattered across the tables and chairs. I cleaned in a hurry, imagining Cillian arriving at any moment. In reality, he showed up two hours later. I was still in my suit from work, but he now wore a more casual vest and tie. I should have changed. I ushered him inside.

"So sorry I'm late. The baby was colicky and my sister needed a rest," he explained as I brought him some tea. Seated in my father's old armchair, Cillian looked around and let out a low whistle. I was mortified. He thought my apartment disgusting. "You have a lovely home."

"You're just being kind."

"I meant every word."

"Oh. Thank you..."

He chuckled. "You always assume the worst, Theo."

"Why would you think that?"

"How long have we worked together? A year? A little more?"

"Perhaps?"

"I've gotten to know you rather well, I think," Cillian

said with a wink that made the heat rise in my face. "Now, tell me what was bothering you this morning."

I reluctantly explained what had transpired with Freddie's neighbor. By the time I'd finished, Cillian had set down his tea and joined me on the couch. When I was out of words, he took my hands and gave them a comforting squeeze. His hands were rough but gentle, and up close, he smelled of bergamot tea and sandalwood.

"You poor dear." He grimaced. "I'm sorry about Freddie. Did you know him well?"

"I'm not sure I really knew him at all. He was the last person I'd suspect of murder."

"Some people are good at hiding the darkness within themselves."

"I don't believe that. Surely there was something I missed, some hint of what was to happen."

"Don't blame yourself, Theo. I saw him too, and I suspected nothing."

"I suppose..."

The room was quiet for a long moment. Cillian had yet to release my hands. His thumb stroked my knuckles. I glanced up, and our eyes met. His eyes were such an intense green it made my head spin. I blushed and looked away, and he let go.

"Well," he said, clearing his throat. "Should we get to work on that phonograph?"

"Y-yes, please."

I stood, and he followed me to the stand where the phonograph lay waiting. I took off the wooden top and laid it aside. Cillian unscrewed the handle and opened the box. The insides were dusty, with a few flecks of something black and dried. Cillian oiled several components and soon proclaimed it in working order. I gave him a towel to clean his hands and then set up a cylinder record of "The Sidewalks of New York." Music filled the apartment. Cillian grinned and offered me his hand.

"Dance with me?"

"*Me*?"

He laughed. "There's no one else around."

My face heated, and I accepted his hand. He pulled me close, and when I froze like a fool, he gently placed his arm around my lower back, leading me in the steps. I tightened my grip on his hand, praying I wouldn't step on his toes. Thankfully, Cillian was as skilled a dancer as he was with repairs, and he avoided my clumsy feet.

"Relax," he said. "It's just the two of us."

"Why are you so nice to me?" It was a burning question I had wanted to know for the past year.

"Isn't it obvious?"

"Not to me."

He sighed, and his hand on my back guided me even closer. Our hips were nearly touching. At any moment, I would no doubt have an erection and ruin the whole thing. When he dropped my hand, I knew it must have happened. Before I could apologize or flee, Cillian cupped my cheek, arresting me with his eyes. I felt faint. Surely, I was dreaming. Despite the crushing fear in my chest, I leaned down.

We kissed, and I knew then it was no fantasy. His lips were soft, and his five o'clock shadow scratched at my cheeks. I was stiff and awkward, but he coaxed me onward until we moved as one, exploring each other's mouths. He tasted of honey and lemon.

"I've wanted to do that for ages," Cillian explained, resting his forehead against mine. His fingers were entwined in my hair, his breath ghosting my burning cheeks.

"Truly? But I—"

"—*I invited Cillian over for tea. He came to me eagerly, expecting carnal delights. We escaped to the bedroom, where he proceeded to undress. That was when I had him—*"

The sound came from the phonograph. We stared at each other, brows furrowed in confusion as it continued on.

"—*I produced the knife—*"

Oh god, was that grainy voice mine?

"—*The first stab came as a shock. He looked at me, his mouth a perfect O of surprise as the knife hung from his stomach. Then came the blood, leaking from the wound—*"

"Is this some kind of joke?" Cillian pushed me out to arm's length, his face pale, his lips pressed to a thin line.

I clung to him, or rather, I tried to. "Th-that's not me!"

"But that's your voice!"

"I didn't record it! I'd never say such horrible things—"

"—*I took the blade and slit him from ribs to groin. His organs slipped out onto the carpet, hot and stinking—*"

"This is sick," Cillian said, turning away.

"Cillian, please! It's not me!"

"—*Highmore had said only one of us could continue on at the Second Chance, and I would ensure it was me.*"

The record turned off with a click. Cillian started for the door. I ran to stop him, grasping him by the shoulder as he took his coat from the hanger. He slapped my hand away.

"Don't touch me," he hissed, fixing me with such a glare it made my blood turn cold.

I backed off, shaking my head. "It's not true. I'd never—"

"Isn't it? I knew Highmore was up to something. I just didn't know you would sink to such lows to keep your job."

"But I was going to—"

Cillian slammed the door behind him. I started to go after him, but how would that look to the neighbors? If I went after him, it would no doubt look like a lover's quarrel. Someone would call the police, and we'd be arrested. Hot tears streamed down my cheeks, but I scrubbed them away with my sleeve. My mouth still tasted of Cillian.

What had happened?

It was the phonograph. I turned it back on, and "The Sidewalks of New York" began playing again. Impatiently, I skipped to the end. Instead of a horrid monologue, the record ended naturally. I tried it again, listening to the entire song this time, but the result was the same no matter how many times I played it. Finally, the neighbors banged on the walls, demanding that I stop. They must have thought I was going mad.

Was I mad? Was I going to end up like Mother? My stomach clenched in dread. I could still smell the fear, sweat, and urine of the asylum. The howls of the inmates. Mother screaming, her nails raking my hands as Father dragged me away... No. Cillian had heard the phonograph as well. It had definitely happened. Perhaps this was simply a nightmare. I pinched myself and discovered I was wide awake.

THAT NIGHT I dreamt of Cillian.

We lay in bed, naked and tangled in each other's arms. He kissed me, his mouth hot and yearning, and I threaded my fingers through his hair. My back arched as he moved on to my throat. Cillian's erection pressed needily between my thighs. Mine was hard between our bellies. His stomach was taut and muscled as he lay atop me.

"Theo, please," he begged, his teeth nipping at my neck. I reached between us and palmed his straining member. His flesh leaked at the tip. "Please, I want you inside me."

I blushed. I had never been on top before, even in fantasy. Still, I'd never deny him anything. He straddled my waist, hovering above my erection. I readied myself to enter him, slipping past the tight ring of muscle until I was inside. I gasped, squeezing my eyes shut as I gave him time to adjust. White-hot pleasure shot through my body with every little movement.

He stilled my hips, shaking his head. "Not like that."

"How?"

"Like this," he replied and handed me the knife.

I stared at the wooden-handled kitchen knife, open-mouthed. Cillian inserted his tongue. He tasted like a copper penny left out in the snow.

I turned my head away. "Cillian, what is this?"

"Please," he repeated.

My hand tightened on the blade. Of its own accord, it inched closer and closer to Cillian's chest. "No," I said, shaking my head and trying to pull away. My erection wilted inside him. "No, stop!" My arm twitched, but it was no use. The tip of the knife pressed against his sternum. "*Cillian*!"

My hand stilled.

Panting, I focused every ounce of willpower I had into withdrawing the knife. This was my dream. I would not hurt him. Not Cillian. Never Cillian with his beautiful jade eyes and his gorgeous, toothy grin that he seemed to save just for me. I'd sooner kill myself.

Mottled arms enfolded me from behind, dragging me deeper into the bed. Everywhere they touched burned. One hand wrapped around my wrist and pushed, its grip like iron. The blade sliced down Cillian's sternum, opening his chest and biting deep once it reached his belly. I screamed. The flesh separated and blood splattered onto my face—

I awoke, nauseous and sweating, my stomach sticky with jism. My slickened fingers stung abominably. I rolled over and discovered my hand clenched around the blade of a kitchen knife. I yelped and dropped it, splattering blood on the bed. I turned on the gas lamp, hissing through my teeth. I had cut myself.

Oh God, I was going mad.

I went to the bathroom to bandage my fingers. Luckily, the cuts weren't too deep, but they bled with a vengeance. I had done this to myself, I thought as I wrapped my hand in bandages. Perhaps I'd recorded that message and was simply unaware of doing so. Mother had done things without being aware of them, hadn't she? I didn't remember; it had been so long ago. But as I finished bandaging my fingers, my pajama sleeve slipped, and I noticed the bruise on my forearm.

In the shape of a hand, the purpled fingers encircled my wrist. It lingered in the same place I had been grabbed in my dream. I shook my head, unwilling to believe it. Simply a nightmare, nothing more. When I came back, the bloodied knife was still on my bed, staining the sheets. I couldn't look at it, much less clean it up.

So I went into the kitchen and fixed myself a cup of

coffee. I was wide awake. There was no helping it. Not that I wanted to go back to sleep, terrified of my dreams, of what I might do next in the waking world. My hands shook as I stirred in cream and sugar. Wanting to distract myself from my thoughts, I decided to read one of the newspapers that had been piling up.

WOMAN POISONS DINNER PARTY leapt out at me from the front page. I dropped my cup. It cracked, and piping hot coffee spilled across the table and onto the floor. Some of it dripped onto my pajama bottoms, but I was already on my feet, dishcloth in hand to mop up the liquid. I had to salvage the paper. I had to see the drawing again to confirm it was her:

The woman I'd sold the phonograph to.

I stared at her for a long while. The ink ran until the article was no longer legible, and the woman's eyes and mouth melted into blackened smudges. I dropped the dishcloth—my fingers bleeding anew—and strode into the living room where the phonograph awaited me.

It was such a benign thing. Wood and metal, the sort of device found in homes across the country. I leaned in close to examine it in detail, taking in the pitch-black horn and the mahogany box and handle. My own distorted image was visible on the polished surface.

What was that?

I listened, frozen in place, and heard nothing aside from my own labored breathing. But something was wrong. I felt it in the base of my spine, the way the hairs on my arms and back of my neck stood straight to attention. I placed my ear to the horn and listened.

Someone else's ragged breathing echoed back.

KILL YOUR DARLINGS  - 25 -

I yelped and darted away, tripping over the coffee table. I toppled to the ground, landing hard on my backside. The phonograph loomed above me on the end table, and I scrambled backward, crablike, to get away from it. My bloodied hand left stains upon the hardwood floor. I could no longer hear the breathing, but I knew it was there.

There was only one thing to do. I grabbed a bath towel and threw it over the phonograph. Only then could I bear to touch it. I cradled it in my arms and took it outside to the curb one block away, where the trash cans waited. I opened the lid and tossed the thing, towel and all, into the can. Then I walked home, nursing my bleeding fingers.

CILLIAN WASN'T AT work the next day. I stood in the entryway waiting for him, wondering what I would say, but after an hour passed, Mr. Highmore emerged from his office and barked at me to get to work. Too late, I remembered it was Cillian's day off.

"You look terrible," Highmore said. "And that's no excuse for leaving the phonograph on the stoop this morning."

It was as if all the warmth had escaped from the room. "Wh-what?"

"The phonograph," he said, overenunciating each syllable. "The phonograph! What the devil's wrong with you, Maxwell?"

"Show it to me!"

Both of his thick eyebrows shot up, but I pushed past him and entered the back room. There on the table, it waited for me. The veneer was chipped, and it smelled of garbage.

A deeper scent, of rot and copper, emanated from inside the horn. I felt the color drain from my face. My fingers were so cold they tingled. On the verge of vomiting, I sucked in a breath.

"Maxwell?" Mr. Highmore grasped me by the shoulder, and I jumped like a startled cat. Alarmed, he released me immediately, placing a hand over his heart. "Sweet Jesus, Maxwell! Are you insane? It's just a phonograph!"

"I threw it away!"

"What do you mean, you threw it away? That's company property—"

"Last night, I threw it away!" I grabbed Mr. Highmore by his burly shoulders and shook him. "I threw it away!"

"Let go of me!"

"Why the hell is it here again?" I shouted.

The two customers in the shop stopped perusing and stared at us. Mr. Highmore smiled at them and dug his meaty hands into my shoulder. He then dragged me fully into the back room and closed the door. I didn't want to be locked in the room with it, but Mr. Highmore spun me away from the phonograph and slammed me up against the wall.

"What is wrong with you?" he hissed through his teeth.

"I threw it away!" I babbled, craning my neck to keep the phonograph in view. "I threw it away!"

Mr. Highmore slapped me, hard. It was only by a miracle that my glasses didn't fall entirely from my face. My cheek stung, and I rubbed it with my bandaged hand, which Mr. Highmore just then seemed to notice. "You've cracked, Maxwell! Go home and get yourself sorted before you show your face here again," he snarled.

"You can't sell it! It's too dangerous! You can't—"

The next thing I knew, I was out on the street, the shop door slamming shut behind me, Mr. Highmore explaining to the customers that I was sick with fever and there was nothing to worry about. I paced before the Second Chance. What should I do? Whatever was happening to me, it all had to do with that phonograph. The deaths, the dreams, my sabotaged relationship with Cillian—I needed to apologize to Cillian, to explain what was going on. I hurried down the street.

I knew Cillian's address, having heard it from Mr. Highmore some months past. "He lives in a slum" were his exact words. Unfortunately, Mr. Highmore wasn't far off. Horse excrement and mud lined the streets, and the closer one came to the tenement housing, the worse it smelled of boiled cabbage. The apartments themselves were falling apart. Cillian's stoop had a broken board on the step, which was no problem to step over with my height but was most certainly a difficulty for Cillian and anyone else of his stature. I knocked on the door, and it creaked open.

I soon realized the apartment was broken into individual rooms with a shared toilet. Muffled conversation from behind closed doors filled the hallway. A roach skittered past my feet, and one of the doors had a strong odor of cat urine emanating from within. My skin crawled. As I walked past, the door that reeked of cat opened, and a stocky, white-haired old lady peered out at me. The smell increased tenfold. Seeing me, she started to close the door.

"Wait! Excuse me, ma'am, but I'm looking for the McKennas?" I asked.

She opened the door just wide enough to gesture to her neighbor before slamming it shut. It echoed throughout the apartment. I heard a latch click.

I knocked on Cillian's door, hoping, too late, I wouldn't wake the baby. After a moment, a short, thin woman with Cillian's rusty-brown hair opened the door. She was young, no older than sixteen or seventeen at most. Her eyes were a clear blue, and a smattering of freckles graced her cheeks. She held a similarly colored squirming toddler in her arms.

"Yes?" she asked with a musical accent like her brother's.

"You must be Mary," I said, offering her what I hoped was a pleasant smile. I twisted my hat in my hands. "I'm Theo Maxwell, I work with your brother at the shop—"

Her face darkened. "Oh. *You*. No, he's not in."

My smile melted away as the lump in my throat grew. "Do you know where he is?"

"No, I don't. And I think it was a mighty cruel trick you played on him, whatever you did. He came home last night in such a state. Wouldn't tell me a thing, other than you and that bastard Hugh Highmore conspired to put him out."

My stomach lurched. "P-please, when you see Cillian, please tell him to come see me."

"I'll tell him you came by," Mary snapped. Like her neighbor, she slammed the door in my face.

I was just leaving, dejected, but as I opened the front door, I found a man carrying a large box. I stood aside to let him in, but then I recognized the hair.

"Thank you," he said without looking at me. The box was big enough to obscure his vision, and he shifted it on his hip and got a look at my face. Green eyes narrowed. "*You*. What are you doing here?"

"Cillian, please, I need to speak to you."

"Well, I don't want to speak to you."

"I—" A wave of sudden dread washed over me. My height had allowed me to catch a glimpse of what was inside the box. "Cillian, that's not..."

"Mr. Highmore asked me to clean it up. Says you threw it in the trash."

"No, you can't bring it here!"

"Theo, what the hell is wrong with you?" Cillian demanded.

At that, Mary and her neighbor opened their doors in unison. The neighbor disappeared again quickly, but Mary frowned at us. "Do you want me to get the police?" she asked.

"No, it's fine," Cillian replied, paling.

Did he think I would tell the police about our kiss? My cheeks grew hot at the thought of betraying him so. "Cillian, please, you have to listen to me. There's something horribly wrong with that phonograph!"

He laughed bitterly. "There's something horribly wrong with *you*."

"I'm being serious. I think it's cursed! You remember what happened to Freddie—"

"Don't bring him into this."

"And that woman we sold it to, she poisoned her guests!"

"Bullshit," he said.

The box must have been getting heavy, for he went into the apartment with it, despite my protests. I followed behind. Mary tried to close the door, but I darted forward, and she ended up closing it on my hip. I winced and made my apologies before hurrying after Cillian to the living room.

The apartment was tidy and smelled of baby powder and Cillian's cologne. A couch was made up like a bed, where I assumed Cillian slept, having given up the bedroom to his sister and the baby.

Cillian placed the phonograph on the coffee table. "Get out," he said, crossing his arms. He was smaller than me, but I had no doubt he could throw me out if he had a mind to it.

I held up my hands in surrender. "Why would I lie to you?"

"You're a sick bastard?" Cillian replied dryly.

"I care about you," I insisted.

Cillian shot a quick glance over at his sister, his cheeks faintly pink. "I said, *get out*."

"Not without that phonograph. I won't let it hurt you."

"You've gone completely insane; you know that?" He shook his head, exasperated, and I winced. "I'll play you a record, and nothing will happen. Then you have to promise to leave our home and never come back."

"No, don't!"

I made a dash for it, but Cillian locked my arms behind my back and held on tight.

"Mary," he said, "play a record for us. I don't care which one."

"No!" I struggled in his arms, but it was no use.

Mary, juggling the baby on her hip, selected a wax cylinder and, after some explaining from Cillian, set it on the mandrel. I slumped against Cillian, half clutching him for support. Debussy's *Clair de Lune* soon filled the apartment. I waited in agony for the song to be over, dreading what would happen next.

"See? It's just music," Cillian said with something like

pity in his eyes. He thought me mad. I could see it in his sister's expression as well. "Theo, I think you need to go home."

"I…"

Nothing had happened.

It wasn't the phonograph. It was *me*. I was mad. Mad like Mother. Cillian released me and went to stand beside his sister. I felt their eyes upon me. I was on the verge of tears.

"I'm sorry," I murmured, my eyes growing misty. "I—"

"*It's her fault that we're destitute.*"

Mary and I turned to Cillian in unison. Her mouth hung open. He looked as startled as she.

"Don't look at me," he said, his eyes wide.

"*—we could have been rich, but no, she wanted the brat—*"

"That was your voice," she said.

"No, it wasn't—"

"*—I gave up my life for her, and what do I get in return? A squalling babe and a couch in the living room. So, who could blame me when I picked up the little bastard and bashed his head upon the floor?*"

"Oh my God," Mary said, staring at Cillian in horror. She clutched her baby in her arms, taking a step backward. Cillian was stark white.

"Mary, I'd never—" he started, but the phonograph was louder.

"*The bitch came next. If only she had kept her legs closed—*"

Cillian picked up the phonograph and hurled it to the floor. The box split open with a resounding crash. The wax cylinder crumpled into the stylus, and the horn popped off, which soon met its fate beneath Cillian's shoe. The phonograph gave a sad little groan and then lay silent, its gears twitching feebly. The baby began to cry.

"Get out," Mary said shakily.

Cillian held out his arms, his face pale. "Mary, I—"

"I said get out, both of you!" she screamed and then locked herself inside her bedroom. Muffled sobs and the shrieking of the toddler could be heard through the door.

Cillian and I looked at each other. There was no longer pity in his gaze, only bewilderment.

"We should leave," I said. "Before the neighbors call the police."

Cillian stood rooted to the spot, his eyes locked on the phonograph. I began collecting the pieces and set them in the box to take with us. We left the building with Cillian following behind, every so often glancing back as though he expected his sister to call him home.

On the way to my apartment, I noticed some homeless men crowded around a trash can fire. I gave them whatever change I had in my pocket and then emptied the box into the flames. The thing hissed and popped, and foul-smelling smoke billowed forth. Cillian and I watched in fascination while the other men turned and fled.


"MAKE YOURSELF AT home," I said as I unlocked my apartment door. After seeing where Cillian lived, my house seemed embarrassingly opulent. What he must have thought of me for complaining about it...

"I've never even thought those things," Cillian murmured, standing in the doorway.

I ushered him inside, and locked the door behind us. "What?"

"My sister, little Thomas; I've never thought those things about them. I love them."

"I know," I said.

"How? You heard it; it sounded exactly like me." He was on the edge of despair. "It knew things; it called Thomas a bastard! How did it know he was illegitimate?"

"It perverts your feelings. It says horrible things about those you love most."

"Did you mean it? What you said about Freddie and the woman poisoning her dinner party?" Cillian was so pale that I wanted to deny everything just to make him feel better. Instead, I nodded. Cillian turned away. "Oh God…"

I laid my hands on his shoulders. "Cillian, I'm so sorry."

"I can't go back there." He turned around and took my hands, squeezing them. "I can't risk any harm coming to Mary or the babe."

"Maybe we broke it. Maybe it's over with."

"How do we know?"

"I don't. You can stay here—" I broke off, the pain of his squeezing my bandaged hand forcing me to remember my dream from last night. "No, I can't risk it."

"What?"

"What if it's not over with? What if I hurt you?"

Cillian let out a dark bark of laughter. "I'd rather you killed me than—"

"Don't say such things!"

The thought of hurting him was too much, and I pulled

him close. I could no longer help myself, needing to hold him, to feel him in my arms. He cupped the back of my neck and brought me down for a kiss. Our lips met as we sought reassurance in each other's touch. His teeth scraped my bottom lip, and I granted him entrance, his tongue plundering my mouth. After we broke for air, he leaned against me, his arms around my waist and holding me to him.

"I thought you hated me," he breathed.

"I love you," I said before I could stop myself, embarrassed but no longer caring. "I've loved you for a long time. And the damned thing was right—Highmore did say that only one of us could stay. I'm going to give up my job for you if Highmore hasn't fired me already. I can't bear the thought of you in the bread lines."

His eyes widened. "Theo, you can't do that!"

"Watch me," I said and kissed him again.

"Maybe it is over with." He chuckled nervously. "Maybe it's broken and our jobs are the only things we have to worry about." He looked up and cupped my cheek. "Let me stay with you tonight."

"You'd be better off in a hotel."

"Please, Theo. I'm afraid." He gave me a helpless grin, his eyes more anxious than before. "I've never been so scared in my life. Don't abandon me now."

"All right." I tilted my head and kissed his palm. "But we're locking up the knives."

That night, anything and everything sharp was taken from around the house and placed in my grandmother's old trunk. I gave Cillian the key, which he hid only God knew where, and loaned him my extra pair of pajamas, which were too long. He offered to stay on the couch, saying it was what he was used to, but I brought him to my bed. We lay side by side, fingers joined under the bedsheets. I dreaded going to sleep.

"What happened to your hand?" Cillian asked, stroking my bandages with his thumb.

I remembered my nightmare with shame and some horrible form of arousal. "You don't want to know."

"Tell me."

"I was...having a dream..."

"A dream?" He rolled over onto his side and propped himself up on his elbow. His eyes glittered in the darkness. "What sort of dream?"

"It was about you," I admitted.

"About me?" Cillian grinned. "Was it a naughty dream?"

"Y-yes."

He snickered, his fingertips ghosting up my arm and down my chest. My member twitched as he neared my hip. "But how did you hurt your hand?"

"I woke up clutching a knife."

Cillian's grin melted instantly. "Jesus Christ."

"Would you like me to sleep on the couch?" I asked, sitting up.

Cillian gently pulled me back down. "No, we've locked up all the knives."

"Still, I'm afraid to go to sleep."

"We don't have to sleep." Cillian squeezed my hand, careful of my bandages. "We can lie here all night and keep each other awake. Just until we're sure it's done with."

I sniffled and then let out a helpless laugh. "I thought I was going mad."

"You're not mad."

"My mother was. She used to hear things, see things that weren't there. My father had her locked away in an asylum. We never spoke of her again; it was like she no longer existed. She was just a shameful family secret to be kept."

"Do you know why I left London?" Cillian asked suddenly.

I shook my head.

"I was an under butler, my sister a maid for an earl of some renown."

"You never told me that."

"I felt it wasn't my secret to share. That's all over now. Anyway, I grew up in service. My father worked with the horses, and my mother was a maid. But that ended when the earl's son took advantage of my sister."

I gasped. "He didn't—?"

Cillian gave me a grim smile. "She was fifteen, he twenty-seven. Of course, he promised to marry her. That was why she carried on for as long as they did. I had no idea. I was in a rather heated relationship with a footman from another household. I blame myself for not paying more attention to her, for not seeing the predatory looks he gave her. I was so afraid of being arrested myself. But I digress; soon enough, she was with child."

"And he didn't marry her?"

"No, he didn't. And when my father went to the earl, my entire family was threatened with dismissal should we breathe a word about it to anyone."

"How dreadful."

"He got his comeuppance, in the end. Fever swept through London. He died. And without issue too. He being the earl's only child, you can guess where this is going. They wanted the baby. They offered Mary a hefty sum, provided she bugger off and forget the whole incident. My parents agreed. They said it was a chance for a fresh start."

"She couldn't do it?"

"She was going to. The adoption papers were all drawn up. But then she changed her mind. Said Thomas was hers and she wouldn't give him up for anything. So, my parents disowned her, and the earl came after her with his blood-thirsty lawyers. She had no choice but to run away to America."

"And you came with her."

"I couldn't let my baby sister go to the New World on her own. Not after I'd failed to look after her the first time."

"You're a good man," I said.

"You're the first person to call me such."

"I think I've gotten to know you well in the last year." I repeated his earlier words to me.

Cillian's mouth curved into a smile. He drew me close and kissed me. "I know how to keep us awake," he said with a devilish grin.

At once, I thought of my dream. My manhood swelled despite my trepidation. Cillian noticed the growing tent in the sheets and laughed. It assuaged some of my fear. We exchanged languid kisses, holding each other in the darkness. I stiffened when he began kissing my neck.

"What's wrong?" he asked.

"You did that in my dream."

"Did I do this in your dream?" He began planting kisses down my chest. I squirmed, weaving my fingers through his hair. Next, he came to my hips; I let out a strangled gasp as he slid my pants down and took my head into his mouth. He looked up at me then, his tongue swirling over the sensitive head, and took me in deeper. He didn't retch like I would have. I bit my lip to keep from crying out, lest the neighbors hear.

Cillian's head bobbed over my lap, licking and sucking until I was a writhing mess beneath him. His mouth was hot and wet. I was no stranger to a quick fumble in a back alley, but I'd never had such an act done to me before, had never even imagined such pleasure could be possible. I wondered if this was how it was done in London.

Finally, I could take no more. The pressure building in my groin exploded in a sea of stars behind my eyelids. I let out a wanton moan, my fingers clenched in Cillian's hair as I came. He swallowed it. A thin trickle of jism leaked down his chin, and he licked it away, smirking at me. I pulled him up for another kiss, tasting myself on his tongue.

"Have you ever…?" he asked, and I nodded, still dizzy with excitement. "Do you want to?"

"Yes."

He leaned in, his lips to my ear. "Ask me to."

I shivered. I wasn't used to talking dirty. "Please, t-take me."

Cillian grinned wolfishly. "As you wish, my darling."

Some cooking oil from the kitchen served as our lubricant. He slicked himself generously. I would never think of olive oil the same way again. I squirmed as he introduced his finger.

"Relax," he said soothingly. "It's just me."

"Yes," I breathed. "Do it, I want it."

He kissed my thigh as he inserted a second finger,

stretching me to what I thought was my limit. I gritted my teeth and held on. Then he pressed against something deep inside, and another spasm of pleasure rushed through me. My flaccid cock twitched feebly. Cillian kissed it, making me squirm even more. Next, he positioned himself at my entrance, his head teasing.

"I'll go slowly," he promised.

Before I could wonder if it would hurt, he pushed himself inside. I choked on a gasp, gripping the sheets tightly. Unbeknownst to me until much later, my fingers began bleeding again. His lips muffled my cries as he slipped fully inside, and by God, I was stretched to breaking.

"Relax," Cillian groaned, resting his forehead against mine. "God, you're so tight."

"I'm sorry." I blushed.

"Don't be, it's wonderful. You're wonderful."

I loved him. I loved him more than anything else in the world, more than life itself. Panting, he began to rock his hips, and I strained to take him in deeper, to show him how much I cared. I was past all pain. He had found that wonderful spot again and drove at it mercilessly. Cillian moaned, his breath coming in short spurts. When he climaxed, he shuddered atop me, his member pulsating as his hot seed flooded my body, marking me as his own.

"I love you, Theo," he murmured, dropping to my side as he slid out of me. I was sorry for the loss of him as his spend, wet and sticky, oozed down my thighs. I pulled him close, and he rested his head against my chest. We lay tangled together in mutual, blissful exhaustion. Before I knew it, I was asleep.

I awoke hours later, my fingers around Cillian's throat.

He struggled in my grasp, digging his fingers into my wrists. My full weight bore down on him. I blinked. What was I doing? Good God, what was I doing! My grip slackened as I came to my senses, and he brought up his knee, jabbing it into my stomach. I wheezed as the air was forced from my lungs, and I crumpled to his side in pain.

"Theo?" he asked, his voice raw. He reached for me in the darkness. "Theo, wake up!"

"I'm awake," I said, once I could breathe again. "Wh-what happened?"

"You tried to kill me!"

I let out a pathetic moan of terror. "I'm so sorry, I— It's not over."

"It bloody well isn't!" Before I could apologize again, he held me in his arms. "I'm sorry, Theo," he murmured in my ear. "I'm sorry. I know you didn't mean to."

"No, I'm sorry. I never should have brought that damned machine home!"

"It's not your fault, it's—" He froze suddenly, staring at me without seeing. "It's..."

"What? What is it?"

"It's Highmore. Where *did* he get the bloody thing?"

I had no answer for that.

We lay awake for several hours, too afraid to fall asleep again. When the sun rose, I saw the full damage I had inflicted upon Cillian. His eyes were bloodshot and bruises ringed his throat. I wanted to cry, but the tears wouldn't come.

"WHAT IN GOD'S name happened to you?" Highmore demanded as we entered the shop that morning. He was still dressed in his coat and hat, having just unlocked the door.

Cillian ignored the question, scanning the tables before approaching Highmore directly. Cillian's clothes were severely wrinkled, and though he'd pulled his collar up, I could still see his bruised throat. Having barely slept in three days, I looked only slightly less disheveled.

"Where is it?" Cillian asked.

"Where's what?" Highmore crossed his arms, scowling at Cillian's tone.

"*The phonograph*," we said in unison.

Highmore blinked, his eyes darting between us. "What's this about?"

We ignored him and searched the shop. I finally found the phonograph outside buried in snow. It was decidedly worse for wear, the wood charred in some places and the metal blackened, the whole thing wet from the snow. It shouldn't have survived at all, but the fact that we had damaged it gave me some hope.

"What did you do to my phonograph?" Highmore shouted, jabbing a finger at me. "That was company property! Now look at it—"

"Where did you get it?" I asked, setting the phonograph down on the nearest table. "This had to have come from somewhere."

"That's none of your business—" He broke off when Cillian grasped him by the lapels. "What the hell are you doing, McKenna!"

I locked the door and shut the blinds.

"Maxwell? What is going on here!"

"Look here, Highmore," Cillian said, getting right in his face. "Frankly, I don't care if you believe us or not, but we've got a curse on our hands, and if we don't do something soon, more people will die."

Highmore grasped him by the wrists and shook him off. "That's preposterous!"

An idea came to me suddenly. "You had me erase something on the phonograph. A record, not one of ours. What was it?"

At that, Highmore flushed a guilty crimson. "It was nothing." He looked away.

"Damn it, Highmore!" Cillian exclaimed. "My family is in danger here!"

"I don't see how that has anything to do with it!"

"Mr. Highmore, *please*." I tried to appeal to a better nature that we all knew he didn't have. "Our lives depend on it."

"Confound it, Theo; if he's going to play dumb, then there's nothing for it," Cillian said, fetching some rope from the back room. "We'll just have to return with some whiskey and matches. Let's see it come back from *that*."

"What! You wouldn't dare!" Highmore blanched.

"Try me," Cillian snarled, advancing with the rope. I couldn't tell if he meant to tie Highmore up or hang him with it.

"All right, fine! It was a suicide note!"

Cillian and I exchanged a look of horror. He cursed under his breath in Gaelic before turning back to Highmore. "You erased a *suicide* note?"

"*Maxwell* erased it—" Highmore started, and it felt like a nail in my coffin. Guilt twisted up my insides, and I leaned against a table for support. This was all my fault.

Cillian wasn't having it. He threw the rope at our boss in disgust. "Someone's last words, and *you* erased it? Jesus, Highmore! What did it say?"

"It was vulgar." Highmore sniffed, but when Cillian advanced upon him, Highmore tripped over the rope in his haste to get away. "It was something about not being able to live without a man named Charlie—Charlie Harris, I think!"

"How is that vulgar?" Cillian snapped. "Some poor girl pining—"

"The speaker was a man!"

I avoided looking at Cillian, a guilty flush on my cheeks. Cillian coughed. Highmore had a look of "I told you so" on his face.

"We'll need the address of the person you bought this from," I said, glad that my voice came out evenly.

"It's in my office." Highmore paused, staring at the phonograph. "You don't really believe that thing's haunted, do you?"

"Would you like to try it and find out?" Cillian asked.

Highmore puffed out his chest and opened his mouth, only to close it abruptly. He looked rather sheepish. "No."


THREE HOURS LATER, we stood outside a modest, two-story home several blocks from the Second Chance. It wasn't the address we had been given, but it was the right spot to find Charlie Harris, according to the unfriendly woman at the first address. It reminded me of the neighborhood I'd grown up in, which brought along another pang of guilt as I thought of Freddie. If I hadn't erased the recording, would he still be alive? As if sensing my thoughts, Cillian laid a hand on my shoulder.

"We're at the right place," he said, giving me a comforting squeeze. "It's almost over."

His voice was raspy from the attack this morning. I bit my lip and nodded, not because I believed him, but because I didn't want to worry him further. He strode up to the porch and knocked. I waited behind him, carrying the phonograph. The wail of a violin radiated from somewhere inside the house. I didn't recognize the tune. Cillian knocked again, and the music halted. After a few minutes, a haggard looking blond man in his early thirties opened the door. He seemed oddly familiar, but I knew for a fact I'd never seen him before.

"Yes?" He stared at us, no doubt taking in our rumpled clothes, the shadows beneath our eyes, and the bruises around Cillian's neck.

"Are you Charlie Harris?" I asked.

He frowned. "Charles Harris. No one calls me 'Charlie' except—" His mouth twitched toward a grimace. "What is this about?"

"A suicide note," Cillian said, and Harris paled.

"*Honey? What's going on?*" came a call from inside the house.

"Nothing, darling, just some salesmen," Harris replied, then stepped outside and closed the door behind him. His lips pressed into a thin line. "He left a note?"

"He?" Cillian said.

"Don't play dumb with me," Harris hissed. "Marion Owens. That's who you're here about, aren't you?"

Marion Owens.

Finally, a name to the thing that haunted us. I shuddered, clutching the phonograph box tighter. It felt unnaturally warm in my arms for such a cold day.

"Yes, Marion left a note," Cillian said. "You were mentioned in it."

"How much do you want?" Harris pulled out his wallet. "I'll only pay once, so—"

"We're not here to blackmail you!" I said, aghast. "We only want to know what happened."

Harris's anger melted into confusion. "Why?"

"We have reason to believe that Marion isn't happy in the hereafter," Cillian explained, loosening his collar for emphasis.

I also showed him the bruise encircling my wrist. It had turned a dark purple, the ghostly fingers clearly outlined on my skin. Harris paled. He reached behind and grasped the door handle as though he meant to escape back into the house.

Cillian took him by the elbow. "Let's go for a walk, shall we?"

Harris nodded. I left the phonograph tucked away behind some bushes alongside the porch. Cillian motioned for me to flank Harris as we walked. He looked like a man on his way to the gallows.

"I suppose I knew," Harris murmured. "I've been having dreams since he died."

"Explain to us what happened. Who was Marion to you?"

"I tutored him in violin. He was a brilliant student. I'd known him since he was young…"

Cillian frowned at that. "His note said he couldn't live without you."

Harris stopped, his face an angry red. "Wh-what are you implying?"

"Now who's playing dumb? We're not here to turn you in, Mr. Harris. We're here for Marion."

Harris chewed at his lower lip, his eyes narrowed at the two of us, and then he sighed. "Very well. We had a... We were..."

"Having an affair?" Cillian suggested.

"*Yes*," Harris hissed, glancing about as though he expected his wife to hear. "I broke it off, and Marion couldn't take it. He was obsessed with me; he wanted me to leave my wife and move in with him. He'd rented some rathole of an apartment. At first, I humored him. He was only seventeen and knew nothing of the world, but when it became apparent he was serious..."

"And you weren't serious?" Cillian asked dryly.

"Men like us can never be serious. I tried to teach him that, but he wouldn't listen! After he showed up at my house, *when my wife was home*, I told him never to contact me again. I meant it too. I even pushed him away. He fell in the street, and I didn't bother to help him up. I just...left him there." He swallowed thickly. "A few days later, I heard he had shot himself."

I saw Marion Owens, a small boy with mousy hair and dark eyes, sitting in an armchair by the phonograph. Despondent as he dictated his last words to the world. He finished the recording without listening to it and then picked up the gun from the table, a Colt 45 pistol. He pressed the barrel to his temple and then squeezed his eyes shut—

"—*Theo*?"

Cillian watched me with concern while Harris looked confused. I stammered that I was okay, but inside I was reeling. How had I known what Marion Owens looked like? I didn't just imagine it, I *knew*. Just as I knew the gun had been his father's service revolver from the War of the Rebellion. That the chipped veneer near the phonograph's name plate had come from an errant shard of Marion's skull embedded in the wood. The phonograph had been cleaned up and sold to Highmore, who hadn't respected Marion's wish for Harris to hear his message. I *knew* these things.

"He loved you," I said suddenly.

"Don't you think I know that?" Harris snapped.

We'd arrived at his house again. His wife peered at us through the window curtains. Harris waved her away with a flick of his wrist.

"Look, I'm sorry he's dead, but I wasn't about to ruin my life for him."

"You ruined his life well enough."

Cillian raised both eyebrows. "Theo!"

"He seduced him. Told him he loved him. Made promises he never kept."

I could see it now, just as I had seen Marion's death. The teasing touches as Harris placed Marion's fingers in the correct position on the violin. The way he put his hands on his shoulders as they read the sheet music. The first kiss, how it had stunned Marion. How after some reflection, he'd wanted more. The games they would play once Marion's mother was out of the house... I felt those mottled hands from my dream on me once again, arms wrapped around my chest, hands at my throat, suffocating me.

"Theo?"

They couldn't see him, but I felt him. Marion was behind me, his cold breath on my neck.

*"Why didn't you keep your promise, Charlie?"*

The voice wasn't my own. It was younger, the pitch lighter. I clamped a hand over my mouth, but it was too late. Harris blanched, his eyes wide, and his jaw hung open. Cillian grasped my shoulder, studying my face.

"You need to listen to the record," I said, my voice normal once again as Marion's presence receded.

"Theo—"

"No, Cillian. It's what he wants. What Marion wants. He'll never leave us alone until Harris hears his final message."

"But Highmore erased it?"

"He didn't erase *him*. Marion's spirit is still in the phonograph."

We turned to Harris in unison.

He shook his head, chewing at his bottom lip. "I can't," he said weakly.

"Don't be a coward," Cillian said. "He was your lover!"

"Keep your voice down!"

"You want him to go away, you need to listen to him one last time."

"All right, *fine*. If it will get him—and you—to leave me in peace!"

He strode up the porch steps. I followed behind and retrieved the phonograph from the bushes. It was still hot, as though it had been warmed by a fire. Harris snatched it from my arms and went inside. Cillian started to follow, but Harris blocked his way.

"No, this is private," he said.

"Mr. Harris, there's a risk to your wife—"

"You leave my wife out of this," he snapped.

The woman in question appeared behind him, curiosity and apprehension on her face, but he barked orders for her to go visit the neighbor. I thought she would argue, but instead, she turned on her heel and left. The kitchen door slammed behind her.

"People have died, Mr. Harris," Cillian said.

"Marion would never hurt me," Harris sneered. "I'll take my chances."

"I'm afraid we have to insist."

"I won't have your wife's death on my conscience," I added. "Do you have any weapons in the house?"

"No," he said, a little too quickly.

Cillian and I exchanged a glance. We couldn't just leave. What if Harris tried to hurt someone? What if he merely threw the phonograph in the trash and abandoned us to our fate? *Well, it would just turn up again at the shop.*

"Come inside," Harris muttered, standing aside.

Cillian took off his hat and followed Harris to the living room, where he set up the phonograph.

"Jesus, what's happened to it?" Harris said. "I bought that for him as a Christmas present... No, never mind. Just play it."

Cillian started to wind up the machine. Before setting the playback stylus, he paused and looked over at me. I nodded. *Clair de Lune* echoed throughout the house. Harris turned to us, obviously confused, but I ushered him on. It felt like forever before the song ended, though I knew for a fact the recording could only hold two-minute-long segments.

Suddenly, the song dropped into a minor key. The notes dragged on and on, slowing to a mockery of the original tune. Harris went pale.

I expected to hear Marion's voice, but instead, whispers echoed forth from the phonograph's horn. I couldn't make them out, but Harris stood rapt to attention. The air grew cold enough that I could see my breath. Cillian came forward and grabbed my hand, fear in his eyes.

"I can hear him," Harris murmured. He drew closer to the machine, enraptured by it. He then bent on one knee, pressing his ear to the horn. "Marion?"

A shudder went down my spine. Harris's assurance that Marion wouldn't hurt him aside, there was a decided malevolence in the air. I tightened my grip on Cillian's hand. This was what Marion wanted. Poor, obsessed Marion, pining away after his lost love—and damn anyone who got in his way. We were alike in that regard. I knew what was coming, and I allowed it to happen for Cillian's sake.

Harris lurched forward, his mouth a perfect *O* of surprise as the horn's opening suctioned itself to the side of his face. He screamed briefly before his head disappeared into the depths of the horn. Bone crunched as his shoulders soon followed. Blood oozed from the sides of the machine as his body was squeezed into an opening no larger than my fist. His legs, kicking feebly, disappeared last until there was nothing left of him but a leather shoe.


WE RETURNED TO the shop. It was just before closing, and Highmore emerged from the back as we entered, paling as he saw us. There was no one else in the store.

"What do you two want?" he asked. "You're both fired, as of this morning."

Calmly, I set the phonograph upon the nearest table and took off the lid. The bloody horn glittered in the gaslight. Highmore gaped, his eyes locked on the blood. Cillian stood in the doorway, watching me with a grim curiosity.

I grasped the handle and began to wind the thing. "I think you want to reconsider firing us, Mr. Highmore."

"Why would I want to do that?"

"Because if you don't, I'll sic Marion Owens on you. He's not happy that you erased his suicide note."

Highmore's face went white. "You're bluffing."

I beckoned Highmore closer, but he wouldn't budge. Garbled notes of *Clair de Lune* echoed forth from the bent horn. I raised my voice to be heard over them. "Are you a superstitious man, Mr. Highmore?"

Highmore shuddered. I knew then that I had him. I turned off the machine just as the song ended. Highmore looked relieved.

"If you ever threaten us again, I'll be back with this," I said, jabbing my finger at the phonograph. "Understood?" Highmore nodded, and I smiled. "Good. See you at work tomorrow."

Not wanting to press our luck, we left before he could reconsider. Cillian burst into helpless laughter after the door closed behind us. I let out a breath I didn't realize I'd been holding, the phonograph heavy in my arms. Cillian waited until we were a block away before speaking.

"So, it's over?" he asked, glancing nervously at the machine.

I shifted the phonograph to my hip and then lifted my shirtsleeve. The bruise around my wrist had vanished. Cillian beamed at me. I suspect he would have kissed me, but we were still in public, and neither of us wanted to risk arrest. It would have to wait until we got home.

Cillian escorted me to my door and then paused as I unlocked it. "What are you going to do with that?" He gestured to the phonograph at my feet.

"I'm going to lock it up in my great-aunt's trunk."

"Good. I suppose I should go home and check on Mary," Cillian said, frowning. "She'll believe me, I think. She's always been the superstitious sort."

"You'll come back later, won't you?"

Cillian grinned, his eyes sparkling. "Every day. For as long as you'll have me."

"I'd like that," I said and pulled him into the apartment for a kiss.

# ABOUT THE AUTHOR

Ridley Harker is an up-and-coming horror author who delights in all things gay and spooky. Influenced by Billy Martin (Poppy Z. Brite), Clive Barker, and Gemma Files, his favorite books are those with enemies to lovers, great villains, and queer main characters. Horror-romance is his favorite genre. He currently lives in the Middle of Nowhere with his two dogs, a grumpy old snake, and a host of pet tarantulas. Please follow him on Twitter @RidleyHarker, or chat with him on his website www.ridleyharker.com.

Facebook
www.facebook.com/ridley.harker

Twitter
www.twitter.com/RidleyHarker

Website
www.ridleyharker.com

Pinterest
www.pinterest.com/ridley_harker

## OTHER NSP BOOKS BY AUTHOR:

*Parasite*

# EXHIBITION

## LAUREN JANE BARNETT

WARNING: Depictions of voluntary confinement of the MC in a small exhibit space and a panic attack.

FOR KAELYN

THE HOLES DRILLED in the Perspex offered Emily the feeling of fresh air moving through her space along with the sounds of visitors and—most importantly for the gallery—the questions of interviewers. Today's interview was with a webzine she had never heard of.

"You aren't the first artist to be a living installation in the gallery," the interviewer commented, looking at Emily as though he had asked a question. Out of politeness as much as self-promotion, she pretended he had.

"Performance in a gallery is as old as the Happening itself. Think of Yoko Ono sitting in a room while people cut her clothing. Or Joseph Beuys who locked himself in a room with a wolf. They are inspirations and pioneers for my work and works like mine." Emily paused to assure herself that the man was listening, even if everything she said was already in the press release. "The real difference in my piece is what I'm trying to achieve."

"And what are you trying to achieve by locking yourself in a box?" he asked with an air of boredom. Emily forced herself not to roll her eyes.

The man on the other side of the glass had already read the press release explaining the reasons behind her work. He already knew that the dimensions of the box represented the average personal space in a refugee camp. He knew that everything in the room, including the cot she slept on, came from one of the camps. He knew her family had been immigrants two generations before. So why, she wondered, did he ask these redundant questions? It made her feel invisible, even as clusters of people stared at her.

Burning with humiliation and frustration, Emily went over the information again, as passionately as she could, while remembering to say the gallery's name as often as possible. The interview felt like a game. He nodded and she spoke—a rally in tennis—but they weren't really communicating. Another invisible wall in addition to the Perspex. The wall of human indifference. The very thing she was trying to challenge with her artwork.

When she finished, he glanced around, one eyebrow arched. "It looks like a prison," he said.

"Yes," she replied. "Yes, it does."

It never ceased to amaze her how many people read articles about refugee camps, saw news reports, shared stories on social media or "liked" a post about the crisis, yet were astounded when they saw a representation of it. And her version was comfortable by comparison. She was cushioned with layers of care from the gallery's climate control, light, and security to the nuances of health and safety regulation, which ensured she was never in danger. They even insisted on making the box bulletproof. As though anyone in London would bring a gun to an art gallery. Besides an artist.

Boredom was perhaps the only thing she suffered to

make up for luxuries like heating. While the refugees might be among family or speak to people, she was truly isolated. In the day, the gallery staff brought the appointed meals, and some chatted briefly, but she was genuinely isolated in her installation. The staff didn't want to disrupt the artwork, visitors always talked at or around her as though she couldn't hear—and, naturally, she couldn't say anything back. Even to the student whose sole comment was "Well, anyone could do it", she managed to keep herself from replying, "Then why don't you?" by digging her nails into her hand.

At least, she sighed, the days offered distraction. She could eavesdrop on the visitors and get caught up in their brief passing conversations. Occasionally, an interview or a chatty gallery assistant made her feel human again. At night, she faced only endless silence. The gallery agreed to stay open twenty-four hours a day so anyone could see that Emily was still abiding by life in her box, but few people bothered to check. A few security guards joined the sole gallery assistant on the night shift, all of whom focused on their own work, and almost entirely silently.

The guards rotated throughout the gallery, but they always stood at the corner of her room. Occasionally, she might catch their eye or even share a word or two, but for the most part, they looked right past her, like any other work of art on the wall. Maybe it was professional; but it felt cold. It also made her watch the guards more intently, as if noticing how they shifted their weight or tapped their knuckles might connect her with them.

That night, the first guard in her room was her least favourite. Darren, or Daz. When they met on his first shift, he'd laughed and said, as if to the air, "So this is how spoiled rich kids spend their time." She knew better than to respond, but she didn't forget. Darren appeared in the open break in the wall leading from her room into the hall. With a look around the room—and through her—he shrugged and leaned his back against the partition wall as though he didn't even want to be in the same room with her.

It couldn't have been later than 9:00 or 10:00 p.m. when he made a noise. She was focused on her evening food ration and took a moment to realise he was speaking. When she looked up to see who he was talking to, she saw his eyes boring back into hers. His shoulders were tensed and his body alert.

"Did you make that noise?" he accused.

"What noise?" she replied automatically, her voice having involuntarily slid up one octave.

"The buzzing," he replied impatiently.

"I didn't buzz," she sighed. "What am I, a bee?"

When he didn't respond, she listened too. "I don't hear anything."

"Wait." Darren raised his hand sharply, keeping the rest of his body poised.

Slowly, he backed out of the room, stopping just before the entrance to the gallery opposite them. The phantom noise drew his attention to the left, down the hallway that led to the entrance, the giftshop, and the office. His body was taut, straining to hear any faint resonance.

After a beat, without looking back to her, Darren stalked off down the hall. She listened to the echo of his footsteps fade, reverberating off the high white walls as he made his way to the front of the gallery. It might have been a trick of the acoustics, but to Emily's ears, his gate stopped dead after ten steps. Only then did she wonder why he hadn't alerted the guard in neighbouring gallery.

Left with nothing but the empty space and a lone wooden bench opposite her, Emily began to imagine things that made a buzzing noise. Her first thought was of the gallery assistant's phone. Visitors rarely were so considerate with their mobiles, but gallery assistants always set their phones to vibrate, to pretend they were being courteous, but they created a tremor loud enough that she could occasionally hear the buzzing from across the small room. But she doubted the thrumming of even the loudest mobile would travel as far from the reception desk as the galleries.

Her next thought was of humming. If Darren thought she'd made the 'buzzing', she reasoned, it was probably more of a hum than a buzz. For all the professionalism of the staff, a boring empty gallery at night could make anyone want to fill the void with a hum or even whistling. But if this phantom frequency had come from a person, surely, she would have heard it.

Her final guess, and the most likely option, was some electrical noise. Electronics always seemed to buzz. But she couldn't picture what could have caught Darren's attention. It certainly wasn't an alarm—the alarms blared with a ferocity no one could ignore (including the person who'd set it off). Therc were some systems in the gallery which emitted periodic moans and trills throughout the night. The CCTV system, the cameras, and the backup power all had their own signature hums. Even the retro intercom at the front desk—apparently installed for its appeal—fizzled and cracked. Yet, none of these were true 'buzzes', and certainly didn't warrant a guard leaving his assigned room. It didn't make any logical sense.

Like the sudden lifting of fog, Emily realised the buzz had just been an excuse for Darren to leave. Emily could imagine him joking to the assistant at the front desk: "Anything for ten minutes away from the girl in the box."

As she grimaced at the thought, another guard came through the doorway. Dyed blonde and over fifty, Lynn was the only female guard on the shift, and the only one to actually speak to Emily.

"Did Daz leave already?" Lynn asked.

"He went down to the front desk a little while ago," Emily replied. "What time is it?"

"Shift change, 11:30."

"Oh, he left closer to ten," Emily realised out loud. "Have you run into him in the last hour or so?"

"No, I haven't seen him since we got in. But I'm sure he found a reason to stay up front with the newest intern." Lynn laughed and shook her head.

Emily felt a pulse of warmth spread over her chest, melting the claw of fear that had been slowly gripping at her. If Darren chose to skip guarding her, it wasn't any of her business.

"How's the shift tonight?" Emily asked.

"Odd." Lynn made her way to the box, lowering her voice. The look on her face reminded Emily of her mother when she was excited to share a piece of gossip about her friends. "Have you noticed no one has come in since 8:00 p.m.? Not one person. Not even to ask for the loo, or directions."

Emily thought back over the past couple of weeks.

There were only one or two nights where she could remember no one coming into her gallery, but even on those evenings, she usually heard the sound of footsteps in the other spaces or the faint murmur of voices at the front desk.

"I think that's happened once or twice before," Emily ventured. "But I can never really tell in my corner of the gallery. All I ever see is this room and the lights in Gallery 2."

"You aren't missing much." Lynn laughed. "But we always get someone through the doors. A lost tourist, someone curious and coming off a late shift. One night, a drunken stag do wandered in and tried to order food."

"What?" Emily cursed her isolation once again, begging for the story.

Lynn was happy to oblige with all the details she could remember, including the moment where the groom tried to crawl under the front desk and go to sleep. Hearing the story filled Emily with a sense of bliss; she hadn't talked to anyone since the interviewer, if it could be considered a conversation.

"The gallery manager had to come in and push him out of the desk with a broom," Lynn exclaimed, her face flushed pink with pleasure. Emily snorted at the image. She was about to ask what happened next when Lynn's head cocked as though she heard something behind her.

"Back to work." She smiled and returned to the edge of the gallery, standing straight as a soldier. She stared into the hall for a beat, perfectly still, before her smile fell and her eyebrows creased.

"I thought I heard someone," Lynn said, turning back to the gallery. "Did you?"

"I was laughing too loud." Emily tried to smile, but

something in Lynn's face made her lips waver.

Lynn moved to the entryway and peeked around the corner into the dead space between the galleries. "There's nothing there."

"Did you hear footsteps?" Emily guessed, uncertain why she felt the need to fill the silence.

"I'm not sure..." Lynn trailed off.

Before Emily could ask anything else, a head and shoulders appeared in the entryway. Emily recognised one of the other guards, Kareem, leaning around the corner of Gallery 2. Darren had called him K-pop in a joke Emily failed to understand.

"Was that you?" he asked Lynn.

"Me?" Lynn turned to Kareem.

"The noise just now," he replied with a smile.

Lynn glanced at Emily before turning to Kareem and shaking her head. "No, but I heard it too. The hall looks clear. Maybe someone dropped something." They exchanged shrugs, and Kareem departed into the orange lighting of Gallery 2.

Lynn turned to Emily, keeping one foot in the hallway. Framed in the large entryway, Lynn appeared as a strange echo of Daz. Before Emily could share her thought, Lynn spoke.

"It could be Daz playing a joke. He does things like this. Makes stupid noises to scare people, or hides around a corner and jumps out at you. He once put exploding candles in a birthday cake."

Emily cringed at the image of cake exploding over a room full of guests. But then, she could imagine Darren finding other people's misery funny.

"I'm just going to check up front to see if he mentioned anything to the girl at the front desk." Lynn nodded and headed off, her features frozen.

Silhouetted in the strange lighting between the two galleries, Lynn glowed momentarily, like an angel in a medieval painting, before disappearing behind the vast emptiness of the gallery wall.

Abandoned in the silence of the gallery, Emily was engulfed by the sudden sensation of slipping into the dampening eerie silence of deep water. At least when a guard was in the room, she could anchor herself to the shore of noises. She could listen to the waves of their breathing, the shuffle of shoes on the polished wood floor, the movement of cloth against cloth as they crossed their legs.

Desperate to tear herself out of the stifling quiet, Emily tapped mindlessly on the Perspex. The acrylic coating reverberated in her fingernails and made her smile. Such a large, empty space should echo, she thought, yet it seemed to devour sound.

She traced the edges of the box and made her way to the small circular holes. When the gallery explained for health and safety inspectors that the box would be made of bulletproof glass, she'd laughed, but she said nothing when the same health and safety regulations required them to drill a series of holes in it for adequate air flow. It was now as bullet-resistant as a cheese grater. And yet, it was a shield. Guests might send verbal jabs her way, but they weren't likely to rush the glass. There was safety in enforced distance.

Emily shivered. The distance might feel safe, but it was the guards who protected her. And she had spent too much time alone tonight. Glancing around the empty room, she felt certain Lynn had been away for too long.

"Lynn," she called, keeping her voice steadier than she felt. The returning silence made her stomach wobble uneasily. "Lynn!" Her voice strained like a bow.

The cry died in the expanse of the space, but it was followed by the pad of footsteps. Her throat unclenched at the welcome thudding of boots on wood.

Kareem walked in calmly, but his eyes darted around the room. "Were you calling for Lynn?"

Emily could only get her thoughts together enough to nod.

Kareem looked around the room with his eyebrows furrowed. "She should be here."

"She went to check with the front desk about the footsteps we heard earlier," Emily explained, her mouth dry.

"Footsteps?" Kareem seemed surprised.

"You heard them too." Emily's throat rebelled against her breath. "You looked around the corner and asked if the noise was Lynn, remember?"

"I didn't hear footsteps; I heard a noise." Kareem looked at Emily with a strange reserve in his eyes.

"Whatever, I don't know. I didn't really hear it." Emily thought back to what she'd heard, but her mind swayed. "It doesn't matter. I called for her because it seems like she's been gone for too long. Maybe even half an hour."

"Half an hour?" Kareem drew himself up, adding unseen inches to his height. "That's not like Lynn." In firm, quick movements he glanced down the hallway and back into Gallery 2 before making a call on his radio for Lynn. There was no reply. Kareem tried a second time. And then tried Darren. The stretch of silence grew ten, fifteen, and then twenty seconds as Emily's stomach clenched.

"Must be broken," Kareem grumbled, but the veins in his neck pulsed visibly as he slipped it back into his belt. Emily could feel the tension spread across the room, sucking away their air.

"You said she went to the front desk?" Kareem asked again, his face now as stony as the rest of his body.

"Or to find Darren. I wasn't certain, but she said she was going to the front desk." Emily was babbling.

"I'll go check." Kareem strode towards the door.

"Wait!"

"What?" Kareem demanded, the word brimming with impatience.

"It just feels too strange." Emily took a breath to steady herself. "First, Darren went into the hall because he heard a noise, and then Lynn went after him. Now you. They both haven't come back. It just doesn't seem right for you to go too." She could hear how strange her own words sounded. Like a child having a nightmare, she sounded unreasonable and lost in nonsense. There had been no sounds of struggle, no screams or cries. She had no reason to feel the way she did. But her hands were also shaking.

"It's okay." Kareem softened slightly. "I'm sure my radio is broken. But listen, the rotation changes in ten minutes anyway. I'll just check in with the front desk, and we'll sort this out."

She nodded and watched Kareem walk away with a sickly cold in her stomach. When Kareem reached the hall, he hesitated. The gesture should have lasted only a second, but he remained suspended with one foot not quite on the floor and his eyes fixed on something Emily could not see. Finally, he took two steps forwards before halting. Every muscle tensed as he squared off with the invisible threat.

"What?" Emily asked urgently, desperate to see what Kareem could.

"Shh!" He hushed her, not moving a muscle except his lips, his entire body focused on something beyond her vision.

Hands still shaking, Emily pressed herself up against the glass and craned her neck until the tendons strained. She grunted in frustration, unable to see more than an inch into the hallway. Instinctively, she glanced behind her to the wall just beyond glass. Camouflaged in the wall behind her was a secret door to the back office. The original plans for her exhibit placed her box against the wall so she could access the door in an emergency. The gallery decided to move her enclosure to the centre of the room to ensure no one would accuse Emily of sneaking out at odd hours.

At the time, she had thought nothing of the change, but now she wished she could hide in the fluorescent safety of the back room. Instead, she was surrounded by Perspex with the only exit an elaborate series of hinges and locks on the left wall. As she thought of it, she automatically edged towards the locks on the movable wall. As if reading her mind, Kareem reacted sharply.

"Stay in there," he commanded, his voice reverberating off the walls.

"What do you see?" Emily asked urgently.

"Just stay in that box," he barked and stepped beyond the white wall, out of Emily's gaze.

"Kareem," she called after him. "Kareem!" But her cries

dissolved into silence.

Emily shivered, her body trying to exorcise the last few moments. Something in Kareem's tone had been unsettling. Even Darren had never spoken to her so forcefully. And how had he known she was thinking of leaving her box? Had he guessed? Or was he simply reminding her that the safest place in the gallery was the bulletproof cage she'd made for herself?

Her stomach squeezed, and acid ran into her mouth. What had he seen to make him change so quickly? A flash brought up the image of Lynn's body lying on the floor, followed by a trail of blood leading to the front desk. The air wedged in Emily's mouth, refusing to go down her throat. Like a fire catching and spreading over her imagination, morbid images fluttered before her eyes—Darren strangling Lynn; a man with a knife; the cold, black circle of the end of a gun.

She gulped, trying to pull the air deeper into her lungs. Her hands found the edge of the glass, eyes not registering what she was seeing. She banged the side of her hand against the glass.

"Kareem!" she cried out. "Lynn!" Her voice cracked. Her vision pitched sideways as though she were on a boat. The ceiling went left. The floor broke up. She stepped back, trying to get away from it, but the floor had moved. She heard her own strained breath and tried to grab for anything. Her fingers only found the smooth unyielding pane of Perspex as the world went black.

AND THEN THERE was a sound of breathing. And tapping. Somewhere above her. Emily woke to find her cheek pressed against the floor. Sitting up, her eyes focused on the fuzzy image of a person before her. One of the gallery assistants was looking down at her from the other side of the glass. Her face was calm, with perfectly arched eyebrows and gleaming, smooth blonde hair. It took a moment for Emily to realise it was Laura, the gallery owner's right hand.

Laura kneeled, revealing the shining buckle on her Manolos. They looked as though she'd never worn them outside.

"Sorry to wake you, Emily." She smiled brightly. "There's nothing to worry about, but we thought you should be aware. Some of the guards seem to have left during their shift."

"What? No—" Emily's throat spasmed, stifling her words.

"Oh, don't worry. I am sure it's just a miscommunication," Laura interrupted. "You know how it is. One needs to leave early, and someone else does, too, but no one recognises it was on the same day."

"Wait, wait…" Emily waved a hand between them to derail the gallery assistant. "That's not what happened. Lynn went missing." Emily wrestled to put her head together, reaching desperately for the words in the haze of her unsettled consciousness.

"No, Emily, I think you're confused. I woke you up too fast." Laura paused and gave Emily a moment to get to her feet. "Now." Laura smiled brightly and looked directly into Emily's eyes with an irritating calm. "Lynn checked in to work on time, so no one was missing. She just seems to have left a bit early. And two other guards as well—"

"Laura, wait!" Emily interjected firmly, her head now balanced and the clarity of what had happened settling onto her shoulders. She needed to make the next words count. Laura might have saved her from whatever was happening, but she needed someone to know what had happened that night.

"I'm awake, and I know what happened," Emily began, the tenor of her voice commanding Laura's attention. "Something happened to all of them in the hall. Darren first, and then Lynn went to look for him, and last, Kareem. All of them went into the hall, or maybe the front desk. Kareem at the very least, saw something—"

Laura tried to interrupt, but Emily smacked her hand against the Perspex to demand her focus.

"Check the CCTV cameras, Laura. The hallways first. Kareem saw something. And whatever it was, it scared him."

"Okay," Laura replied in a soothing hospital tone. "Unfortunately, the CCTV is down, so we aren't entirely sure what happened. And when I arrived, none of the three guards were here, so I shut down the gallery. We are safely locked in, and while we wait for the backup crew to come, I need you to tell me what happened slowly and clearly." Laura's serene voice had the strange effect of making Emily feel that she was in trouble.

"The first guard on duty in the room was Darren," Emily began. "He left...for some reason."

"Do you remember why?"

"I'm not sure." Emily's head ached as she tried to remember. It seemed days ago. "Yes, he heard something, a noise."

"Well, the gallery is open."

"He heard something that made him leave," Emily shot back in frustration. "And I don't know what it was, but he said it was a buzzing."

"Was this before or after Rebecca left?" Laura asked, lips pursed.

The words stunned Emily briefly. "Rebecca?" she managed to ask in a whisper.

Rebecca was missing, too, which meant that only Laura and herself were in the gallery. And Emily was stuck in a box. If someone had done something to Rebecca and the others, the only person it could have been was Laura. The thought caused Emily's knees to become heavy and loose. She couldn't tell Laura another word. She couldn't reveal that she knew anything. But, she reminded herself, she had already given away too much.

"Emily? Pay attention." Laura breathed in. "Do you know when Rebecca left?"

"No," Emily managed. "I didn't know she was gone." She suddenly felt lightheaded again.

"Okay," Laura continued, the muscles of her face relaxing. "So, Darren leaves because of a...buzzing. Then what?"

"Um, Lynn came in for her shift." Emily struggled to pull in a deep breath—had the air conditioning been turned off?

"And you said she went missing too." Laura nodded. "Did she hear a noise too?"

"Well, actually I'm not..." Emily stumbled to the edge of her cot to sit. "I'm not sure.

"Emily, are you okay?" Laura's tone swiftly changed. Her voice seemed to float in the air between them.

"Um…" Emily tried to keep her focus as a feverish flush spread through her face and across her limbs. What had Laura done to her?

"Stay there; I'll call the medic." Laura's voice was etched with sharp concern. The sudden worry made Emily's vision click into place. Laura looked scared. The gallery had a medic on call in case something happened to Emily, but it was clear from the look on Laura's face that no one in the gallery ever expected to need him.

The sight of Laura rushing from the room seemed to steady Emily's breathing. Laura disappeared around the corner, followed by a sharp, hard thud. The sound of a body hitting the floor.

Emily's vision snapped back to perfect clarity. Her muscles tensed, and her spine stiffened. Tingling, she shot up and ran to the Perspex wall in front of her.

"Laura!" she screamed, smacking the flat of her palm against the clear wall. She hit it with surprising force, but the pain did not echo in her hands. Her face pulsed with cold and hot all at once. "Laura!"

Silence loomed over her, threatening her with the horrid reality that whatever had been attacking them, it wasn't Laura.

Again, Emily banged her fist against the wall, the skin now red with the effort. "Help!"

She wailed, her voice scratched and stretched, pitching to an unearthly shrill. "Help! Help me!"

The words filled the room with the heat and humidity of her breath while the sound pounded against the Perspex, causing it to tremble. But there was no reply.

She dove to her knees in the corner of the side wall,

where the pin and latch system held her in. Her hands flung for the lock and shook as she carefully unhooked the mechanism. It took longer than it should have, but she could only barely feel her hands.

Her breathing echoed in her ears as she finished, and the lock pinged open. She looked up to the lock in the ceiling corner. Once she had it undone, she could force the wall open on its hinge. Wildly, she scanned the sparseness of the room. She needed a ladder. The cot would have to do. She jerked the cot into the corner and watched it bounce off the wall, opening it barely an inch where the lock had come undone.

Her breath echoed in her ears as she climbed on top of the cot. Her head swirled enough to make her pause. She needed to get a grip. She clutched her hands by her sides and closed her eyes, aching to slow her breath. She listened to its ragged rhythm soften until it became barely a whisper in her ears.

And in the silence, she heard the buzz. She knew instinctively that it was the sound Darren had commented on before. Her ears strained to meet the noise. Too loud for breathing, too slow to be mechanical, but she couldn't place it. It wasn't a bee, or an alarm, or even the fuzz of a radio. It was a buzzing whirr, steady and unmoved. Inhuman.

She glanced around her as the thrumming grew, searching for the answer. The room revealed nothing unusual. Certainly nothing that could make that uncanny tremor. The walls were empty and bare, with their sharp white matte. The only other object in the room—a wooden bench—didn't seem to be vibrating. Her ears stretched to pinpoint the source.

It was coming from the hall.

Emily's eyes fixated on the crisscross of light and shadow that filled the empty entryway to the room. A large, square void cut into the wall revealing a scattering of lights in the hall and gallery beyond. There was a fluttering among the lights. The soft, tinned buzzing made its way towards her. It grew as it approached, filling the room.

In a panic, she dove beneath her cot, curling herself into a ball to block out the noise that reverberated through her bones, gripping her from the inside. Even worse, something within a hidden corner of her mind recognised the sound. It was familiar but not, like a doll of a close friend, the face distorted but familiar. She couldn't place it, but the hint of a memory that it touched caused her entire body to shake. It ran through her hands and then convulsed into her chest, shaking violently against her muscles, forcing her tighter into a ball.

The shiver coursed through her body, a cold, sharp river, causing involuntary spasms of fear. She gripped her eyes shut and tensed her back, trying to stop the motion, trying to find in the corner of her mind an origin for the terrorising clatter.

As the vague shadow of the secret came into shape, her ears picked up a change in the pitch. The reverberation grew cleaner and softer, revealing the distinct rhythmic undulations beneath the hazy flurry of sound.

It was in the room with her. Coming towards her, a gentle whirring that creeped towards her, carrying no other sound. She forced her eyes tighter, pulled her knees deep into her chest until it hurt. Her palms twitched and strained against the skin of her throat. Her tears blazed fiery tracks along her cheeks. Her mind fought with itself, straining to hear and not wanting to know, tearing itself in a cacophony of splitting agonies.

THEY FOUND HER that morning, crying and curled under the cot, the only soul in the building. All that remained of that show were the interviews. The gallery closed shortly after. The Perspex box was recycled.

And in that moment between awake and dreaming, when the mind is engulfed by the unexpected jolt of falling, Emily remembered where she heard that sound before.

# ACKNOWLEDGEMENTS

Thank you to NineStar Press for support and editorial eye.

# ABOUT THE AUTHOR

Lauren is a London-based horror writer with work in magazines such as *BFS Horizons* and *Horrified* and the *Duplicitous* (Inked in Gray Press) and *Bloody Good Horror* (Hellbound Press) anthologies. Her first non-fiction horror book, *Death Lines: Walking London's Horror History*, is coming out in 2022 with Strange Attractor Press.

### Email
info@laurenjanebarnett.com

### Website
www.laurenjanebarnett.com

### Instagram
@laurenjanebarnett

### Pinterest
www.pinterest.com/DrLJBarnett

# ON THE OTHER SIDE OF SOUND

## JON JAMES

WARNING: Depictions of gore, children imperilment, family drama, mental illness, cannibalism, and trauma.

To my kids, whose baggage will hopefully never compare to those in this story.

A GRATING SOUND, a whining whirr, it never went away. Ever since the accident, it has plagued me. Always.

Like any day, I was driving home from work. It was one of those freak things, one second, driving the normal route down I-69, and the next, the brakes in front of me flashed, and I didn't glance up from my phone fast enough to react.

I was in the hospital for weeks. Asleep for most of the time. They said my head swelled up to twice its normal size. Lex and the kids slept there with me the first few nights. My parents stayed at my house with the kids the next few. I was alone after that.

They put a metal plate in my head to replace the splintered bone where my skull was. The scars had already healed before I even opened my eyes for the first time.

The first thing I remembered—after thinking *oh shit* and slamming on the brakes too late—was the sound.

Like machinery, or a rapid beeping, or something between the two, or both, it was all around me. I heard the sound in both ears. I couldn't hear the doctors when I woke up. *What?* I said repeatedly. They scanned my brain for damage to the temporal lobe, but it lit up just fine. *I can't hear you over this whining sound. Is there, like, a fan belt slipping?*

They couldn't hear it. I've always had sharp hearing, I told them. Just, get a mechanic to look at the vents.

They couldn't find anything. They switched my room, but the noise was still there. *I'm sorry, but there's nothing we can do. There is no sound.*

Fine. I could deal. It was just... distracting. Hard to focus.

My neurotrauma specialist told me it wasn't uncommon for people like me, *victims of traumatic brain injuries*, to experience *neuropsychiatric effects such as auditory hallucinations.*

*When does it get better?* I asked him. He didn't have an answer. He talked around it, some non-answer gibberish such as *most patients experience a full reversal of such effects within the first few months.*

I rubbed my ear, opened and closed my mouth as if pressure just needed to be relieved. The noise ground on in my head.

*Are...are you sure you can't hear it? It sounds so real...*

He shook his head. *Don't worry, we will get you fixed up in no time.*

I nodded, but I was hardly paying attention. The tone fluctuated and made it hard to follow his words.

They let me out of the hospital early. I still had to go in for physical therapy, but I was walking again sooner than expected, and I had hardly lost any speech ability once the swelling went down.

It was hard on Lex and the kids. Tristan was too young

to really understand. *Daddy will be... Um, I'll be all better soon, okay, big guy?* I told him, but by the end, I was looking up at the ceiling to the left, my ears ringing with tones the boy couldn't hear.

Lex kept it together for me, but I heard them crying in bed when they thought I was asleep. I never told them how hard it was to get to sleep with the grating, grinding noise going all the time. I'd always had the radio on when I slept, but this was different. I couldn't not listen to it. The sound demanded attention.

Like waiting for someone to message, feeling my phone buzz in my pocket. Suddenly, in the middle of conversation, the thread is gone, lost.

Or getting robocalled by my insurance company and hearing my voice echoing back on the other end, slightly delayed. Impossible to ignore, and always. Always.

My youngest, Freya, wanted to use me as a jungle gym. I tried, but I didn't have the endurance to stand there for long. *Hey, honey, give Daddy a rest, okay? I'm not feeling all the way better yet, okay, princess? Soon, you can climb all over me again, but right now, I'm...not there yet.*

Of all of them, Maddie took my issue the hardest. She'd idolized me. She loved asking questions; she loved chatting. Whenever I didn't know, which was a lot, I googled the answer, and we'd talk about it. Or we'd get sucked into a rabbit hole, and soon it was way past her bedtime, and we were digging up reviews of aubergine inks on fountain pen forums.

*Daddy, why does it only snow in the winter?*

*Well, honey, that's because...of...um... Remember the water cycle? Um, the clouds...crystallize the rain...*

*That's not what I asked! I know what the water cycle is; we learned that in third grade! I want to know why snow doesn't fall in the summer if the stratosphere is always cold!*

*Oh. Right… Sorry, honey, it's…hard for me. I can't… This damned noise! I can hardly hear you over it! Don't you hear it? Is the furnace on? The TV? It…it sounds so real. I'm sorry, honey. I'm so sorry. I can't…*

*Can you just give me your phone so I can look it up, then?*

I passed her the device. Seconds later, I reached into my pocket to add a note to my shopping list to get her a tablet for her birthday, but my pocket was empty. I felt like a fucking idiot when I saw that the phone I was trying to get out was already in her hand.

*Maybe I should get another scan*, I finally told Lex one night. *It's not getting better.*

*Every one has been better than the last,* they said. *You just have to wait. You're still healing.*

*…What? Sorry, it's…hard.*

*I know. I know.* They rolled over and didn't say anything else.

Words broke through the buzzing and whirring while they thought I was in the garage.

*…I want…back…to talk to him like before…miss him.*

*Maddie…getting better…needs…time…*

*No!* Maddie's shrill scream pierced through the haze of noise. *He's not!…just as bad…worse…*

I couldn't eavesdrop anymore. I came in, picked her up. I held her close. *I'm right here, baby. Right here.*

She whispered something in my ear, but I couldn't hear

it. She said it again, but the damn sound still drowned her out. *What...?* I started to ask, but the sound was moving, circling my head, ear to ear, shifting in pitch, in timbre. I looked around for it. I realized my arms had let Maddie go, that she'd slipped back to the ground, that she stood there watching me as I looked around the kitchen at nothing while she tried to talk to me, begged me to listen. I caught a glance of her face, raining tears. I forced myself back to her, like breaking through ice on the surface of a lake.

*I'm sorry. I'm here. I'm sorry.* But it wasn't enough.

My appointments slowed. My motor skills improved, my reflexes, my speech. But the noise didn't leave. It was my guardian angel, my personal demon. It didn't leave me for a second.

*Are you sleeping better yet, Robert?* asked some doctor or physical therapist or psychologist.

*No.*

*We can give you something for that. A stopgap.*

*It won't help.*

*It might. But it's entirely up to you.*

I stared off into the corner of the office. I could almost imagine that the sound was coming from the air vent there in the ceiling. A squeaky rotor or something in the HVAC. All this time, and it still seemed so real.

*Robert? Robert?*

*Yeah. Pills. Yeah. Whatever might help. It's not stopping.*

They didn't help. They made me tired, but I was already so tired. I took two before bed, lay down, stared at the orange *X*s on the wall cast by the streetlamp through the trellis. Lex breathed slowly next to me, their body radiating heat under the covers. I couldn't hear them breathe.

Sirens outside. Maybe. Or just the sound. It had no pattern. Sometimes it was high, sometimes low. Pulsating or steady. One ear, both. The only thing the sound wasn't was quiet. It was always there. The more I tried to focus on something else, to let myself slip into peace, to meditate, the louder it got, the more intrusive. I took three pills, four. Nothing helped. The sound chewed at my ears. I was afraid sometimes it would damage the little hairs, getting so loud. I tried earplugs. but they only drowned out everything else. I tried music, white noise. I tried drinking. Nothing stopped the sound. Sometimes it was almost music. Other times it was a scream.

I started writing about it. A journal, kind of. My therapist suggested a journal, but whenever I tried to write, I couldn't think. My thoughts were interrupted by a spike, a tone, a trill. So I wrote what I heard instead.

At first, I was just writing text. A diary of the sound. *Now it is high-pitched with a slight warble. It reminds me of the fan belt in the car I still need to fix. Now it is a deep tremble, barely audible, more felt than heard.* I kept the notes on my phone. Whenever the sound got to be too much, I pulled out the journal, tried to describe what I heard.

I developed a shorthand. A code for it. Kind of reinventing the wheel, maybe, but I was never good at reading music. *P^E2. S-S73. T4.*

If I couldn't escape from the sound—and it was slowly becoming clear that I couldn't—at least I could make something of it. I documented every moment of it I could. And since I was on disability from work, there were a lot of moments I could document. I started leaving the TV off. Even with closed-captioning, I couldn't focus on it.

My neck was sore from looking down, my eyes dry from the constant glare of the screen. Sometimes, I switched to a notepad and pen. Nothing mattered. It wasn't anything. Just a way to feel in control again, even a little. Maybe, if I could write something, if I could name it, I'd have some power over it.

Lex and the kids, watching TV, eating dinner. I was there, but I wasn't. Even when I wasn't writing the notes, I was listening. Sometimes I just translated them in my head.

*Why isn't Daddy answering me?*

*RR28.*

*Daddy? DADDY!*

*Y.6c.*

I started to study it, the journals, the code. It almost felt like... No, that was crazy. Even to me, where I was, it felt crazy. But I couldn't shake the impression that there was some intelligence behind the sound.

Maybe the doctors were right, and the whole thing was mine, all in my head, my brain trying to get my attention or feel in charge or something. It seemed silly, but there was only one alternative: it wasn't all in my head. A separate intelligence, trying to communicate through the metal in my head.

I looked over the letters and numbers and symbols. I rearranged them, turned them around. Substituted letters for words, sounds, syllables, pictures. I could look at them and recreate the sound in my head. I sped it up, slowed it down, looked for something of meaning in it. Anything to make my suffering have a purpose.

And then, I found it.

A cypher hidden in the sound. A message. My code, translated correctly, could be turned into text. Meaningful words.

It was convoluted, but once I found the pattern, it became everything. A syllable here, a word there. Some tones were concepts, others just a letter. Some changed the emotion, like speaking with a smile versus a frown. Some were punctuation. But there it was, meaning emerging from the tumult.

Every moment was the sound, and it was telling me something, and after all this time, I was finally starting to learn its language.

Either my phone or my notebook was out constantly. Freya screeched in my ear, pulling my hair and stacking up McDonald's toys on my belly. Tristan played with army men, using my knees as the battlefield. Maddie avoided me. Lex drank. I wrote.

And slowly, it emerged. There *was* a pattern hidden in the noise. It consumed me. There was a purpose to this torture. Somewhere, something was trying to communicate. I listened with intent. I closed my eyes; I hummed along.

*Daddy, play with me!*

But I sang along to the noise.

*Daddy, how do fish breathe in the water?*

I heard the words sort of far away, like a TV show with the volume down, not really watching while scrolling through the feed on my phone.

*Daddy, let's wrestle!*

But I wrote what I heard.

And then, I had it. A key. The answer to the noise.

*Lex! It means something! Maddie, come here! Freya,*

*Tristan! Daddy found it! It means something! A key! Look!*

*That's great, honey.* Lex took another swig of wine.

*Does that mean we can play again?*

*Yeah, buddy. Soon. Real soon.*

I looked over my notes. My mind raced, attempting to translate the persistent sound even as I tried to tell my family how excited I was.

*What is this? This means nothing.* Maddie looked over the paper. *You're a piece of shit! This means nothing!*

*No, baby, no, princess, look. It's a key. A code. It means something! They're trying to tell me something! It all means something!*

Maddie scoffed. But the sound had me again. It was talking to me. I felt like I was learning ancient Babylonian, a dead language with a foreign context; mostly gibberish, but slowly, words taking meaning. Things clicking. Exponential growth.

It was coming together. Letters and numbers filled my notebooks, unopened envelopes, Maddie's homework, book margins.

*I... It's...a recipe?* I announced one day. Nobody came. They returned the attention I gave them. *A recipe. A fucking... A pizza recipe! It's a fucking recipe for making fucking pizza!*

I screamed, and the sound grew to a buzz, a deafening roar. I couldn't hear my words over it, but it repeated in its alien cipher: *3 cups flour. 3 cups flour. 3 cups flour.*

*No! Fuck you! Fuck you!* I screamed over a sound nobody else could hear. Freya cried. Tristan cried. Maddie turned up her radio.

*1 cup warm water*

*1 teaspoon salt*

*Stop! Shut up! Leave me alone! Why won't you leave me alone?*

A wine glass broke, but I barely heard it. In the cipher, it made the sound that meant ampersand.

*1 tablespoon olive oil*

*1 ½ teaspoons sugar*

*Why? What did I do? Why!*

A door slammed. The letter *M*. More crying. E4E4E4. Lex cursed.

*2 teaspoons dry yeast*

*Just stop. I'll do it. You want me to make you a fucking pizza, I'll do it. Just stop. Will you stop if I do it? Stop! Let me hear again. Let me hear silence. I'll make you a fucking pizza. Three cups flour. Here, I'm making your pizza. Stop!*

*15 ounces tomato sauce*

*6 ounces tomato paste*

*1 tablespoon oregano*

*2 cloves minced garlic*

*Fuck you, Dad! Shut up!* The radio, louder still, blasting pop songs. Screams of G8*((^ST+p3#.

*1 teaspoon paprika*

*8 ounces shredded mozzarella*

*½ cup pineapple chunks*

*Pineapple. Got it. Mozzarella. I'm going to have to go shopping, but yes. I got it. I'm making it, okay?*

*12 human ears*

*A dozen ears. Yeah. Let's go. Wait. No. No. Please. No.*

*12 human ears*

*Will you stop? After I make this, will you stop? Please, stop!*

*12 human ears*

I put on my coat. Nobody noticed. Keys jangled to the nonsense of @**(===.

I drove. I bought what I needed, everything except the last ingredient. Where would I get those? Twelve human ears. They were all I needed, then it would stop. The sound would stop and I could hear quiet again, the sweet sound of nothing. I could have my family back, my life.

*Twelve human ears. Twelve human ears,* repeated in my mind. I couldn't tell if it was the sound or my own thoughts. I couldn't tell if they were even any different. I bought a sharp knife and some pills. I paid at the self-check-out. The *beep, beep, beep* of my items scanning said *rose, rose, rose.*

I carried the bags back to the car. A man sat outside the door, shaking a can with coins in it. *Anything helps, God bless*, he said. *PPPPP,* said his can. *PPPPPPPPPPPPPPP.*

*I, um, excuse me, sorry*, I stammered.

*Hey man, you got any change? Anything to spare? PPPPPPPPPPPPPPPPPPPPPPPPP.*

*I just, let me just.* I set down my bags.

*PPPPPPPPPPPPPPPPPPPPPPPPPPPPPPPPPPPPP PP*

*PPPPPPPPPPPPPPPPPPPPPPPPPPPPPPPPPPPPPP PPPPPPPPPPPPPPPPPPPPPPPPPPPPPPPPPPPPPP PPPPPPPPPPPPPPPPPPPPPPPPPPPP*

*Could you fucking stop it?*
*PPPPPPPPPPPPPPPPPPPPPPPPPPPPPPPP*

I opened a bag. I pulled something out of it.
*PPPPPPPPPPPPPPPPPPPPPPPPPPPPPPPPPPPPP PPPPPP*

*Ah! Fuck, man! Help! Someone help! My ears! Ahhhhh!!!!*

I was driving home. I was wet, sticky. *Ten human ears.* I whistled notes that said *Silence, quiet, peace. Peace. PPPPPeace. PPPPPPPPPPP*

I sped up. Had to get home. Had to make it. Ten human ears. Ten human ears.

I slammed the door to a loud *@@@*. I locked it. I went to the kitchen.

I made the crust. Put it in the oven. Stirred the sauce. Spread the toppings.

The timer chimed a sad warble, a sound that meant something like nostalgia.

I put some water in the kettle, got four mugs from the cupboard. Dropped two pills in each of them to the clink of an *I-I*. Crushed them against the bottom with a spoon.

*Honey? Kids? Can you come here? I know I've been...off lately. But it's going to be better soon. I'm making pizza! Come on, to the kitchen! Soon, it'll all be back to normal, okay?*

They came. *Smells great! Thanks, Daddy!*

*Here, have some tea.* I gave mugs to each of them. Soon they were asleep in their chairs.

*Ten human ears,* I hummed as I cut. *Eight human ears. Six human ears. Four human ears. Two human ears.* I sprinkled cheese on top of the sauce. Spread pineapple. Pulled the ears out of a baggie in my pocket and placed them neatly in a circle. *Two human ears.*

I lifted the knife to my own ears. I could barely feel the pain over the ecstasy of the music. It was a chant, a hymn, as I placed my last two ears onto the pizza and put it in the oven. I stepped over my sleeping, bleeding family to set the timer.

A noise from outside. A shrill, repeating noise, rising and falling. ```````````````````>>>>>>>>>>>>>> ``````````````````>>>>>>>>>>>>> ``````````````` ```>>>>>>>>>>>>>

The timer ticked down. Voices, amplified. Lights. The sound, continuing, echoing. Disrupting the music. The pizza was ready.

Banging on the door. *YYYY! YYY YY YYYYY!* More voices.

I pulled the pizza from the oven and placed it on the stovetop to cool. I got a pizza cutter from the drawer.

The door bowed inward with each strike of the ram. It creaked and groaned in moans of *!@#$%^\**. The walls shook. Photos and knickknacks rained to the ground. I swallowed the first bite of pizza as the door burst in a wave of splinters, shards of wood cascading to the tile floor of the kitchen.

*There. I made the pizza. I ate it. I did the damn thing. Is it over?*

The sound grew louder, louder, and raised in pitch, a whine, a scream.

*Is it finally ending?*

It became impossibly loud, impossibly high. It crescendoed more as the police swarmed in around me. They pointed guns at me. I stood in the kitchen and set down the slice.

*Do you hear that? What is it? Some kind of noise weapon? Shit, it's disrupting the radio! Cuff him! See if you can find what's making that goddamn sound. Jesus, it's terrible!*

I sank to my knees. The noise was higher than ever, and louder. But it hadn't stopped. *Why? Why! Why are you still here?*

*I can't find anything. Just put him in the car; we'll have bomb squad check it out. And get these poor damn kids in an ambulance.*

In the back of the car, they frisked me, hit me. *What do you have? Where are you hiding it? We will not hesitate to check everywhere when we get to the station, if you don't tell us now. What is it? A goddamn bomb? What's making this fucking sound?*

The trial was done remotely over a TV. My mic was only unmuted for as long as my plea.

THEY PUT ME in a box, far away from everyone. Once a day, a guy in earplugs drops off my food. All I have for company is the sound. Forever, now. My family doesn't visit. All I have is the sound, and the code, and the recipe it still screams at me day and night.

*3 cups flour*

*1 cup warm water.*

Today, the man in earplugs leaves me a pizza.

# ABOUT THE AUTHOR

Jon James has a million hobbies, and writing is one of them. Accordingly, he doesn't spend long in one particular genre or even one form. He likes weird stuff, which you will probably quickly figure out if you read anything he has written. He has a spouse and two kids.

Jon James studied English literature at Michigan State University and currently traffics his time to an insurance company as a technical writer, though he tries not to let that rub off on his other work.

Email
jon@jonjameswrites.com

Facebook
www.facebook.com/spaceyjdjames

Twitter
spaceyjdjames

Website
www.jonjameswrites.com

Instagram
@spaceyjdjames

TikTok
@spaceyjdjames

# HER LITTLE JOKE

Kitten and Blonde, Book One

## EULE GREY

WARNINGS: Depictions of historical homophobia.

*Bury a husband, board him up.*
*All day long,*
*You'll get*
*Good luck.*

BLOG ONE
*Random fact of the day: a green wig is hanging on a hook in our office.*

Hello! This is Mave Kitten reporting for the Litten *Echo*, our very own free version of the *New Yorker*. Over the next few months, we'll be offering weekly broadcasts about issues that matter to *you*—our lovely residents of Litten Vale.

When the boss 'asked' mc to run a blog, I almost died from shock. It had been another uneventful afternoon. I was sorting the *Echo*'s files and sorting the *Echo*'s files. Round and round in a forever loop. The office cat snored, and our Lisa was gliding, quite skilfully, on one leg.

I'm nervous of 'she who must be obeyed' and, at the

same time, hypnotised by her idiosyncratic behaviours. Still, I had to ask. "What're you doing, Lisa? Ice skating?"

It's true to say we're wary of each other. Life has taught me to be cautious. I talk too much and don't notice hints. I'm not everyone's cup of tea. On my first day as junior reporter, I noticed and looked. Lisa reciprocated. Now, we're trapped in a bizarre cycle of wariness and looky-looky.

In response to my question, Her Highness hurled some wipes onto the floor, placed her foot on top, and continued skating. "Cleaning the floor."

I winced, started talking, and then couldn't stop. "Wipes are no good for the environment. The cloth takes five hundred years to biodegrade. Haven't we got a mop? Shall I buy one? We need cat treats too. I'll get the pricey kind. Kitty doesn't eat the crappy ones you get. Shall I get organic? Or how about that mice kind?"

Lisa grimaced, as if to suggest I'd twisted off her arm. "Did she tell you she doesn't like the crappy ones?"

I shook my head. "Not exactly. But—"

A firm expression took hold of Lisa's face. "No pricey treats. The cat can stand the cheaper brands if she knows what's good for her. You, Ms Kitten, are about to record an interview down at Ellison. Too busy for mops! If you run, you can catch the two o'clock bus."

Record an interview? I'd have been happier if she'd told me to join the army. "No! Interview actual people and make broadcasts? I couldn't possibly."

"Yes," she'd said. "Definitely. I want a weekly blog about local urban myths."

Dear listener, I died a death of horror and then came back to life and got on with it. Mauve Mave's like that.

*Listen to this,*
*Too good to miss.*

Less than a day later, and the first blog's being broadcast. My sensitive nature isn't equipped to contradict six feet of muscle and blonde. Between you and me, I call her the 'Lisanator'. Blonde, like the beer. Big, strong, and got a kick. Her words, not mine. Our Lisa isn't one to argue with, but don't snitch on me. She never listens to broadcasts or the news. If you don't say anything, she won't know.

A little personal info before frying the chips of journalism. I'm fifty-two years old and am a proud Littenite. I love cats, documentaries, cheese and onion flavour crisps, and the colour purple. Very important, that. Fluffy cushions and wind chimes also make me happy. Friends call me Mauve Mave, and so can you.

What don't I enjoy? Tight spaces and flapping wings. Urgh. I know it's a daft thing, and you can blame it on my sister, Tamara. When did it start? All I remember is a bird or butterfly flapping in my face and a lot of girlish screaming. Tam says we were in a library lift, and it broke down. When we got out, a big sea gull appeared and *flapped at us*. Witches Tipple beer! So horrible.

Reporting for the *Echo* means a lot to my girlish heart. I was made up when Lisa offered the job. Literally, crying with joy. I still don't know why she picked me from hundreds of applicants. I don't ask in case it was a mistake.

I'm nothing to write home about and have had too many thankless café and cleaning jobs. Not that there's anything wrong with that! As Dad says, any work's work. Bless him; he's always been a pub philosopher. Just don't get him onto fracking or craft beer. Not if you want to get to sleep that night.

Our first blog will be—hopefully—of interest to Litton folks and especially anyone from down Ellison way. By now, you'll have guessed what I mean because everyone's talking about it. Yeah, that's right. *The sound*...

According to Lisa, it's something of a local legend. Kids have made memes, and the neighbourhood app is abuzz. Like all good scares, the noise began during a dark and stormy Tuesday night. Right after *Coronation Street*, and before *Holby*. Some heard a buzz and others more a scratch. A few claimed to sense a vibration coming from underneath the house.

Weird, no? Irritating, certainly.

By next morning, the noise had vanished along with the good tempers of Ellison. Tired, confused, and spooked, people got on with their day and forgot about it... Until a few nights later when the same thing happened.

Now the sound is a regular occurrence, despite residents doing their best to get to the bottom of things. They've called the council, plumbers, electricians, and a roads expert. The area has been tapped, dug, poked, and prodded. Nothing has worked, and the noise persists.

Of course, rumours are rife. Lisa told me some old story about the canal, as eerie as spaghetti in a stew.

Get a brew on, and make sure you've a biscuit at hand, dear reader. Are you ready?

The story goes: On the canal bottom lies a secret, hidden door. Locked from the outside. Nobody remembers who put it there or why, but there's a rhyme about a woman who locked her husband in and left him to die.

Nasty, no?

Before they built the canal, folks steered clear of the area because of scratching sounds. Interested yet? *Scratch, scrabble, scratch.* Urgh.

*Listen to this,*
*Too good to miss.*

Random coincidence. A month ago—when the noise began—I started getting headaches you wouldn't believe. Absolute stonkers that left me trembling and weak. Freaky shot of simultaneousness? Maybe.

On with my reporting duties. The boss suggested I start by having a good look around Ellison. "You could get the bus."

"Nah. I'll bike."

I haven't got a car and never did pass my driving test. All those decisions and junctions—argh—just wasn't me, being more decorative than functional. Give me a set of instructions, and I'll bugger it up. After the third failed test, my slightly hysterical driving teacher shoved me out of the car and drove off as fast as a flea in a blizzard. Hasn't answered my messages since. It wasn't my fault red resembled green. An easy mistake anyone could've made.

It was nice on my bike, Bertha. Afternoon winter sun with a hint of evening. Many people hate autumn, but I've always loved the time of year. The way summer slips into the clouds and mists of Litton that's mysterious and ancient. Profound, as my mum would say, bless her.

No doubt you, dear listener, will know Litton was built around the river Ellison and the canal. In years gone by, a busy network of commercial barges and boats crowded the waters.

For that reason, I decided to start with a gander along

the canal path, easily wide enough to push a bike. Lots of streets and estates nestle on both sides of the water. Lisa calls it Ellison-on-Sea. It's a quiet area with a good reputation. When I was looking at houses with a view to buy, I considered it because of the good bus services and affordability. Too late. The houses were sold long before being built. Long story short, *that's* why I'm still living with my parents. Mauve Mave's a stayer; that's what Mum says.

Down on the canal path with birds and greenery, it felt like a holiday. The path was very pretty and scattered with comfy benches. The water peppered with boats. The area seemed safe and loved.

Quite quickly, the canal led to a series of complicated-looking locks, one higher than the rest, with water far below. If anyone fell, it'd be the end.

After, the path branched into an area closed off to walkers by red tape. It looked as if the council had visited and left behind a small cement mixer and some bricks. At the far edge was space enough to squeeze illicitly past the barriers.

Mindful of being the new girl, not wanting to disappoint our Lisa, I, however, leant my bike against a tree, and then carefully made my way beyond the red tape. Not much to see. A few yellow waistcoats and a scattering of litter, and yet, I was compelled to keep looking. A headache started. Something similar to hunger gnarled at my insides.

I crept beyond the machinery to a bricked-in tunnel. Cold and deserted. Other-worldly. Water dripped on my face. A bird flapped its wings.

Properly freaked, I crept to the edge of a circular wall and peered down into a deep, slimy hole, which smelt as horrible as the opening to hell. No, I don't mean the

Lankersby Arms on a Saturday night, ha ha.

A blast of filthy and foul air gushed out. Strong enough to make me heave. Blurgh!

For the first time, I heard the noise properly. Flapping, scratching, tapping, and shuffling. Totally hurl-worthy. Nastier than Brussels sprouts.

That was enough. I stumbled back through the barriers and managed to knock over a safety panel.

I peddled, with haste, across the bridge and into Locke Street. The noise faded. Locke is a pretty place, with gardens well maintained. Half expecting to see vampires or something unnatural, I mooched around. A passing lady told me about an offer on apples in the nearby shop. A man and a toddler went past, hand in hand, singing *The Wheels on the Bus*. So sweet.

I told myself what I'd experienced was only an overactive imagination. The hole was only a hole. The headache faded, and that was when I noticed a woman, wrapped in a long, green coat. She leant against a wall with elbows forward and one hand outstretched. I mistakenly thought she wore a cloak, but it couldn't have been, could it? Not in 2022. Cloaks went out with Sherlock Bones.

The headache returned with a vengeance. A bird swooped down. Witches Tipple! My adult part knew a bird could do no harm. My inner tiny kid was terrified, stifled, and panicked. Flapping, swooping, coming to eat you!

The woman must have sensed my presence because she turned towards me. I wish she'd had the eyes of a goat or a mouth like *Scream*, but to be honest, she was too far away to tell.

"Get lost," she said.

Rude. I hurried away just as the bird landed on her arm. I supposed it was a spectacular and interesting sight, but I couldn't care less. Bertha and I rushed back onto the canal path and sank gratefully next to an old guy wrapped up in a long scarf and woollen hat.

"Afternoon. Slow down! You all right?" he asked amicably.

"Hello. I'm Mave from the *Echo*. Can I interview you?"

I was shaken and disappointed I'd have nothing much to report to Lisa except a big hole and an obtuse woman in green. Looking back, my introduction was abrupt, perhaps even rude. The man (who I'm going to name Bill) didn't seem to notice. If he did, he was too polite to say. Actually, he was keen to talk and interested in the *Echo*. And, yes, he'd heard about the noise and claimed to know of its causes.

I soon forgot about the hole and the strange woman, although the headache didn't fully disappear. With birds trilling and a gentle breeze, it was difficult to imagine there could be anything wrong. A constant stream of parents and buggies, joggers and cyclists, and even a chap on a unicycle careered past.

Early on, I noticed something unexpected about Bill. He held no discernible aura. Very strange. He was kind, friendly, and yet absent. As if not there. Maybe I was tired. It was probably nothing.

As I said, Bill was eager to get going and didn't waste time with chit-chat. "What do you want to know, miss? I'd love to be in the papers."

I got out my recorder. "This noise everyone's talking about. Some say it's electrical. What do you think?"

Bill's old face lit up like a paper lantern. The pale beams

against his weathered skin made it appear etched onto ancient parchment. I imagined I could see his cheek bones, but it was maybe just a trick of the light.

He began in earnest, with eyes of far away. It was clear the events he described were clear and fresh in his mind.

"Go on," I urged.

"What people are talking about isn't a noise at all, but a haunting. Revenge, if you will. Anger don't die with people. It finds a place, and it waits. When times are right, it'll tiptoe back. It's a hungry, greedy thing."

I was surprised and taken aback at such eloquent wording. "Anger? Revenge? A *haunting*?"

Bill paused and grinned cheekily. "That's right. Oh, I know what you're thinking, ducks, and I don't blame you. Ghosts and ghouls—all rubbish. Mostly, I'd agree. Except, I've lived a long time, and by the end, you've seen a few things which don't make sense except by acknowledging the things out there—call it memories or echoes—from another time and place."

I was hooked. "I know what you mean. I've often thought I can catch a whiff of the past in some buildings. Schools, for instance. Community halls."

Bill nodded as if he wasn't surprised by what I'd said. "Yes. I can see you would, my ducks. Everything moves in circles, and nothing is new. People talk about the sound as if it's new, but I can promise it's been going on for hundreds of years. Long before the canal was here. When I was a kiddie, people called it 'her little joke'."

He uttered a rather sinister chuckle. I'm afraid an unprofessional shudder rippled across my coat.

Bill noticed and patted my arm. "Now then, miss, no

need for alarm. Back then, folks knew more; if you get my meaning. Not about dolphins, or books, or medicines. No, I don't mean those. They knew more about the 'other'. Things you can't see but are there just the same.

"A better question might be, why isn't the sound louder? Because it's about murder and death, you see. Of him and of her. They killed her. Stopped a love, and for what? Bigotry, ignorance, and hatred. Because she was poor."

My mouth fell open with shock. "Bloody hell, Bill."

"I'm getting away with myself, and I can see you're scared. Sorry, and please don't be afraid of me—I'm nought but an old man, and I mean no harm. Especially not to you."

I must admit, I'd been expecting him to talk of his family, maybe, or the council. Certainly not murder. "No, you go on. I'm fine! You're doing great!"

He rubbed his head. "It was long ago. When there were bargees coming and going, and this canal was a busy marketplace. Sometimes when it's windy, you can hear the callings between folks and the laughter of kiddies. Those things live in the bricks and curves of the canal. In its curves and structures, and the very timbre. Places have memories, and this one has plenty. Expect you'll hear, too, if you let yourself listen. This canal is in your bones, the same as it is in mine, my ducks."

*This canal is in your bones.* Maybe I should have asked how he knew. Like many local people, my ancestors were bargees. I didn't realise anyone but family members knew of it.

Bill rumbled on. "There was an Ellison town leader called Sidney Bradshaw. I forget which year. Ellison was a booming place then. Sidney had all the riches and power anyone could wish for, while others had nothing. It's the way of things. You were either born lucky, or you weren't. Nought to be done. The mayor's family had three children, and the oldest was a boy named Robert. You won't find anything about him in the museum, so don't bother. I expect his parents are there, grinning in their Sunday best and butter wouldn't melt."

Frankly, the world hadn't progressed. Inequality was still ingrained in our society. "Yeah. I wish the world was different."

At this point, Bill took my hand. Looking back, it should have seemed more awkward. "Robert wasn't like the other boys. Didn't notice the same things. Maybe he didn't care? His sweetheart wasn't some rich girl with clean nails and silly manners. Robert was friends with a bargee called Lilly Pryce. Always together, they were, chattering and singing, laughing and mucking about. For years, they were thick as thieves, and nobody thought much of it. I expect Robert's parents told him to make more appropriate friends. He wouldn't have cared less."

"Aww," I said, always a sucker for a soft story.

"I don't know when it happened. Does anyone? When a best friend becomes something else. Something better and more. It starts with a look, don't it? *You* know what I mean."

He grinned and nodded at me, cheeky bugger. I thought about our Lisa and blushed. "Mm. You could be right. Go on."

"I don't know how long they managed to keep it hidden. As long as they could, I expect. Sidney found out, and Lilly's family was told to go. Move off. Never come back here. Be gone! So. Robert and Lilly disappeared. Run away, you see. Couldn't stand to be parted, and why would they? Love won't be ordered about." His voice shook with emotion.

I was caught up by his passion and felt angry on Lilly and Robert's behalf. "That's sad. Why? I'll never understand people if I live to a hundred."

"Dogs barking and men braying. Hunted them down. Horrible. The mayor was an evil man. He wouldn't stop at nothing to get his own way. Robert was sent off to the army. He weren't seen round here again, so don't you go looking. Leave the dead alone.

"Rumour has it they buried Lilly under the disused tunnel. In a watery grave. I expect you saw the access tunnel the workers disturbed last month before the noise. You did? Those workers should never have started, so they shouldn't."

My eyes welled up, and I fished in my pocket for a tissue. "They killed her? Poor, poor, Lilly."

"In a way. Death wasn't the end, so don't you fret. Lilly and Robert didn't give up. They fought back in whatever way they could. Some say the noise is the ghost of poor Lilly, buried in that hole. Secrets deeper than graves and bones. The answer—the real one—is in your heart. But you know this already, my ducks."

Bill's words chilled me to the bone. Murder, young love, and ghosts!

On the ride home, all I could think about was the scratching noise and Bill's final chuckle.

"Her little joke. Ha ha ha."

## BLOG TWO

*Random fact of the day: my bike is named Bertha.*

Hello! This is Mave Kitten reporting for the Litten *Echo*. I'm amazed so many of you tuned in to listen to my first broadcast. 'Gasted with flab', as Mum would say. Hundreds and hundreds. Forty, at least. Lisa keeps saying it's down to me, but I think people are glad to hear about local news and things which affect us all. These days, our world is so fragmented. It's nice to bring people together.

Fess up time—I'm no journalist. I did a free course as a girl is all. I've always loved reading the papers. We all know how cruel the media is; I won't be though. My broadcasts will report. Nothing more. It's down to experts and residents to decide what's best for Ellison. Lisa agrees. I'll get better as I go.

Anyway, thank you from the bottom of my purple heart. Like all local newspapers, the *Echo* is on its last legs. I'll try my very best to keep on reporting, and hopefully, we can keep the *Echo* going for another year or two. Since my podcasts, Lisa's been much chattier, and things are looking up.

I relayed Bill's story with more than a dabble of nerves. He'd upset and unnerved me. I hadn't expected such depth of emotion. To the outside, he's just a nice old fella, but once he got talking, his was the spirit of a much younger and very passionate man. I forgot the time and date and could think only about the horror of the story, and of the poor girl they killed.

*Listen to this,*

*Too good to miss.*

An interesting thing. When Lisa and I started talking about Bill, my headache returned. "I can still hear it. That thing. Something has crawled inside me and is gnawing on a bone like a bone."

"Fuck a duck," Lisa said with her usual articulate flair. "It's one confused story, Mave. A lot doesn't smell right. Anyone would think Ellison was a hotspot for murder. We need to visit the museum."

We said goodbye to the office cat-cum-security guard and locked up. Like always, I left some treats and my cardy for her to snuggle. "Don't let anyone in, Penelope. There's a dear."

The museum is an old, decrepit building on the corner of Gauge Street. We wandered from room to room, looking for anything relevant. Have you visited? Lots of framed prints of men on horses and regal-looking dogs.

"Stuffed shirts and snobbery. Fuck's sake," Lisa said with an appreciation for art not often seen outside of le gay Paris.

Some rooms are laid out as historical reconstructions. I loved the old shop with scales and the pinafores you can try out for a laugh. We had a happy time until the volunteer told us frostily it was normally only children who partook.

"Why?" Lisa asked with a pinny tied round her head and a plastic cake in her hand. Why, indeed.

I could have spent all day playing. Her Majesty grew bored, so we entered the last room, a library of stained books of births and deaths. I had shimmied into a sad daydream about having and losing so many children when Lisa summoned me to her side.

"Mauve Mave, look!"

She'd found a list of Ellison's mayors, their families, and children. We followed the rows until finding a Sidney Bradshaw with three children and a wife. It was weird seeing his name in black and white. Proof of what Bill had said. I shivered and began to feel a tad weak. At the far edge of my hearing, the noise started up. *Shuffle, shuffle, scratch, scratch.*

"Might be getting a cold," I said.

The Lisanator gripped my shoulders suddenly and squeezed until I all but evaporated from the pressure.

"Lisa! Put me down?" I wheezed.

She became agitated and started jumping up and down. It was more than a little disconcerting, attached to her side as I was. Truthfully, I haven't had as much action in years. Not since Aggie Turner snogged me round the back of the gym when I was fourteen.

"Do you see it?" Lisa hissed.

Right then, a woman appeared at the doorway and told us it was time to close the museum. "You can come back tomorrow. If you must. Kindly put that woman down."

We staggered outside, laughing. Lisa dragged me round the corner of the building into a narrow alleyway, all the time checking to see if anyone was listening. Very cloak and daggers. Not like her at all. To be honest, it reminded me again of being a teenager and sneaking off maths for a crafty smoke with Aggie.

Lisa gripped me by the shoulders again and lunged. "Did you see? The answer's right there."

Her breath was warm and tickly. Though a surprise, the closeness wasn't unwelcome.

But I had no idea what she was on about. "Sidney and

his three children? Yeah. I'm starving. Do you want to go halves?"

My stomach gurgled like a drain. I needed soup! Butternut squash and ginger. Tomatoes and courgettes. Lisa would provide the bread. I might be shit at a lot of things, but soup wasn't one.

"There was no Robert. Sidney had *three girls*," Lisa hissed.

"Eh?" I said, still thinking of snogging round the back of the gym and of how nice Lisa's hair smelt. *Vanilla? Coconut? Mops? Soup?*

"Robert Bradshaw. He was a woman. Don't you see? It's your answer right there. The secret they're trying to conceal. Signed up to the army? My arse. I bet Lilly and 'Robert' did a runner and loved it up. Good for them! Let's hope they slit Sidney's neck."

Anyone would've been impressed at such Sherlockian deductions. Were official records of deaths and births ever wrong? And if so, it didn't explain why Ellison had succumbed to the scratching hounds of hell.

We hurried back to the office and then spent an enjoyable afternoon bickering. There was naught like a heated discussion, with soup, to get the brain ticking over.

By day's end, I'd go as far as saying we'd connected. Started looking at each other full-on. True, Lisa beat me at arm wrestling.

Between you and me, I let her win.

## BLOG THREE

*Random fact of the day: Lisa loves pickles and will defend them to the death.*

Thank you to everyone who called or sent emails! I'm blown away you want to know about Ellison and shocked you're enjoying my broadcasts. Please clarify—you're not my mum and aunty? LOL.

To answer the question about Bertha, the bike—I promise to include a photo in this week's edition of the *Echo*'s print. My baby is yellow and sturdy. Bought with redundancy money, and she's worth every penny. There hasn't been a week since when I haven't cycled out into the hills on a Sunday. Each time, something different. Shadows on leaves. Birdsong. Coughing sheep. As a gal who suffers from the stress monster, having a bike helps.

Aggie Turner—oh my god! It's so good to hear from you. Five kids and a tarantula? Email pictures, please.

Anyway, back to gritty journalism. After our trip to the museum, things turned a shade darker. The noise took root in my head and nothing would shake it. *Scratch, scratch, scratch.* I'd tried ginger, vinegar, painkillers, and a swig of Mum's rhubarb gin. It looked as if *the demon underground* knew about me and the *Echo*.

Maybe it wanted my attention? Or to spook and scare me off?

*Listen to this,*
*Too good to miss.*
According to residents who kindly called, the noise

transformed overnight from a hum into a roar. Some said they couldn't cope with it anymore and would move out unless the council took action.

Lisa remained unconvinced. "It's a ruse. You better get back down to Ellison and interview someone else. I would come, but there's this report to write."

I'd always been a fair-weather cyclist. "It's raining."

She gave me a look that could easily have curdled lard cake. Dutifully, I fed the office cat and then cycled to Ellison.

I'd done my research and found out where the descendants of the two families Bill mentioned live—Pryce and Bradshaw. Maybe they'd shed light on Bill's story? Explain the anomaly in the birth and death book?

I hated to leave Bertha unattended, but there was no choice. I padlocked her to the stand near the locks. Nosiness made me nip back into the area cordoned off by red tape. There was nobody about. Like last time, the pathway felt safe. Hah! It was what *I* thought.

*Looky-looky*. Behind the tape, the birds became silent, and the wind stilled. Uncanny. Unnatural. The whole place had an ecosystem all its own.

Anyways. It took a while to build the courage to walk to the edge of the hole. I kept looking behind and around, sure someone was watching. The hairs on my neck bristled worse than on a hedgehog. And *the noise*—I wouldn't know how to describe it. Shuffling, and scratching, and flapping. Not loud exactly. Resonating inside my head. Was I imagining things?

One cautious step at a time, I inched closer to the maw of hell. The world stopped.

It began in my right ear. A voice. Roared and shouted

and vibrated until I felt sick and weird and dizzy as a dandelion in the wind.

*Listen to this,*
*Too good to miss.*

What felt like a pair of hands suddenly shoved me from behind. I stumbled and almost went over the wall and down into the hole. My biking shoes saved my life—thank you, Bertha! One of the cleats got caught on the path.

By the time I scrambled back up and swivelled round, the track was empty and the noise gone. No footsteps. I'd imagined the whole thing.

Still, it was bloody freaky. I ran back onto the path, glad to feel wind and hear birds. Relieved not to be dead. I phoned Lisa and blabbed.

She was gratifyingly horrified and choked on a pickle. "The fuck! Someone pushed you? I'll kill them. Get back to the office!"

I rather enjoyed the rage in her voice. It'd been a long time since anyone—especially a gorgeous, buff woman—jumped to my defence. "I imagined it. Nobody was there."

"Mave!"

"I'm on the street now and there are loads of people about. Stop worrying." *Please don't*, I thought. *Please don't stop.*

Eventually, I found the house listed as belonging to Mrs Pryce. A polite woman opened the door and asked me in. She gave me cherry cake and tea.

She hadn't heard of the podcasts and was, indeed, a bargee. She insisted I use her proper name on the recording and gave me full permission to repeat the story she told me. (Thanks again, Mrs Pryce!)

Her aura was glowing and light. Translucent. Sunshine underneath clouds. Warmth behind laughter. I sensed kindness and honesty. Although the interview didn't take long, she made me welcome.

"I don't know much of the story about the buried body, but I shouldn't think it's anything to do with the noise," she said. "More likely to be power grids. The workers have been poking about. It never does any good to go looking into the past."

I wanted to put her at ease. "Just tell me your thoughts about the noise and the area. It'd be great!"

She sipped at a cup of tea. At first, she spoke haltingly, but she soon got into the swing.

"I come from a family of bargees, though I was born in this house. My dad left the barges when he was young and would only talk about it once he'd been to the pub. Not shame. Far from it. Those memories made him yearn for a life not possible these days."

I knew exactly what she meant because some of my relatives were the same. We understood how hard it must've been to live on a flimsy barge. Didn't stop us missing our roots and the community we once shared. "True. It's a long time ago."

"Nowadays, the kids stay in school, the way it should be. Back when my dad was a nipper, you went to work at fourteen and before, if you could get away with it. Each morning, him and his sister went to work in the town and then came back to the canal. You earned what money you could, and it kept your family in food. It's how it was."

She kept on flickering looks at me. I guessed she was building up to saying something important, and I tried to reassure her.

"You're doing great! And the cake is gorgeous. What do you know about Bill? Have you heard of Robert and Lilly?"

She warmed and offered me more. "Help yourself. Bill? Never met him, though I've heard of Robert and Lilly. It happened long before my time. I don't know much about them. In my opinion, you should stop wasting your time, my dear, and go and look for a different story. There's no ghost or any such nonsense. Why do people always want more than the truth?"

Mouth filled with plump fruit, I probably would've agreed to anything. "Yeah. I know what you mean."

"Here. Take some cake with you. I'm sorry I haven't got anything more. Would you like to see the ducks? There are some mandarins. Very beautiful."

I left with a big chunk of cake. Who do you think ate it, along with more pickles? It wasn't Penelope!

*Random fact of the day: Lisa bought a mop!*

Hello, this is Mave Kitten reporting from the *Echo*. Once again, thank you from the bottom of my purple heart for listening in! According to our Lisa, we've had two hundred likes and have secured funding for another year. Two hundred people interested in what I say? Literally more people than I've spoken with my whole life. When I asked Lisa if two hundred was an exaggeration, she offered me a pickle. Say no more.

*Listen to this,*
*Too good to miss.*

More news. The council finally rang to say work on the tow path wasn't going well. Expensive equipment had been stolen. They couldn't find construction workers, and employment agencies wouldn't help. One of the previous workers claimed he caught flu from the hole, and another insisted the noise caused genital warts.

Yes, I admit Lisa and I did have a little laugh at that one.

The council wanted to help Litten, but admitted they didn't know what was causing the noise. They believed someone was tampering with their efforts.

Exciting, no?

Of course, after the 'shove' near the hole, Lisa demanded a full and vigorous health and safety discussion. It lasted all of five minutes and consisted mainly of some eying up and blushing from my end. Not sure our Lisa's a blusher.

"Just be careful. You're doing so well, Mauve Mave.

When we did the interview, I knew you were the one," she said.

"Aw," I said, donut dipped in sugar.

A sizzling second commenced. *She* started vigorously dry mopping the floor, and *I* hammered random letters on the laptop. It was surprising I didn't knock the keyboard into China.

"Why is everyone telling you to stop investigating? It's suspicious, and I won't have it. Never be told no," Lisa finally said very firmly.

I enjoyed the *rushy-roily* sensations and tried not to melt into the cat. Penelope wouldn't appreciate it and neither would Lisa, even though we'd bought a super mop with a rotating head.

"What do you mean?"

"Bill told you to stop poking, and so did Mrs Pryce. Even bird woman. Why? You'd think they might encourage you to get to the bottom of the noise. I can understand them not wanting the council round, but not my Mave. It's not right."

*My Mave.*

I hid the blush by crossing my eyes and humming like a bee. "*Bzz*. True. And it's why I have to keep looking. *Bzz*. And for the extra funding."

"We should tell the police about the shove. If not the army. Maybe the queen?" Lisa said.

I hid the blush by being horsey. "Neigh! I'll give Her Majesty a ring, shall I? Neigh. Nobody was there. I imagined it. Stop worrying." *Really, don't.*

Lisa guffawed. "Why are you making that noise? You sound like my boiler."

We reached a compromise whereby I'd call once I

reached Ellison. Any sniff of trouble, Lisa would ring the police, or possibly the prime minister.

Once I'd stopped neighing, Lisa pretended to take notes. "Who are you interviewing today?"

"Thought I'd try Iris Bradshaw and the council workers. They've asked for an interview. Seems Ellison is dying to get in on the action."

Lisa narrowed her eyes. "Sounds like shit to me. I don't think you should go on your own. If you wait till tomorrow? I would come today, but the funders are due, and we can't miss them."

"What do you mean 'it's shit'? It's a good thing people want us to investigate, isn't it?"

Our Lisa wasn't convinced. "It's nice you think the best of people."

It took a bit of flattery, but in the end, the boss agreed.

Bertha and I set off back to Ellison like *Knight Rider* without the leather, sex appeal, or hairdo. Still, with the wind behind us and the heat of one too many pickles, we were gorgeous, just the same.

Once in Ellison, I locked Bertha to the stand. I fought the urge to visit the canal path, even though council workers were there, and the towpath was crowded.

Iris Bradshaw's house was easy to find and impressively massive, with a large garden and space for several cars. I wiped my hands clean before knocking.

She appeared suddenly, ushered me inside, and checked to see if the neighbours were watching. "I've been expecting you."

I grinned like a scary doll. "Hello."

She jumped and twitched. "You can go ahead and interview me, though I'll not be of much use. I don't know anything."

I got out my recorder and hoped she'd calm down. "What are your thoughts about the noise?"

She pulled a face as sour as a lemon. "Awful. Here at the edge of the cul-de-sac, we don't get it as bad as the other streets, but it's started to bother us too."

I tried to win her over with a show of empathy. "Too bad. Have you heard the rumours about ghosts?"

"No such thing. We all know what's caused it. Pylons, up on the hill. They built them about four years ago. I expect it's electricity. It builds and builds and then—*bam*! An explosion, and it's us who have to suffer."

I gulped and tried to hide my disappointment. "Pylons?"

She chuckled rather wickedly. "Sorry. If I were you, my ducks, I'd go on up the hill and have a look-see. The whole area hums with the electric. I suppose it gets underground. One of the council electricians told me what we hear is an outpouring of natural power such as thunder and lightning. It's all it is, ducks. No need to listen to any silly gossip."

I glanced aside at the rows of framed photos lining her shelves. "But what about your uncle Sidney?"

Iris shook her head as if to indicate she couldn't hear me. "What?"

"Uncle," I said.

"You want to know about my uncle? Well, all right, but I've got things to do, and my family are nothing to do with the noise. Anyone who says so needs a thick ear. Has anyone said so? Have they? What did they say? Nothing much?

Good, then. I don't want to have to go visiting with my poison."

To my horror, I laughed. (Unprofessional, I know.) "No, you don't."

"I've heard from my grandma, Sidney was a cold man. She and her sister were round the house a lot as kids. All they got from him was shouting. Out at work all day, then down the pub every night. Not that his wife minded! She was glad when he wasn't around, and it's the truth."

I became confused and interrupted. "Grandfather? I thought Sidney was your uncle? Eh? Which was it?"

Iris ignored me. "It was a shock when it all blew up. After what happened. Well. Things carried on. Life's just so. Things were different, yes."

"What happened to Sidney after the murder? Did he get into trouble with the police?"

"What? Did Sidney get in trouble for what he did to Robert and Lilly? Well, no, love. No, he didn't. That I know of, anyway. How could he? He wasn't seen after the night Robert went missing."

I was so shocked; I dropped the recorder. "Shit."

Iris giggled as well as a schoolgirl. "Oh, now. I can see you're shocked. Have I spoken out of turn? I assumed someone had already told you. They haven't? I should've shut my trap. I don't know where he went, and I don't care. It was a long time ago. Everyone assumed he'd joined up, like Robert." Her eyes filled with tears.

I felt terrible and wished heartily I'd never applied for the bloody job at the *Echo*. "Are you all right, Iris? I shouldn't have come round here stirring things up. I'm sorry."

She smiled kindly. "It's not you. Go and look at the pylons, ducks. And no need to be sad for Lilly and Robert. I tell you, they're happy. True love won't be told no."

She pushed me out of the door and then locked it behind me. She was super nervous, and it rubbed off on me. Her aura was skittish and changeable, and it made me say stupid things. Was she trying to get rid of me? Or to keep me from finding out more?

## BLOG FIVE

*Random fact of the day: a hedgehog named Twinkletoes visits our garden every night!*

Hello! This is Mave Kitten reporting for the *Echo*. I'm bowled over by your support. Our engagement figures have more than tripled. I know we started on a low, but still. I couldn't be more pleased. Thank you for listening in and for all the encouraging emails.

To the woman who left a voicemail singing 'Bat out of Hell', all I can say is thank you. You have an awesome, gravelly voice! Better than Mr Kipling. On par with Count Dracula.

After Iris, I felt awful. Still do. This journalism lark isn't a game. Real people are involved. Sometimes, journalists forget, even fake ones. If Iris is listening, I want to apologise and thank you for teaching me this important lesson, which I won't forget. I don't judge what people say or what happened. There's enough sorrow in the world without me adding to it.

Dear listener, I can't sleep. Every time I close my eyes, the awful noise comes back. Scratching and scrabbling. Urgh! All around and inside me. When I asked my parents if they'd heard it, they said no. What can this mean? Am I losing the plot? Has the 'ghost' followed me home? There's a constant ringing in my ears.

My belief is whatever has caused this phenomenon is inviting me to get to the bottom of it. Poking, if you like. Tapping into my antennae and actively demanding I go after it.

Lisa and I threw soft darts at the Velcro board. She won. "One hundred and eighty! Tell me about it?"

"What?"

"Being an empath. It's what they call it, don't they?"

I possessed no special powers. Though I wouldn't have minded! Hearing our Lisa—the most straightforward person on this planet—say *that word* almost caused my purple hair to fall out. I was torn between wanting to agree and being worried I'd scare her off. Like always, the conundrum left me in a chaotic place Dad calls 'Maveland'.

"Urgh. I don't know if it's exactly. But. Urgh. Mm."

She raised her eyebrows at my articulate purple self, swivelled across on the one good chair we owned, with the grace of a heron. "Calm down. You're all right, you."

It was the best thing anyone had ever said to me, and not least because *she said it*. The Lisanator. Lisa Blonde. Like the beer—big, strong, and got a kick. Her words, not mine.

"Aw. Thanks," I said. "So are you."

Auras were exchanged. Just as swiftly, she swivelled back to her safe place while I tapped out a furious paragraph of incoherent nonsense.

Couldn't I have asked her on a date? Pushed things along a little? And the answer was *noooooooo*. If things were going to happen, they would, according to Dad's philosophy.

After a bit, Lisa opened the pickles and the exciting-awkward-brimming atmosphere disappeared.

"What's clear is there's a lot of covering up at Ellison," Lisa said. "Robert being female. Sidney Bradshaw's disappearance. Poor Iris's blunders. I'd hazard a guess Robert and Lilly are still alive. But none of it explains the noise."

I rubbed my ear. "We need an unbiased view. Today, I'll talk to the council. They've left two more messages. I was so worn out after Iris I went straight home. Do you hear scratching?"

Lisa rubbed at her ear. "No scratching, but I've got an earache."

She came to the bike stand and watched me attach my mirrors and check the lights. When she gave Bertha a loving pat, my heart lurched.

"Aw," I said, donut-dipped-in-sugar stupid.

"Switch your phone on. Call me regularly."

With windy sunshine and Lisa euphoria, my head cleared, and the noise faded. Being on Bertha was invigorating. By the time we reached Ellison, I was raring to go and even thought to have a peep down the hole.

I locked up and hurried towards the red tape and two workers. One dug while the other tapped at pipes. He laughed constantly. To tell you the truth, it was a bit annoying. They saw me coming and nudged each other.

"It's the paparazzi. I'm Julie, and this is Tony," the woman said.

The man laughed.

"Sorry about him," Julie said.

But they were okay. (Dear listener, I know what you're thinking and the answer is yes. I did indeed peer into the hole.) But with Julie and Tony around, nothing happened. And yet...my stupid heart started fluttering, and the bloody scrabbling came back. Even through Tony's braying.

Scratching, always scratching.

"Can't you hear it?" I asked.

"Rats," Julie said. "Go ahead. Ask whatever you want."

I brought out my recorder and tried not to wince at Tony, who insisted on doing handstands against the well. "Tell me what you think is the problem."

Julie slapped Tony around the head until he stopped. "You can fuck off with your stories of ghosts. We haven't seen nothing, though it's dismal work down here. In my opinion, it's all rubbish made up by locals wanting this stretch of the canal listed as a place of historical importance. Hasn't anyone mentioned it? There's a petition and group. If successful, a big pot of funding. They're nasty buggers too. We think it's down to them the other workers have refused to come back."

I'd never seen or heard of the petition and couldn't believe the hole was historically important. "Really?"

Julie nodded vigorously. "I'm an engineer of canals and dams. Could be a blockage which forces refuse and rubbish back up into the streams which feed in here from the river. In turn, it creates a lot of trouble for the fish and other river creatures."

I tried to concentrate on Julie rather than Tony, who crammed two chocolate bars up his nostrils. "But why would it cause a noise?"

Julie handed me a map of the pipes and systems beneath the canal. "Why? Well, it could do. If, say, the underground pipes are blocked and interfering with the electricity. I've seen stranger things. This area hasn't been excavated for hundreds of years."

I was genuinely fascinated by the map and leaned across to look. "Wow."

Julie pointed at lines and grids. "Can you see how the

sewage and piping lead into a bowl? Looks like an amphi-theatre, doesn't it? It's quite possible the noise comes from the fermenting effect. Bubbles and fizzes. Who knows? Maybe it's what causes the noise. Imagine if you increased the volume of a glass of freshly poured lemonade. How loud would it be?"

I thought of volcanoes. "I don't know. I was crap at science. I failed my exams three times."

Julie pulled a face at Tony, who laughed at my admission. "It'll be something technical, for sure. Intensive work, and the canal path will have to be closed off for months. The cost would be astronomical. It's why locals want us gone."

I thrust the recorder forward, ready for my killer question. "And you've no doubts?"

"None whatsoever. I've heard the rumours and stories. Ghosts and dungeons. Nothing new. You'd be surprised how many spooky tales we hear doing this job. People are territorial. In my opinion and experience, there's nothing amiss in Ellison except some forceful residents. If I were you, I'd fuck off home and forget about it, love. Ghosts, my arse."

At this point, the scrabbling and earache got so bad, I had to take painkillers.

*Random fact of the day: the Echo senior is a cat called Penelope Sardine. She's a semi-stray, and our Lisa's scared of her.*

Hello! This is Mave Kitten reporting for the Litten *Echo*. Thank you forever for the support. I've never been one of the in-crowd. So honestly, I'm bowled over.

To the man who sent a recording of *The Four Seasons* using nothing but a saucepan and wooden spoon, thank you. Talent such as yours makes our species the colourful thing it is. And yes, you should certainly try for *The X Factor*.

And to the lady who can make shadow vampires from her toes—so cool! Lisa and I have had a go, but yours are way better.

I'm in a quandary. After the last trip to the canal, I don't know what to think. Am I and the residents of Ellison experiencing a group hallucination? Can the noise be explained away by engineering theories?

Lisa gazed longingly at her comfy chair, currently occupied by Penelope Sardine. "Totally to both."

Her sureness was irritating, and I wasn't going to stand for it. "There's more to it. Like the bird woman and the contradictory warnings. Why would people try to scare me off unless they're hiding something?"

Technology couldn't be responsible for the dread which seized my heart every time I was near the hole. There was more to life than bricks and facts—fact. I tapped into things not visible, even when I didn't want to. Some people drained me. My blood dripped away until only skin and bone were left. Why? My theory was they carried so much sadness it stole my own light.

I could sense from an email when the sender wasn't bothered. How? I was born so. Intuition, or empath, or whatever.

Something horrible and sinister happened at the hole, and the repercussions or aftershocks were still being felt. While I'd been messing around with interviews and visits, an entity was creeping up and getting closer and closer. A presence from the darkness.

Why didn't I say this to Lisa?

Because, dear listener, of the oldest reason in the book. I didn't want her to think I was an oddball, or to stop her from looking at me *in that way*. Words such as 'entity' weren't heard in Litten. She'd think me a drill bit.

Her Highness leapt suddenly and landed heavily on her swivel seat, which Penelope Sardine had vacated. "We'll find out soon enough. Julie said they were close to the bottom of the hole. Who's left to interview?"

I took a gulp before answering. "The bird woman."

Lisa laughed and threw an aeroplane bird made from paper. "Sheryl Crow. Right. I'll come with you. I could do with some exercise."

"But yours is a motorbike. Hardly exercise," I pointed out.

Lisa donned her leather trousers.

I'll repeat it, shall I?

*Lisa donned her leather trousers.*

I dissolved into little, thrilled pieces.

Before we set off, Penelope Sardine stalked to the door

and stood on guard. Wouldn't let us leave. When Lisa tried to sneak past, our kitty let out a howl that could've woken the dead.

*Listen to this,*
*Too good to miss.*

It wasn't typical Penelope behaviour. What she loved best was to bully Lisa off her chair and then snooze, with frequent snacks. She climbed in and out of the broken window at will, and didn't take much notice of either of us.

I bent down and tried to stroke her. "What is it, puss? What are you trying to say? Are we in danger?"

"She's an ungrateful beastie. Offer the pricey treats. Sack under the window," Lisa said.

My eyebrows shot up into my purple hair and traversed my head. "The *pricey* ones? A whole sack? But you said?"

Lisa shrugged sheepishly and offered—threw—Penelope some treats. "No, I didn't. You imagined it."

When the cat grudgingly moved, we bolted through the door like the hounds of hell were after us.

"Bit odd," I said.

Lisa argued the walk to the bike stand could be counted as exercise. I wasn't about to argue. Not with those leather trousers.

"You set off. I'll follow," she said.

Once on Bertha, I put on a bit of a spurt. Showing off to the leathered hottie riding behind. Who wouldn't?

Once at Ellison, we locked Bertha to Lisa's motorbike.

"Aw," I said, donut-sugar.

I led the boss down to the canal, feeling absurdly as though it belonged to me. With pride, I pointed out the landmarks. "And here's where I interviewed Bill."

We played around, saying which duck we most resembled. She chose a mallard and I, the mandarin. She tickled me under the chin with a branch, and I giggled like a kid's toy. The sun came out, and some joggers said hello. We sat on a bench. Close to her, I was ten years younger than before. At least, it was how it seemed.

Sadly, the fun didn't last. My headache soon started up, and the noise grew louder. *Scratch, scratch, scratch.* I leant against Lisa's reassuringly sturdy shoulders and wished she'd put an arm around me. "Do you hear it? It's louder down here. I wish I knew what it was."

"Not a thing. Just a vague headache."

From the corner of my eye, something green moved and then disappeared into the bushes lining the canal. I shaded my eyes with a hand. "Did you see her? It's the woman and the bird."

"Where?"

We rushed down the towpath in the direction of the hole, looking from left to right. Dense trees and bushes line the patch of canal, so it's possible she could've slipped behind the foliage.

The woman was near the locks, on the other side of the water. With the sun behind, her green coat lit up like a lantern.

Mindful of the bird, I kept close to Lisa's side. "Excuse me! Can we have a word!"

"Who're you shouting at?" Lisa asked.

By the time we arrived at the barriers and crossed the bridge, the woman had vanished.

Frustrated, I kicked at the wall. "Bugger! We missed her."

Lisa placed a hand on my forehead. "There's nobody, Mauve Mave. You've a temperature. Are you coming down with something?"

Disappointed and confused, I pushed her hand away. "I saw her. Don't you believe me?"

She didn't answer. We trailed over to the hole, me scuffing at the pavement and Lisa bristling with concern or irritation. I was too headachy to know the difference.

Julie was packing up the barriers and placing them into crates. "You again? We're off. Done all we can. There's nothing here but imagination. Tomorrow, we'll collect the last of the equipment."

"But what about the noise? You can't just leave," I said.

Julie laughed. "What noise? I never heard no noise except Tony. You should get off now and investigate something real."

Determined to show Lisa I hadn't been making it all up, I led her over to the hole and made her look down. "Well? Don't you feel it?"

Strangely enough, even I couldn't sense anything. No fear or flapping, and no interviews. I suppose I should've been glad. The residents of Ellison certainly would be.

Lisa placed my arm firmly through hers, and we wandered back to the bikes. "It's over. The end."

She fiddled with my lights more than was necessary. Bike lights, not the other—more exciting—kind of lights. By then, I'd started to feel woozy. Sick, fuzzy, and misty. Not right. I lost a bit of time.

...

...

I'd never seen Lisa so worried. "Mave? Are you all right?

Talk to me?"

"Yeah," I said.

"Do you want to? For a drink? Go. With me, that is. Are you well enough? Do you?" Lisa said in a rushed flurry. Blonde, like the beer—big, strong, and got a kick. Her words, not mine.

Dear listener, I did. I really, really wanted to. But my stomach was churning and my poor head was in bits.

About then, I threw up. The afternoon ended with a bottle of water and a slow pedal home, followed by Lisa on the motorbike. I got into bed, shaking and dizzy, and felt as if the flu had got me.

"Urgh. Must have been my lunch."

I closed my eyes, and the scratching took over. Shut me in, locked up forever.

...

...

*Random fact of the day: This is a live recording. Woohoo. Didn't expect that, did you, dear listener? My head's banging like a horse with a drum, and things are kind of fuzzy...my phone signal's low.*

I dunno...what's going...it's six o'clock, and I'm on the canal path. There's enough light to make it to the hole. Just about.

...

Why am I here? A really good question. I got home and went to bed. Woke up again.

Had a genius idea!

How marvellous it would be to go down to Ellison and broadcast a live show.

And here I am.

Am I scared? I don't know. I mean, it's creepy and quiet, yeah. No different to the toilets in the King's Arms really, ha ha.

I want to have one last look before they seal the hole. I'll know I did everything I can. 'Mauve Mave's persistent' is what nobody says.

My phone keeps going dead.

...

I'm walking along the path towards the hole. There's no one about, which is odd. The water's dark and still and looks solid as coal. Do fish sleep? Can you hear the owl? My signal's in and out.

...

I'm not scared or alone. Bill's here, just as I dreamt.

Funny, that. I'd forgotten the dream until now. Standing by the oak tree. I remember now; it's where he was in my dream.

He's not pleased. "Whatever are you doing here? I don't know, I'm sure. It's not too late to go home. I'll walk you to your lady. She's a good one, and you'll be safe with her."

"Do you think so? I bought her with redundancy money. Everyone said she was a waste of money."

"I don't mean the bike."

Dad said I'd never do it. Ride a bike. Not with my lack of coordination.

"Miss. You need to get home, now."

I want to stop and talk. He's a nice old fella even though he's... My phone signal is low...

...

...

Dear listener, I'm at the hole. It's quite dark. I won't stay. A quick look, and then I'll be gone.

I had to feel by touch. Okay, I'm at the low wall. It's—

...

I'm going to hold my phone into the hole so you can hear what I can.

Do you hear? *Scratch, scratch, scratch*. So horrible! It's loud and getting closer.

What's at the bottom? I'm sure I've never seen it before. Is it a coat? I'm leaning over the wall and holding my phone inside to take a photo.

...

Argh! Help me!

...

Down.

...

It's such a long way, and I'm fading in and out.

...

Shit! Dear listener. In the hole. I've gone down.

...

It'll be all right. Be all right. I fell through a long way. To the bottom. There's a false bottom, and I fell through. Twisted my ankle. It's agony. I can't... It's so dark down here, and my phone's almost gone. I fell through and then fell, and fell. I can't move. I'm at the bottom, and there's not much room. I'm squashed up into a ball, and my leg's gone backwards.

...

The scratching. Flapping. Beating my ears; flapping, always flapping. Get away! Get away. A million of them flapping at my face. Been locked up so long, so long, and now they're free.

...

I'm going to call Lisa if my phone...

...

There's a door! It's a door. I've kicked it backwards, and it collapsed. I think there's a tunnel under the canal. Scratching! I can't move, and it's coming.

...

Argh! Get away from me, get away, get away, fuck you, get back.

...

A skeleton.

...

Help me. Help me. Help me.

...

...

Hands on my face. Kisses. She's got ropes and a plastic thing.

"Blonde," I say.

"Like the beer."

...

...

*Random fact of the day: fucking, fuck, fuck!*

Lisa Blonde here, reporting for the *Echo*. From Mave's chair because Penelope Sardine's taken mine. Blonde, like the beer—big, strong, and got a kick. My words, not Mave's.

I've left her in Litten Royal Hospital. She'll be okay. A broken ankle and concussion. Poor Mave! The foulest night of my life. I never want to be so powerless again. I guess you've been as worried as me. I'm going to try to explain what happened, but I don't promise to be as good as Mave. Or as gorgeous, and clever, and funny, and sweet. Nobody could.

When she called, I was already packing up my climbing equipment. Don't ask me why. Fuck knows. My Mave needed me! I can't explain any of it. Work it out for yourselves.

I rode the canal path on my bike faster than greased lightning. I don't believe in ghosts, or premonitions. How can I explain a bird which kept flapping and hooting and wouldn't let me stop? An owl. I think it was an owl. It led me to the hole, and then I called the team at Mountain Rescue, where I do voluntary work on the weekends.

Sorry. I know I'm not reporting very well.

I heard her calling my name. Not fireworks at Hyde Park or the Northern Lights. Mave Kitten calling *for me*. In my fifty-five years, I've *never*. What a waste.

Sorry. I'll start again.

I didn't wait for the rescue team, though it's protocol.

Just strapped up and climbed down. It was a long way and stank like the bowels of the earth. Of poison and death and fear. I kept going, driven by the thought Mave was alone.

I kept shouting. "I'm coming! Just wait. I'm coming!" I didn't know if she heard or if she was alive because she'd gone silent.

Somehow, I got to the bottom. My Mave was a mess! She'd crawled into a tunnel and broken up this filthy, old board. When she said my name, every shitty thing that ever happened in life was worth it. Because it turned me into a tough bastard who'd got to her in time.

"Lisa Blonde. Like the beer—big, strong, and got a kick. Blonde and lovely," she said.

Bless her; she was out of it. Pain, I expected. Fuck knows how we got back up the rope. I should've waited for the team! It took everything I'd got. Tears and sweat and desperation. Poor Mave was crying and screaming, and it broke me I couldn't stop her pain.

"Hold on, Mave," I kept saying. "Hold on."

Something gave me strength. The climb should have been impossible for one person. I saw a woman in green, pushing us upwards.

By the time we reached the top, there were sirens and helpers and a stretcher. They whipped Mave off, and the police took me to the hospital. I don't know what I told them, or if anything made sense.

Mave's mum ushered me into a little room and made me tell her. I was too knackered to make stuff up. She listened and nodded and hugged me and said her own mum had been the same way.

"Mave's a hearer. As was her granny."

Heck!

## BLOG NINE

*Random fact of the day: Please donate any spare change you have to the voluntary Mountain Rescue team at Litten. Thanks!*

Hello! This is Mave Kitten reporting for the *Echo* from a hospital bed. Thank you for the flowers and gifts and well wishes. I'm gobsmacked so many of you care. It makes me cry. I'm sorry I worried you. When I made the live broadcast, I honestly thought I'd be home in half an hour, and it would be the end.

I'm trying to work out all that's happened. The council and the police are down at the canal path today, and the whole area has been cordoned off. Sorry residents, but it's for the best. There's a skeleton, after all. Whoever's been in the hole all these years needs to be freed.

The doctor says I've got two visitors, so I'll switch off now and do another broadcast later.

## BLOG TEN

*Random fact of the day: hospital gowns don't cover your modesty!*

Hello! This is Mave Kitten reporting for the *Echo*. I'm still in hospital and propped up with fluffy cushions and a huge, polar bear teddy. I've been inundated with flowers and prezzies, so thank you a million. I promise I'm getting better. Once I can get around on the crutches, it'll be fine, and they'll let me go home.

To the lady who sent a knitted purple skeleton, thank you. It's the most adorable thing ever. And to the man who posted the dog tooth necklace, I really don't know what to say. How cute.

Dear listener, you want to know about the noise. I think I've worked out what's been happening, but you'll have to bear with me. It's not simple.

We're dealing with at least two stories. Linked, of course, and yet separated by hundreds of years. The first, and most recent, is of Roberta and Lilly. They've given me full permission to broadcast what they know and have spoken with the police.

They came to visit me yesterday. Beautiful women. Funny, wise, and kind. They've adopted five children and showed me the photos. Grandchildren too.

I recognised them as soon as they came into my room. Lilly and Roberta. I'm so happy they're alive and well. After being down the hole, I couldn't have coped if Lilly had ended her days there.

To be honest, Lilly and Roberta are both so gorgeous, I could have talked with them all night. We chatted about things close to our hearts.

When Roberta asked me to record her, I didn't think it was a good idea. "Are you sure?"

To ensure their safety and be respectful of the investigation, we've changed some details.

Roberta nodded and took Lilly's hand. "Oh, yes. It's stuck in my memory as if it happened yesterday. Sidney, my dad, chased us onto the towpath. We were terrified. I held Lilly's hand tight, and she held mine. No angry man was going to ever come between us, especially not that old bastard."

She stopped to kiss Lilly, and then, they both kissed me. So lovely!

"Go on," Lilly said.

Roberta took a deep breath. "We ran. I remember thinking if we could get as far as Banton—the next town—we could find work and a place to stay. Mum had given me all the money she had, so I knew we'd be all right. The plan was to get established and then let Mum know so she could come and bring my sisters with her."

"You must've been so scared," I said.

"We were! Scared, but also determined. Young, and in love. What's stronger? We ran and ran. Obviously, the bargees knew me, and when they saw us, I suppose they guessed the reasons why. Maybe they saw Sidney? He was a big bleeder with a red, puffed-up face and a filthy tongue. He was no father to me or my sisters."

I sipped some water and cuddled the polar bear teddy. "He sounds horrible."

Roberta nodded. "Some bargees joined in the chase. All the way to the locks. Honestly, I don't know if what happened was planned. I don't see how it could have been. No one knew what was going to happen. If we did, we'd still have done it. It's the truth, and you can put me in prison for it for all I care."

As Roberta spoke, the strength she had showed all those years ago was clear. Such horrors she and Lilly had faced. Yet, they hadn't lost their decency or glow.

"There we were. Two girls running, and Sidney coming after. A lot of shouting and swearing, and the light was fading fast. It was the time of year when it seems it's still summer, but winter's fast on your heels.

"I didn't know about the well. It was hidden by bushes and scrub. When Lilly's dad thrust aside the branches and told us to hide behind the low wall, we did as he said."

She paused to hug Lilly.

"It happened very quickly, like they say on the crime shows. One minute, me and Lilly were crouching down and trying not to breathe. The next, Sidney scrambled over the wall. He slipped and went down into the well. We shouted, but there was no answer. One of the bargees brought ladders and rope and climbed down. Sidney was dead."

The room became silent and cool.

"It was an accident, and nobody was sorry. If Sidney had lived, he'd have made our lives a misery. Old bastard. Gah. All I felt was relief. I remember saying thank you, thank you, over and over."

"I'm not surprised," I muttered.

"The bargees attached a false floor so Sidney wouldn't be found. They made sure to nail the lid of the well too. Later on, Mum spread a rumour Sidney and I—as Robert—joined the army. Nobody questioned it. Litten protected us with a web of lies. I'll be forever grateful."

"They were good to us," Lilly said. "People are so unkind about bargees, and travellers. They showed us kindness and empathy."

The three of us shared another lasting hug.

"Lilly and I moved to Banton. We were, and are, happy. Our community covered our tracks. Expect you've met my aunty who works at the museum? I know you interviewed Mrs Pryce and another aunty, Iris Bradshaw. Good people, all. Litten saved us, and that's the truth. Rich or poor. It doesn't matter. There are good people, and there are bad. Some won't condone hate and bigotry, even when it's the law. Sidney was a poor husband and a worse father. He got what he deserved."

When Lilly and Roberta left the ward, I knew I'd met new friends I'd love forever.

## Blog eleven


*Random fact of the day: Lisa's wearing the green wig!*

Hello! This is Mave Kitten, reporting for the *Echo* from home. I'm overwhelmed by the gifts and flowers. I didn't know it was possible to fit so many into one room. Thank you so much! Please give yourselves a sticky kiss from me, and know you've made me very happy.

The man who sent the eighty-year-old unopened tin of cat food—thank you. It's truly amazing. Truly. 'Mazing.

The woman who sent the crate of pickles—you rock! Seriously. I've never seen our Lisa so happy.

*Listen to this,*
*Too good to miss.*

The best news of all is the noise has stopped. I expect you've heard by now the police have finished with their investigations and have exhumed the whole area. It's been in the media, so I guess I'm allowed to report what we know and what we can only surmise. This will never be a case with solid conclusions. Maybe it's a good thing? What do you think?

As always, I'll lay the facts bare, and the rest is up to you. I'm happy the sound has gone and delighted Lilly and Roberta are safe and well. They've invited Lisa and me round for tea next week. I'm so excited!

The ending of the noise coincided with a few key events. The completion of the work at the pylon station. Maybe the problems were down to electricity, after all? Maybe the scratching and booming had nothing to do with the hole at

Ellison or the ghost of Annie?

Ellison has been a crime scene, and I expect you're sick of the fuss. Specialist police excavated the well. They found Sidney's skeleton. I landed on it as I fell. Urgh. They dug into the passageway, revealed when I kicked away the board. Behind lay a tunnel which led all the way under the canal into a chamber.

This is where the going gets seriously sinister. Dear listener, make sure you've got a cat to snuggle and a strong hand to grip. I've got Lisa's.

The chamber had long ago been padlocked shut. Inside, they found the ancient remains of a man. The walls were lined with scratch marks where he'd tried to claw his way out. Double urgh. Triple *eee*.

They also investigated the old rhyme about Annie, but couldn't find much. It's been too long. Records from the time are patchy. An old man came forward and showed workers a gravestone with the inscription:

*Annie,*

*Daughter to John and Faith, and wife to Timothy. She loved birds and always liked her little game.*

Julie was right. The tunnel eventually led to a bowl-shaped area. As she said, it amplified the sounds of fermentation and water. The specialists have cleared out the tunnels and swept the pipes and sewers.

Could it be the noise was a combination of factors? Faulty pylons on the hill, along with gigantic fermentations under the canal? Or an echo of the ghostly woman in green? Angry because workers had disturbed her husband, buried for bad behaviour. Maybe it wasn't time to let him free, and she was warning me off? Perhaps she deemed him naughty enough as to warrant a few hundred more years locked under the canal?

*Scratch, scratch.*

Perhaps the spookiest thing of all is the first person I interviewed—Bill—seems to have vanished without a trace. Ellison residents have phoned and written by the sackful. Not one person knows who he is, though a few claim to have often seen the ghostly woman and the bird.

Is Bill the guardian of the canal? A friendly ghost tasked with protecting Lilly and Roberta, or anyone needing help? Is he linked with the woman and the bird? He certainly led me up the garden path, as Mum would say.

We might never know. If you're listening, Bill, thank you for keeping Lilly and Roberta safe.

To the woman and the bird, I hope you find peace. If it's what you want. Lisa insists you helped her to climb out and rescue me.

I leave the rest to you, dear listener. Draw your own conclusions, and have a strong brew.

One last thing. Lisa says we've had a call from a resident down Piner way. They want to know if I'll take a look at the myth of the ice lady.

Over and out. Until next week.

Mave Kitten and Lisa Blonde.

# ACKNOWLEDGEMENTS

Thank you NineStar Press and Elizabetta McKay

# About the Author

Eule Grey has settled, for now, in the north UK. She's worked in education, justice, youth work, and even tried her hand at butter-spreading in a sandwich factory. Sadly, she wasn't much good at any of them!

She writes novels, novellas, poetry, and a messy combination of all three. Nothing about Eule is tidy, but she rocks a boogie on a Saturday night!

For now, Eule is she/her or they/them. Eule has not yet arrived at a pronoun that feels right.

### Email
Eule8grey@gmail.com

### Facebook
www.facebook.com/eule.grey

### Twitter
@EuleGrey

### Instagram
@eulegrey

### Website
eule8grey.wixsite.com

Tiktok
@eulegrey

Volcano Chronicles

*I, Volcano*

*We, Kraken*


Sapphic Eco Warriors

*A Pinky Promise*

# M/OTHER

R.B. THORNE

WARNINGS: Discussion of possible abortion, unwanted pregnancy, loss of a husband and baby, body dysphoria, death of infant, panic attack, mold and rot, car wreck, semi-graphic description of a dead body, ghosts, water/drowning, thunderstorm, discussion of infanticide and postpartum depression, and gothic/horror elements.

TO THE OTHERS, THE MOTHERS, AND THE CHANGELINGS

THE NOISES ARE back. Naked branches scratch against the windows. Aged floorboards settle above and below me. And far in the distance, rain has begun to fall, the steady drizzle of an oncoming autumn storm. Beneath it all, a persistent rhythm echoes somewhere inside the house. *Tap. Tap. Tap.* For all I know, these sounds have been present since the day we moved here, and it's only my awareness of them that's new. I used to sleep better, before.

The first few times the noises woke me, I stretched across the bed to nudge him awake, a half-conscious question on my lips: Had he locked the door? But over and over, my fingers found cold, empty sheets, and my whispered words echoed across the cavernous room. And eventually, the habit died.

I rouse myself and slip my icy feet into his well-worn sheepskin slippers. He'd had them long before I ever met him, and he'd given the ratty old things to me when my feet swelled in the final months of pregnancy.

*"They look better on you anyway."*

Now, they threaten to slide off with each step, their

thick rubber soles catching on the carpet as I shuffle up the narrow hallway, past the nursery with its door always closed. I stop short of the bathroom, where windbeaten trees claw desperately at the windowpane, and make my way into the kitchen. I leave the light off.

More than once, I've imagined the scratching might be him, somehow returned, and if I would only open the door and turn on the light, there he would be. Sometimes, I imagine he'd look as he did before—auburn hair, falling in waves around his face and shoulders; warm, honey-colored eyes with the barest hint of laugh lines around the corners; and strong, soft hands reaching—grasping—to caress me once more.

More often, my mind betrays me. The face I see then is the way he looked after. His hair, darkened and matted with blood. His skin, gray and bruised and split along the prominent bones of his cheeks, brows, and jawline. And his beautiful eyes, open, but forever vacant.

He was the first man I ever loved.

Thunder growls outside, quiet and slow, like boulders tumbling down a distant hillside. I fill a glass with tepid water from the kitchen sink and gulp it down, resenting the metallic tang of it. I've never quite grown used to the sensation of living in such an old house. With the ancient pipes, arteries clogged with decades of rust and muck; the creak of every wooden plank and board slowly rotting all around; and the smells, sometimes indescribable—it could drive anyone mad, or screaming out of the place. Anyone sensible anyway. Or anyone with anywhere else to go.

It was a blessing when some distant aunt of his left the house to us in her will, and though, like his family, something about the place always seemed to reject my presence, I've never been one to question a gift, especially not one so desperately needed and so perfectly timed. The first few years of our marriage were not kind to us. With our combined debt and the lousy job market, we were inches from eviction when this ramshackle mansion was dropped into our laps, no strings attached. True, the conditions were somewhere between dubious and downright unlivable, but one can overlook almost anything under such circumstances. It even came furnished.

When I finish, I set the cold, empty glass on the very edge of the counter. My hand lingers on the crystal rim, and I nearly give in to the urge to send it crashing to the floor.

The night he died, I fell. I'd been trying to scramble my unsteady, distended body out of the bathtub, having convinced myself that if I could just get to him, it would all be okay. But even then, I felt my reality splinter, leaving an agonizing rift between Before and After.

I'd ignored the shredding pain in my abdomen until I couldn't anymore, until my sobs turned to screams, and hospital staff escorted me to another wing, away from him, alone. It was time, the doctor had said; everyone was so sorry for my loss, but it was time, and the baby was coming. There was no one to hold my hand, no one in the world to care. He was gone, and I was alone.

And in those agonizing final moments, as my soulmate left the world and our child entered it, I'd wished for a way to trade that small life for his. I asked myself, as I had only once before, whether I'd ever really wanted this baby. I didn't allow myself to answer. The time of second-guessing was long gone. But it didn't stop the aching as love and terror warred in my chest. I knew the answer. Of course I did.

The idea of something growing inside me, a parasite feeding off my tired and imperfect body, had always repulsed me. And the thought of birthing a child and becoming a *mother*—that loaded word with its antiquated ties to the idea of *womanhood*—brought on a dizzying sense of dysphoria I could never quite articulate, especially to him. For all the ways we understood each other, some things must be lived to be known.

How could I have ever made him understand the sense of wrongness that fell over me like a shroud every twenty-eight days, or the fingernail scratching inside my skull every time someone called me "girl" or "lady" and I didn't have the energy or courage to correct them? And more importantly, why would I? None of it was his fault; he had no control over it. All he did was love me, exactly as I was, and completely. We hadn't planned on being parents—each for our own reasons—so why did it matter?

He would have supported whatever I wanted when that test came back positive. I think he might even have been surprised when I said I didn't want an abortion. That had always been our plan, should the odds topple out of our favor. We had the money. But something inside me snapped, or sparked, and all at once, I couldn't imagine not seeing this through. I was never going to be a mother, and then suddenly, I was. We dove into it headfirst, and we were happy.

But none of it mattered, in the end. The baby hadn't lived either. I lost them both.

I didn't drain the tub that night, or any night since, as far as I can recall. I must have, I suppose, but I can't remember actually doing it. I leave the curtain drawn, always, and when I imagine the bathtub, it's full and hot, waiting for me to sink into its depths and forget. He could be in there now, trailing his fingers through the steaming water, his smile soft and inviting.

Or it could be the other him. The wrong one. The one I killed.

And because it's impossible to know which it might be, I never look. Instead, I move through the house night after night as if I am a ghost. Often, I wonder if I might be. I never leave, never speak. Who would I talk to? No one calls; no one comes. Not that anyone would. He was my only family, and I was his.

The clock on the wall reads 9:13. So many hours before sunrise, before sleep might finally welcome me. I haven't slept a single night since I came home from the hospital. The nights are too loud, and too quiet. Every sound in my head and in the house meld and crescendo into one unbearable cacophony, no more soothing than submerging oneself in cold water. The white noise of daytime—life and normalcy that's not wholly unfamiliar to me—has become a welcome refuge from all that noise.

A bolt of perfect white lightning illuminates the kitchen as I turn to leave, and for that instant, it's changed. A thick coat of grime blankets every counter; cobwebs hang from the walls and ceilings in clumped, dusty tendrils. And the fruit, plump and ripe moments ago, is nothing but a shapeless mound of greenish-black mold. The scent of rot curls into my nose and sits on the back of my tongue. I shrink back, gagging. But before the strangled noises leave my lips, the frightful scene has already vanished. The kitchen is tidy, cold, and empty. I scan the room one final time and push that nightmare from my mind as I move back to my bedroom.

But as I lie down again, a new sound interrupts the others—a single, quiet whimper.

A sharp gasp slices through my lungs as I jerk upright. I can hardly catch my breath as I sweep my gaze back and forth, into and between the shadows of my empty bedroom, then slowly, as I bite back terror and heartache, I land on the nursery.

The door is closed, of course, but some inexplicable and dangerous thing takes root in the center of my chest—foolish, unwelcome hope. It pulls me like a marionette out of bed and into the hall outside the nursery door. My heart hammers as I reach out with one sweat-slick hand, twist the knob, and give the gentlest push.

Inside, it's quiet as a tomb. Whatever sound drew me to this forbidden place has ceased. But the second I make the decision to enter, the room is illuminated with the soft golden glow of the star-shaped night-light he placed lovingly on the dresser months ago. Tiny rays dimmed by weeks of dust caress every surface, banishing the shadows that live here.

And as the room comes to life, the sound echoes across the nursery once again.

I run to the cradle, arms outstretched. How could I have forgotten, even for a second? It doesn't matter, I think as I retrieve the infant and kiss its cool forehead, all that matters is that my baby is here, and safe, and we're together. I've heard of mothers falling into a deep depression after giving birth or going mad and doing terrible things. A temporary lapse in memory is nothing. A long, horrible, lonely night-mare. That's all this is. And it's over now.

With the baby in my arms, I lower myself carefully into the rocking chair my husband built for us. Closing my eyes and smiling, I picture his face when he finished the chair, the way he hummed as he hung the folded heirloom blanket over the back and turned the whole thing to face the window.

*"So you'll both have a view."*

Rain runs down the windowpane in thick sheets, and the thunder rumbles ever closer. I don't need to open my eyes to know there is no view, not on a night like this when thick black clouds blot out every star above and dense, low fog obscures the world below. I do anyway, to gaze at the sleeping child. The shadows cast from the rain on the window give the appearance that we are underwater, suspended peacefully just beneath the surface, like a dream. I rock us both, humming a lullaby my mother used to sing to me. The words have been lost with time, but the melody, both mournful and lovely, is etched in my soul.

When I wake again, my chin rests on my chest, and it's dark. Whether it's still dark or dark again, I can't tell. The window is a waterfall, warping the outside world. Inside the nursery, the air is cold and still. I stir, and a familiar and terrifying feeling overcomes me. Emptiness. My arms are empty.

In a panic, I spring from the chair, squinting into the darkness. My hands shake as I peer over the side of the empty cradle. Clutching the side rail until I think it may break, I am only dimly aware of myself. My cold, numb hands. My face, damp with sweat. My breaths, shallow and labored, as if some great beast resides in my chest and squeezes, squeezes, *squeezes* the life from me.

Something terrible has happened. I know it. I know.

Do I?

No. No. No.

The room spins around me. The wood floor heaves and rocks, the boards whining as if they might explode into splinters beneath my feet.

An earsplitting thunderclap jerks me into action. Lightning flashes, turning the nursery into another nightmare room. More cobwebs spread thick over the walls and across the top of the crib in a ghoulish canopy. The floor glitters with broken glass. The smell of mildew and neglect snakes its way into my nostrils. But once again, it all disappears with the lightning.

Uttering a strangled moan, I shove myself away from the baby's empty bed and begin a frenzied, aimless search. Panting and grunting, more animal than human, I drag the furniture away from the walls to better see behind and beneath, then flip the toy chest and rifle through every small, precious stuffed thing inside. My panic reaches a dizzying peak as I pull clothes from the closets, pillows from the couch, and blankets from the bed. Floor by floor, I tear my home apart. I hardly know what I'm doing, but I can't stop. How can I, when the more I search, the more this house becomes a place I do not recognize, and my baby—my sweet infant child—is nowhere to be found? I rip through the bedroom and the nursery twice more, and each time, I come away empty-handed.

Nothing. Nothing. Nothing.

In the middle of the upstairs hallway, I stop and sink to

the floor, covering my face with my hands. This is my fault. Mine. Just like him. Everything I love, gone.

That night comes screaming into my mind. I'd grown increasingly morose, at times volatile, as the final trimester of pregnancy took its toll. He'd drawn a warm bath to placate my cloudy mood and offered to run to the corner store and get me ice cream. A phone call from the emergency room woke me, cold in the tub. I'd fallen asleep. Had to get there right away, they said. A distracted driver, an unnoticed stop sign, and one single mistake had stolen my life away.

He was dead before I got there. The last time I saw him, he was smiling and putting on his coat. He kissed me on the forehead and said he'd be back in a flash. And then he was dead, cold and gray and broken, and gone.

A familiar noise snaps me back into the present. The dripping of the bath faucet. Water landing on water. I lift my tear-soaked face and listen. Something about that sound...

*Drip. Drip. Drip.*

Did I check the bathroom?

I race up the hallway but trip on one of his—my—slippers and crash to the floor. I bark in pain as the weight of my whole body comes down on one knee, but I leave the slipper where it is and rise, my hand shaking as I reach for the bathroom door. The noise grows louder, drowning out the storm.

*Drip.*

*Drip.*

*Drip.*

The brass handle cools my palm. I twist, push, and...

I wake in my bed, breathless and confused, my legs tangled in the sheet. Rain pounds the roof and windows, an endless pattering. The clock on the bedside table glows green, the only light in the room. It's 9:13.

My heart hammers as I try to gain control of my breathing. But the emptiness in my arms, and the feeling that something—someone—should occupy that space, chills my skin. It's all wrong.

I sit forward, still my breath, and listen.

The storm crashes and heaves outside. Underneath it, through it, comes a wailing moan that could be mistaken for wind but for the hitching irregularity of it. I stare out the bedroom doorway and down the pitch-black hall.

As soon as my toes touch the floor, yellow light spills across the hall from the nursery. The soft, sweet whimpering inside makes my cold skin flush with warmth. My fear vanishes as I shuffle, barefoot, into the baby's room. But my sigh of relief fractures into a sharp cry just as it passes my lips; something on the floor bites into the sole of my foot. I glance down, using the lamplight to investigate, but there's nothing.

When the baby cries again, instinct beckons me to the cradle. I pull the child into my arms, sink onto the rocking chair, and release the top three buttons of my nightgown. The motion is automatic; though I can't remember doing it before now, I must have, and the little cries are replaced by satisfied silence and deep breathing. I allow my mind to wander. Outside, the rain has not slowed. The turbulence of the storm strangely calms me; my tempestuous mind made external.

I wish he were here. Every single thing in this place is a bitter reminder of his existence, and his absence. The hollow howling in my chest aches with it. But for the first time since he left, I find myself in a place of welcome nothingness. A brief void. Meditating on the pounding staccato of the rain and the thunder that sounds as though it's directly overhead, I discover in my mind a small, quiet corner in which to rest, finally.

A sudden sharp pain shatters my temporary peace. I glance down in confusion just as it happens again.

I cry out, yanking the little culprit away from myself. Where the infant was feeding, three droplets of blood bead up and roll down my breast. I hiss in pain as I pull my nightgown closed, ignoring the thing's small cries of frustration. Dark blood blooms across the thin white fabric, saturating the cotton threads.

Another flash fills the room with white light, and with it, the baby's face changes. It's as if I'm seeing through a veil and gazing at what lies beyond it. The eyes become hazy and unfocused. The skin, a dull grayish-white, glistens and puckers. The fine brown hairs on that tiny white scalp start to wave as if in a breeze I cannot feel. I barely stop the shriek from escaping my mouth and arrest my arms before they can flex and extend to throw the horrible changeling across the room. This is not my baby. And if this isn't my baby, then...

But as the white light leaves the room so, too, does the vision. The baby is human again, or so it appears. I touch the plump pink cheek with the tip of my index finger—it's warm—and watch the child squirm and whine in my arms. Its distress provides an odd sense of assurance that *this* is reality. I shake myself, willing the image back to wherever it came from. Obviously, I'm half delirious with fatigue and grief. That's all. I hum and rock, and soon, the infant grows silent once more.

The dripping in the bathroom returns, seeming to slow, timing itself with my breathing as my consciousness drifts. The baby falls asleep and is still as death in my arms. My humming fades into quiet sighs.

I force my eyes open, refusing to fall asleep. I can't bear another nightmare. The chair creaks beneath me as my rocking becomes insistent. I hum the lullaby again, louder, trying to ignore the incessant dripping and the scratching and the storm and the itch in the back of my skull that says *something isn't right*. But a question forms in my mind that makes my body still and my skin cold.

Who am I humming to?

My arms are empty, and the room is chilly and neglected. Something glitters on the floor. Glass. I broke a glass on the nursery floor. I recall the tinkling crash as it fell from my hand. It was neither an accident, nor intentional. My hand simply released it, and it shattered.

No, that's not how it happened.

My baby was in one arm, asleep, and I had the glass in the other hand. I watched the water, housed in its perfect prison, and had the sudden urge to free it, to destroy the pretty thing and send the liquid splashing across the wooden floor. And then I did.

No. That can't be right. The baby died in the hospital. They both died the same night.

Didn't they?

No. We fell asleep together in the rocking chair, just minutes ago.

But if that's true, where is the baby now?

Panic seizes in my chest, constricting my lungs until I

grow dizzy. I stumble out of the chair and down the hall, and the noises grow louder. No, not louder. Closer. I grind my teeth as I limp down the hallway, my knee throbbing, my hair growing damp with the sweat of the nightmare and the panic. My hands are cold and stiff by the time I reach the bathroom door. As I clutch it, my lost baby begins to cry in the nursery, a desperate, howling wail. For a moment, my only thought is turning back and gathering the child into my arms. We can ride out the storm together. Just us. But the sounds are too clear, too near—the ceaseless dripping and the low, primal moan building in my chest.

But why? It's the same sound I made standing over my husband's broken body. The same sound I made when...

I throw the bathroom door open, ignoring the scream-ing instinct to go back, to flee from this place, take the baby and accept the lie. Because now, I can't deny that all of this has been a lie. My lie. My fault. Isn't that right?

No. No. No.

The bathroom is still and quiet, except for the dripping and the scratching. The scratching is nothing to fear, just branches on the glass. The shower curtain is closed. The room stinks of mildew and stagnant air.

My hands tremble as another memory seeps into my mind, slowly, like ice dissolving in tepid water. I shake my head, wishing it away, but it makes no difference. Not now that I am here.

Every detail comes rushing back, demolishing whatever barriers I'd built in self-preservation, and I shake with the weight of it.

The tub, deep and white. The water, cold by the time my consciousness returned to my body. My hair, matted and stuck to the sides of my face. The gooseflesh on my arms and back as I shivered so hard that it hurt. Even then, I couldn't remember how long I'd been sitting in that frigid water. I could hardly comprehend what was before me as I slowly came back to myself: The tiny body, suspended just beneath the surface. The eyes, half closed and unfocused. The skin, so much paler than it ought to have been. Ripples from the dripping faucet, casting repetitive shadows across the small, lifeless face. The actuality and impossibility blurred my vision and made my head throb in time with the hypnotic *drip-drip-drip*.

What finally snapped me into focus was a new sound: a low, guttural moan, clawing its way up my throat as my body reacted before my mind could catch up. I knew before I realized. But then, I saw—really saw—and I understood.

Didn't I?

No.

Yes.

"Oh," I whisper, and a black hole opens up in my chest.

The only thing I can't remember—the thing eating away at my insides—is perhaps the least important part. Or the most. Was it an accident? Did my sorrow take hold of my body and kill my child? Did I kill us both? Is this purgatory?

Does it matter?

And though I know what I will find, I must see.

In the nursery, the infant coos, high and jubilant. The only happy sound this house has heard in so long. The walls expand with it, drinking it in.

My heart pounds as I creep up the hallway and into the dark nursery. No golden light chases the shadows away, not anymore. The thunder becomes my pulse, hammering in my ears as I peer over the side of the cradle. The thing that lies there is no longer a baby, if it ever was. The changeling is back; its cruel disguise has dropped away for good, revealing bloated gray flesh and milky, unseeing eyes. And the hair. The fine brown hair waves gently in that same invisible breeze. Not a breeze. It waves as if it were underwater.

The thing in the crib—both mine and not mine—smiles an eerily knowing grin; tiny purple lips stretched around blackish-blue gums.

It reaches for me; I stumble backward and run. The high, unnatural laughter rings out behind me, taunting me. Terrifying me. Thunder crashes, and the house shakes. I barely keep my balance, bracing myself against the wall as my vision begins to blur. Tears flood my eyes when I stop again, just outside the bathroom door.

I set my flat hand a hair's breadth from the cheery yellow-painted wood, push the door open, and step inside one final time.

The thing in the nursery falls silent, and the sounds of the storm and the scratching and the never-ending *drip-drip-drip* fall away, leaving me alone with the sound of my own thundering heartbeat and the intermittent flashes of lightning. I close my eyes and clutch the edge of the shower curtain in my left hand.

With a sharp breath, I wrench the curtain aside. A single plastic ring snaps off the rod and clatters to the floor beside me. I kneel beside the tub as if in prayer. My knuckles turn white as I grip the side, digging my fingernails into the hard white porcelain until my hands ache.

No moan leaves my lips this time. No scream of terror either. The tub is empty. There's nothing to see. Nothing to fear.

But then the power flickers off, and the only light in the room comes from a streak of lightning, and I see the *other* house again. The house just beneath this one, or beyond it. Cold room, smell of mildew, and something...else. And the body in the water. The body that wasn't there, that never should have been there, or here in this house at all. The body that never came home.

The power comes back, and the yellowish light from the bathroom ceiling reflects on the water's surface. The tub is empty again. I reach over to drain the basin. Maybe I ran a bath and forgot about it. My memory has been unreliable at best, lately. But I stop myself, my arm hovering in midair. If I put my hand into that water, if I break the surface, I can't be sure what I might find. Will it be this house, this tub? Or will it be the other?

I sit back on my heels, fold my hands in my lap, and stare at the shadows in the water.

After moments or hours, the storm begins to quiet, and the laughter turns to pitiful cries. With a sigh of relief, I stand and leave the bathroom without draining the tub. I step over the slippers in the hall, and the minefield of shattered glass in the nursery, biting back the wave of panic that washes over me when I peer into the cradle.

The baby is whole, and perfect, except when the lightning flashes. And I don't mind. As I settle into the rocking chair and gaze out the window at the starless sky, an understanding washes over me. I can never leave this place, can never abandon this child, not for a single minute. It's my punishment, or perhaps my salvation. A remedy to my grief and loneliness, whether I want it or not. But I think...

I think I really do.

I swaddle the infant in its blanket and begin to rock, cringing only the slightest bit when the storm reveals its other face. I wonder how long this might last, and whether I, too, have another face. Pushing the thought aside because it doesn't really matter, I hum a lullaby and allow myself to rest, at last.

Outside, thunder crashes and the whole house seems to shake. I wake with a quiet gasp, alone in my bed. Something stirs inside my mind, cold and viscous, just out of reach. And beneath it, around it, through it, a steady rhythm.

The noises are back.

# ACKNOWLEDGEMENTS

Thank you to everyone who read this nightmare piece, and to everyone who helped make it the best worst nightmare it could be.

# ABOUT THE AUTHOR

R.B. Thorne writes slow-burn gothic horror, often with occult and supernatural elements. They can usually be found exploring forests, beaches, and cemeteries along the West Coast of the United States with their spouse.

Rose's other passion is uplifting youth in their community. During the week, they lead an art program at a nonprofit for teens. You can visit Rose at www.rbthorne.com and on Twitter and Instagram at @ThornsAbound.

### Email
rosebwriting@gmail.com

### Twitter
@ThornsAbound

### Website
www.rbthorne.com

### Instagram
@ThornsAbound

# HOLY WATER

## A.R. VALE

WARNINGS: Depictions of school bullying, homophobia, lesbophobia, misgendering, ableism (of a hearing-impaired character), depiction of drowning, and implied CSA.

T'S EARS RING. He stares at the slab of cold stone pressed up against the side of his face, and his ears ring. But it's not his ears. He reaches up a shaky hand and pulls off his hearing aids one at a time. The world immediately becomes quieter, but the ringing stops.

A hand comes down and grips his wrist. Long, painted fingernails dig into his flesh painfully. He releases his grip on reflex, dropping his hearing aids to the floor. They bounce once on the stone tiles.

A shiny shoe descends just inches from his face, smashing the hearing aids to pieces beneath the heel. Pieces of shattered plastic scatter across the flagstone floor. T risks a glance up at his attackers, his vision only slightly impaired by the long fringe falling across his face. The girl standing over him is speaking—he can't hear her properly; her quiet voice sounds more like white noise without his hearing aids. Zoe Monroe with her perfect black hair, her perfect soft face, her pretty blue eyes that stare right into your soul. T knows he is in love with her, has been for a while now; it's one of the reasons she hates him so much.

He hears a soft sound—muffled laughter—from some-where out of sight. She isn't alone. There are three of them.

It hadn't always been like this. For a while, they'd even been his friends.

*

T had been drawn to Zoe on his first day at St. Ade-laide's. He'd felt so lost and alone, sent off to a new boarding school in the middle of the semester. And there she'd been, sitting at an old wooden table in the middle of the common room, twirling a strand of glossy dark hair around her fin-gertip as she chatted with her friends. She'd looked up as he walked in, and their eyes had met briefly before T looked away.

T hadn't started it. He'd never have the courage to ap-proach a girl like her, but he kept finding himself in her vi-cinity, sitting near her at mealtimes and studying in the common room at the same time each evening. He didn't un-derstand it at first, this pull to be near her, but he couldn't have resisted if he'd tried. Zoe had noticed, though, noticed the new girl who never talked and always looked away when-ever they made eye contact. She'd been curious, T thought, or maybe she only pitied him always eating alone.

And what was he supposed to do when she approached him as he sat alone in the corner of the common room one evening? How could he have turned the beautiful, captivat-ing girl away? She'd smiled and asked him his name. He wrote on a piece of scrap paper: "T." That definitely wasn't the name on his school ID, but Zoe hadn't said anything, she'd just kept smiling. She invited him to her table, and his feet started to follow her before he'd even decided to go.

When her friends arrived at their usual table to find T had joined them, Zoe smiled and greeted them as if it was completely normal for him to be there. "This is T by the way," she'd said as they sat down. Like it was no big deal. They glanced at each other, then smiled awkwardly at him and introduced themselves as Imogen and Evie. Introductions made, they got to work as usual—homework and revision. Imogen was struggling with her French, and Evie had a talent for biology. The whole time they studied together, T found himself glancing at Zoe. She was smart, worked hard. She was also not afraid to laugh and gossip with her friends. She had the brightest smile that seemed to light up the room.

It became a regular occurrence after that. Zoe invited him back to their table the next day and the next. As the weeks passed, T no longer sat in the corner alone, instead heading straight to Zoe, Imogen, and Evie's table. The latter two still seemed to find him a bit weird, probably because he didn't talk. And he regularly missed things in conversation—the combination of auditory processing disorder and hearing loss could not be underestimated—but they tried to include him in conversations. And Zoe—Zoe always led the way. She went out of her way to include him as much as possible, insisted the other girls repeat things so he could be included, always took the time to read whatever he wrote for them on his notepad, laughed at his jokes, and nodded at his insights.

One month into his time at St. Adelaide's, Zoe invited him to a sleepover. They weren't supposed to have sleepovers in the dorms. Each girl (and T) had her own room, and no one was allowed in someone else's room after lights out. That didn't stop them from happening though. Girls found ways to circumvent the rules in order to spend more time with their friends, and there were always some teachers who'd look the other way.

T had never been to a sleepover before; even at his old day school, he'd struggled to make friends and hadn't been invited to those kinds of things. He'd always told himself he didn't mind, but when Zoe approached him in the hallway in between classes one afternoon and invited him to join them in Imogen's room that night, he'd been over the moon. He tried not to let his excitement show, putting all his effort into keeping his hands still instead of flapping around and his feet flat on the ground as he nodded his agreement. By the wide smile on Zoe's face—wide enough that he could see the solitary dimple on her left cheek—he hadn't completely hidden his feelings.

That night, he waited until after lights out before slipping out of his room and down the hallway. The school looked different at night. The long, narrow corridors felt everlasting and claustrophobic at once. The dormitory building had photos of previous students lining the walls, black and white going into sepia tone going into full colour. When he first arrived—before Zoe and her friends occupied his time—T had spent a lot of time looking at the photos and imagining what the girls were like (and wondering if they were all girls or if some of them might have been like him). Now, they seemed to watch him from the walls, looking down at him in judgement as he tiptoed down the corridor, making his way to Imogen's room.

Imogen's dorm room was on the floor above his, so he

took the stairs at the end of the hall. The stairwell was cold, the stone-tiled steps leading up and down in a seemingly endless spiral. The steps always echoed any noise, enough so that T could hear it and was overwhelmed every time he had to take them when it was busy. That night, he'd planned ahead by wearing only his socks. It worked, but he didn't like the feeling of cold stone beneath his toes with only a thin layer of fabric to protect them. Still, he continued on, knowing the girls were waiting for him, knowing *Zoe* was waiting for him.

The corridor leading to Imogen's room was much the same as the one to T's own. The doors were plain, apart from small stickers, each with a girl's name on them. Zoe had told him Imogen's room was near the end of the hall. So, on he went, trying not to slip in his bare socks on the hardwood floor. As he neared the end, he paid more attention to the names on the doors, looking for Imogen's; otherwise, he might not have noticed the blank door. It was the only one without a sticker. He looked around to see if it had fallen off and was on the floor somewhere, but it was nowhere to be seen. T took a step toward the door. He didn't know why, but he felt compelled to knock. He raised his hand to the wood and heard a hushed voice behind him.

T shot around to see who was there. Zoe. She wore her nightdress, her long, silky hair falling loose around her shoulders, and stood by an open door three down from the blank door. She was saying something but kept her voice low to avoid attention. T couldn't hear her, but he figured he should probably go to her. He spared one last glance at the blank door before stepping into Imogen's room.

All the dorm rooms at St. Adelaide's were laid out

exactly the same, with a single bed pressed up against one wall, a desk by the window, and a wardrobe and chest of drawers by the other wall. That said, the students were allowed to customise their rooms somewhat by choosing the sheets for their bed, what they displayed on the noticeboard above their bed, and the items decorating the surfaces around their room. T's room was still rather a blank slate. He hadn't brought much with him to St. Adelaide's, and he'd yet to unpack most of it. Most of his things currently sat in boxes at the bottom of his wardrobe, and he had nothing he wanted to display on his noticeboard. Only his Superman bed sheets and the mess of pens and notebooks on his desk indicated that somebody actually lived there.

By contrast, Imogen had taken every opportunity to decorate her bedroom to her liking. Fairy lights were strung around the edges of the room, an assortment of ornaments decorated the surfaces, and the bed was piled high with brightly coloured cushions. Photographs covered the noticeboard. Most of them featured Imogen, and many of them also included Zoe and Evie and other girls he didn't recognise. He was surprised to see one in the corner of himself sitting in the common room one evening with Imogen and Evie. He remembered Zoe had taken that one.

"T! You're finally here!" Imogen smiled a saccharine smile. T smiled back, holding one hand up in greeting. Imogen turned and whispered something in Evie's ear, and her friend giggled. Zoe rolled her eyes and took T by the hand, her soft fingers fitting gently in between his own like they were meant to be there, and led him to sit on the floor opposite the bed.

Evie and Imogen continued their gossiping, and Zoe

joined in. T tried to follow as much of the conversation as possible, but it was hard for him when people spoke quickly and kept turning away. Instead, he found himself focusing more on more on Zoe, how her long black hair fell around her shoulders and the way her little pink nightdress fit around her frame. When he was younger, T might have thought he wanted to look like her, feeling inferior with his short brown hair, which never seemed to stay flat, and his oversized T-shirt and old pyjama bottoms doing anything but emphasising his figure. Now he knew better. Now he knew he was a "he," even if he wasn't sure if he was actually a boy or something else entirely. Now he knew the way he looked at Zoe wasn't envy. He didn't want to be her. He wanted to be *with* her.

"T?"

T startled at the sound of his name. He looked up to see all the girls looking at him. Imogen looked on the verge of rolling her eyes, but Zoe was smiling fondly at him.

"Did you space out, T?" she asked.

T nodded, heat rising in his cheeks. He desperately hoped none of them realised what he'd been imagining.

"We were thinking we could tell ghost stories, unless you're too scared." Imogen smirked at him from up on the bed.

T shook his head. He grabbed his notebook from his pyjama pocket. "I'm not scared," he wrote.

"We know you're not; she's just teasing," Zoe informed him.

T hadn't heard many ghost stories before—one of the problems with never attending sleepovers. He'd read a lot of comics, though, including some spooky ones, and he was excited to hear some new scary stories.

Evie started them off, telling a story about a haunted doll. A shiver ran down T's spine as she whispered, "Three steps coming to get you, two steps coming to get you, one step coming to get you..." as the doll climbed the stairs. They all giggled after she got to the end where the girl's body was discovered with the doll lying next to her in bed.

Next, Zoe took a turn. This time, it was the story of a girl who saw a creepy clown standing outside her house as it got closer and closer. But when she called the neighbours, they couldn't see it. T couldn't help glancing behind him when it was revealed that the clown had been behind her the entire time, and she was just seeing the reflection. The girls laughed at him, and his face heated again with the embarrassment of it.

"All right, enough silly stories." Imogen spoke up. "Now I'm going to tell you a true story."

Zoe rolled her eyes again, and T was tempted to do the same. That was what everyone said about scary stories.

"It's true," Imogen insisted. "And not only is it true, but it happened in this school. This is the story of the ghost of St. Adelaide's.

"Fifty years ago, a new girl came to St. Adelaide's. She arrived in the middle of term, and she didn't have any friends. She was a very religious girl, so she spent a lot of her time in the chapel praying. But bad things happen to girls who are on their own."

"Imogen." Zoe cut in, her voice sounding strained. T was glad he wasn't the only one feeling uneasy about where this was going.

"The chaplain saw the girl kneeling to pray, all alone in

the chapel, day after day." Imogen continued as if Zoe hadn't spoken. "And he became obsessed with her. One day, he approached her and tried to kiss her, but she pushed him away. He grabbed her by the hair and dragged her to the baptism font. He held her face down beneath the water until the poor girl drowned."

T felt sick. His body was so tense he wouldn't have been surprised if he'd stopped breathing. He glanced at Zoe who seemed more disturbed than he did. She looked down, her hair falling across her face, but he still caught a glimpse of the tears in the corners of her bright blue eyes.

"They found the girl's body the next day, lying in a pool of holy water. No one suspected the chaplain. One year later, he was setting things up for morning prayers when he heard a strange dripping sound. *Drip. Drip. Drip.* He turned and saw the girl he'd murdered. She was dripping wet, and her eyes were all black. She pointed at him, and he felt his lungs fill with water, and he drowned right there."

"Imogen?" Evie whispered. "I know you were trying to scare us, but that might have been a bit much."

Imogen shrugged her shoulders. "I told you; it's true. Everything I said really happened. Afterward, they never let anyone use the girl's old dorm room again. It's just down the hall if you want proof. The one with no name on the door."

T froze. The room down the hall? *That* room?

Evie got down from the bed and went to sit beside Zoe, then took her hand. "Imogen, I'm serious. You scared Zoe."

"I'm fine," Zoe whispered. She shook her head, running a hand through her hair, and when she looked up, she was back to her smiling self. She laughed. "It takes more than that to scare us. Right, T?"

T nodded slowly, surprised by the quick change in her demeanour. If she could hide her fear that well, how much else was she hiding from them?

THEY'D LEFT IMOGEN'S room in the early hours of the morning. It had still been dark, but they didn't want to risk getting caught breaking school rules if they'd left when other people were awake. T glanced at the blank door as they walked by, but neither Zoe nor Evie looked that way. Evie and Zoe's rooms were on the same floor as Imogen's, so they didn't have far to go, which left T to go back down the stairs alone.

Somehow, the stairwell seemed even darker now, colder and emptier than before. T glanced over the banister and found he couldn't see the bottom. He took a breath to steady his nerves. They were just a bunch of silly ghost stories.

Still, as he took the steps one at a time, down into the darkness, he remembered Evie's story ("one step coming to get you"). And his mind went back to Zoe's story as he caught a glimpse of his pale-faced reflection in a window.

He got down to his landing. On one side of the landing was the corridor of dorm rooms that would take him back to his bedroom. On the other side was another door, this one leading to another long corridor and, at the end of that corridor, the school chapel.

It was just a story, T reminded himself, heading back to his room.

NO ONE TALKED about Imogen's story after that night, and T told himself not to think about it. He was able to ignore it during the day, but sometimes at night, lying alone in the dark and the silence, his mind wandered back to that night. To the empty bedroom somewhere above him and to the chapel down the hall, across the landing, and at the end of the next hall. To the old stone font near the entrance, filled with holy water. And sometimes, even though he didn't wear his hearing aids at night, he could swear he heard a *drip, drip, drip* getting louder and louder, closer and closer, from the chapel to just outside his door.

Zoe seemed completely unaffected after the sleepover. T had expected maybe she'd be a bit off when he saw her later that day, but she was as warm and smiley as ever.

The only difference was that now, Zoe wanted to hang out with T more. No, not quite. Zoe wanted to hang out with *just* T more. She would frequently ditch her other friends to be with T in one of their rooms rather than study in the common room with Imogen and Evie. T was more than happy to oblige her; he'd always liked Zoe more than the other two girls.

One day, Zoe was in T's room when she remarked on how little stuff he had. He opened the wardrobe and gestured to the boxes tucked away at the bottom. She raised an eyebrow at him. "Don't you wanna unpack?"

He shrugged.

"I can help you if you'd like?"

He didn't care to unpack his stuff, but the idea of Zoe helping him made him smile. It took a whole evening's work, but eventually, all his things were unpacked: comics and graphic novels lined up on top of the chest of drawers, his

Lego Batmobile in pride of place on the windowsill, and his colouring pencils and sketchbooks organised neatly on his desk. He smiled at Zoe when they were done, but she wasn't smiling back. Instead, she was looking at his noticeboard, still empty as ever with nothing he wanted to display.

"Don't you have any photos?" Zoe asked, and T shook his head.

He did, technically—a few of his family and their pets sitting in the top drawer of his bedside table in his real bedroom back home. They might as well be in another world right now. He didn't expect his family would welcome him back any time soon; they considered him more of a burden than a sibling or child.

"I'm sure we can get you something." Zoe turned to him and smiled that warm smile, and he felt a matching smile spread across his own face.

The next day, Zoe approached him after registration and pushed something into his hand. He looked down to see a Polaroid picture she'd taken of them weeks ago. Her arm was around T's shoulders, and he was blushing slightly as they both smiled at the camera.

"For your noticeboard," she said before walking away.

T pinned it to the board as soon as he got back that evening.


IT WAS INEVITABLE, wasn't it? T could only have continued to hide his feelings for so long. And Zoe? Zoe actually seemed like she might return them. She was spending more time with him than with any of her other friends, and she was always tactile with him in a way she never was with them, holding his hand, sitting closer to him on the bed. T knew he wasn't imagining it.

They were sitting in T's room. They'd planned to get some studying done there, but that had soon fallen away to sitting on the bed together chatting. T showed Zoe one of his favourite comics, and she asked questions and waited patiently for him to write out the answers. He loved it. He loved that someone showed an interest in the things he liked. He loved that she waited for him to write the answers out instead of growing inpatient. He loved her.

He loved her.

It was just them sitting on the bed with a comic book in between them. It was early evening. The curtains were shut, and the bedside lamps were the only light they had. Zoe's hair fell across her face again, and T reached up to gently push it out of her eyes.

Zoe looked up, a faint pink blush colouring her pale cheeks. She'd leaned over, studying the comic, and when she looked up, her face was no more than an inch from his. He could see the shine of her pink lip gloss, feel her hot breath against his lips, smell the sweet scent of her strawberries-and-cream shampoo.

He leaned closer and kissed her. She stiffened, then relaxed a little, her lips giving way for T's own. He pressed in, resting a hand on her forearm.

Then she was gone. As quickly as the kiss started, Zoe had pulled away.

She stood from the bed. T was too stunned to move. She gazed down at him, tears in the corners of her eyes.

"Why would you do that, T? Why would you ruin things

by doing that?"

Before T could even think to answer, she pulled open the door and stormed out. T watched as the heavy wooden door fell shut behind her, leaving him alone.

THAT NIGHT, HE'D lain awake in bed thinking about Zoe, thinking about everything he'd done wrong, how he'd misread the signs. She just wanted a friend, and he'd tried to kiss her. What kind of asshole was he?

His hearing aids were on his bedside table. Everyone around him was asleep. It was impossible not to hear the sound breaking through the silence, the *drip, drip, drip*. Louder and louder, closer and closer. He shouldn't be able to hear it without his hearing aids, but he does.

He listened as it stopped moving. A loud *drip, drip, drip* right outside his bedroom door. His eyes were fixed on the door. He watched as the knob slowly started to turn.

No. He wanted to scream, to call for help or yell at whoever it was to go away, but he couldn't. He often felt frustrated that he was non-vocal, but never like this. The doorknob kept turning. The door started to move. T couldn't move.

Then it stopped. The door fell closed once again, and the sound of dripping ended.

T DIDN'T KNOW when he fell asleep that night. After what had happened, he was shocked he was able to sleep at all.

When he woke up, his eyes heavy from exhaustion, he

inspected the door, looking for any sign as to whether what had happened was real or a dream. Everything looked normal, but when he looked down, he saw it. A Polaroid picture.

T reached to pick it up. It was a picture of him and Zoe, different from the one on his noticeboard. He turned it over and saw there was something written on the back.

> *T. I'm sorry I freaked out. Can we talk? Meet me tonight after lights out in the chapel. Zoe.*

It was her handwriting. He'd know it anywhere. Did this mean he had it right? She was interested in him in the same way he was interested in her? T's heart did a flip in his chest, last night's fears forgotten. Zoe wanted to see him.

He looked for her in class that day, but she was nowhere to be found. He passed a note to Evie in biology, asking her where Zoe was. She just shook her head in response. T didn't know how to interpret that.

It didn't matter though. He had Zoe's note. He carried it all day in his blouse pocket, right next to his heart. She wanted to see him.


AFTER SCHOOL THAT day, he sat in his room, trying to fix his hair and wishing he had a proper mirror. Instead, he used his reflection in the window to check his appearance. He didn't usually care much about how he looked, but it felt important that night. He wanted Zoe to like him; he didn't want her to change her mind over something as stupid as his messy hair.

He waited, sitting on his bed, trying to focus on the

reading he had to do for English. No matter how much he tried, the words didn't go in, and his thoughts kept drifting back to Zoe. Zoe's eyes. Zoe's smile. Zoe's perfect loopy handwriting on the back of a Polaroid picture.

At 10:00 p.m., he heard the matron walking down the hall calling "lights out." When the corridor was silent again, he made his move.

He walked down the hallway, socks on hardwood, trying to ignore the feeling of eyes on him as the photos watched him from the wall. He braced himself for the cold as he stepped out onto the stairwell landing. It was so dark out there at night. Then he crossed the landing to the other corridor.

T hadn't visited the chapel outside of mandatory prayers everybody had to attend once a week. It was an old building that they'd built the dormitories around at a later date. The hallway leading up to the chapel was much the same as the others around the dormitory building, long and narrow with hardwood floors and more old photographs on the walls. This time, the photos featured the various school chaplains over the years instead of the girls.

The chapel itself was large for a school chapel—probably because it had never been intended to be one. Large, uneven stone slabs made up its floor, some with letters carved into them, and the walls were carved stones broken up by stained-glass windows. At the entrance, an old stone font, filled with holy water, stood tall, a heavy wooden lid covering it. Rows of wooden pews led up to the altar on a raised dais at the front.

And there was Zoe, standing with her back to him, her long black hair braided neatly down her spine. She turned when he stepped into the empty chapel. It was cold, colder than the stairwell even, but T barely noticed; he was so fixated on Zoe.

"T, you came." Zoe's voice was soft.

T walked down the aisle toward where she was standing, smiling shyly.

Zoe frowned at him. "I was hoping you wouldn't."

T stopped in his tracks, taken aback by Zoe's sudden iciness. Hadn't she asked him to come here?

"I told you she would."

T recognized the voice. He turned to see Imogen and Evie stepping out of the shadows.

"She thinks she's in love with you. She can't help herself."

Evie giggled.

T glanced at Zoe, but she was looking away from him. What was this? Tears stung his eyes. Why invite him here just to humiliate him? Why would Zoe do this?

He turned to go, but Imogen stopped him in his tracks. She stood in front of him and grabbed him by the shoulders. A hand wrapped around his wrist, and he turned to Zoe behind him.

"Where are you going?" she asked.

T stared at her in shock. What was she talking about?

Before he could think what to do next, Imogen pushed him backward. His foot caught on the uneven stone, and he fell into Zoe. She shoved him off of her, and he hit the cold stone floor.

*

T'S EARS RING. He stares at the slab of cold stone pressed up against the side of his face, and his ears ring. But it's not his ears. He reaches up a shaky hand and pulls off his hearing aids one at a time. The world immediately becomes quieter, but the ringing stops.

A hand, Zoe's hand, comes down and grips his wrist. Long, painted fingernails dig into his flesh painfully. He releases his grip on reflex, dropping his hearing aids to the floor. They bounce once on the stone tiles.

A shiny shoe descends just inches from his face, smashing the hearing aids to pieces beneath the heel. Pieces of shattered plastic scatter across the flagstone floor. T risks a glance up at his attackers, his vision only slightly impaired by the long fringe falling across his forehead. Zoe is speaking— he can't hear her properly; her quiet voice sounds more like white noise without his hearing aids. She looks down at him.

He hears a soft sound—muffled laughter—from somewhere out of sight.

Another shoe appears in front of his face. Before he has time to react, it's making contact with his nose. T gasps in pain, shutting his eyes tight.

Then come the hands. Two sets of hands grab him by the arms and drag him to the entrance of the chapel. He lets them. He just wants this to be over.

There's a bang, loud enough that he can hear it even without his hearing aids. He opens his eyes to see that they're in front of the font, and the lid has been pulled back. *Why?* He doesn't understand.

Then the two girls holding his limbs drag him up to the side of the font, and he realises what's about to happen right before Zoe takes him by the hair and pushes his face down into the water.

He gasps. He can't help it. He gasps, and cold water floods into his mouth and his airways. He flails his limbs and tries to lift his head, but their grip on him is too tight. He can't move, can't get out. His lungs start to burn, unable to get enough air. He's going to die here. T is going to die. Drowned in freaking holy water.

Just as he thinks he can't take any more, they relent. The grip on his head releases, and he comes up for air, gasping and choking as he collapses to the floor. Water from his sopping-wet fringe drips into his eyes, and he barely sees three pairs of shiny black shoes walking away as he curls up on the floor.

He doesn't know how long it's been, but he hasn't moved, and his lungs still burn painfully when the chapel doors open again.

T doesn't have the energy to care as feet in shiny black shoes approach him again. But when he looks up, it's not Zoe, Imogen, and Evie. It's a man. One he vaguely recognises from school prayers. The chaplain.

He's a young man, maybe in his early thirties. Blond with a few lines around his blue eyes but not enough to make him unattractive. He's speaking; his lips move, but T never learned to lip read, so he has no idea what's being said.

The chaplain kneels beside him and helps him to sit up. He speaks again, but he must pick up on something from the blank look on T's face because he reaches into his pocket and pulls out a small notepad and pencil.

"Can you hear me?" he writes.

T shakes his head.

"What happened? Are you all right?" he writes.

T just sits there shaking. The chaplain reaches out; callused fingers brush across T's cheek as he pushes his fringe out of his eyes. The chaplain leans closer, his face right in front of T's, and T flinches back, pulling away from him.

The man frowns, and T gets to his feet despite the way his legs shake. He never learned sign language, but he remembers one sign they used at his primary school sometimes. T holds up one hand, palm out flat. "Stop."

The chaplain looks him up and down, then seems to come to some kind of conclusion because he turns and walks away, leaving T alone in the chapel once again.

T gasps out a shaky breath. He's not okay. He stumbles down the aisle and finds himself before the altar, looking up at a crucifix that hangs above the room, watching everything.

T doesn't know if he believes in any kind of God. His family are Catholics; that's why they sent him to a Catholic school, but he's never felt sure about any of that. Still, he finds something reassuring about the church and the altar and the kind eyes staring down at him. After everything that's happened, he finds himself wanting to pray.

*God—Father? I don't know if you're listening. I don't know if you listen to people like me. I'm so tired. I'm tired of rejection, and I'm so scared of what they'll do next. Take me away from here, God. Or...or get rid of them. Just don't let them hurt me anymore. Amen.*

He stands to go, feeling somewhat calmer, then remembers what his mum always told him and makes the sign of the cross.

T WAKES UP with a pounding headache. He wants to roll over and go back to sleep when the sunlight slips through the gap in the curtains, but he can't. They have mandatory morning prayers, and if T isn't there, the matron will come looking for him.

He rolls out of bed. He doesn't know how he's going to manage without his hearing aids or what he'll tell his teachers, but that feels like the least of his worries right now. The thought of seeing Zoe again makes him nauseous. He tries not to think about her as he puts on a clean uniform, ignoring the clothes he'd left on the floor after he'd gotten back to his room last night.

As he makes his way to the chapel, girls keep glancing at him. He wonders if Zoe, Imogen, and Evie have told everybody that he likes girls yet, or if he just looks as bad as he feels.

When he approaches the chapel, there is a crowd of girls standing outside, which is weird because he's definitely late for morning prayers. A teacher stands in front of them stopping them from entering the chapel. T isn't sure what's happening. Some of the girls are turning back while others try to look around the teacher to see whatever is in the chapel.

Is this because of last night? Did he leave something behind?

He pushes his way through the crowd. Short and skinny as he is, it's easier to slip through the mass of bodies, despite how much he hates being touched. When he gets to the front, he catches a glimpse at what's behind the half-open chapel door. There's a white sheet on the ground, but it's not hard to see what it's supposed to be concealing. A man lies on the chapel floor in a puddle of water. T doesn't have to look any closer to recognise who it is.

He turns and flees.

IT'S ALL ANYBODY is talking about that day. The chaplain found dead—drowned. Gossip spreads like wildfire at St. Adelaide's. By lunch, three girls have passed him notes asking him if he knows what's happened.

He knows. He can't get the image of the chaplain's body out of his head (or the chaplain's face so close to his that he can feel his breath). He feels sick.

He makes do as best he can without his hearing aids. He tells his form tutor he lost them, and she tuts and tells him not to be so careless, then passes him a note saying she'll ask the matron to organise for some replacements to be sent straight to the school as soon as possible.

It's not until that afternoon that T has a class with Zoe. He doesn't have butterflies in his stomach. He has worms. Wriggling and squirming and making him want to throw up. As T gets to the classroom door, he braces himself, wondering if he'd be better off skipping. He steps through the door, and his eyes go straight to Zoe's seat. She's not there. Again.

Imogen is in this class though. She glares daggers at him as he enters the classroom, then pointedly looks away when he takes his usual seat next to Zoe's empty place.

He doesn't even try to pay attention in class. He can't hear anything being said without his hearing aids, and his mind is elsewhere. He keeps glancing at Zoe's empty seat.

The bell rings at the end of the lesson. Someone knocks into T as he gets up, and he turns to see Imogen behind him. She glares at him, then glances downward. He follows her gaze to a folded piece of paper at his feet. When he looks up again, she's gone.

It's a note. Not from Imogen. From *Zoe*.

Four words in Zoe's familiar loopy handwriting.

*Did you kill him?*

AFTER LESSONS WERE finished for the day, T goes looking for them. He finds Imogen at her usual table in the common room. Evie and Zoe are notably absent.

He writes out what he wants to say to her before he approaches her, knowing she won't have the patience to sit and wait for him in the moment.

She looks up when she sees him approaching. She opens her mouth and says something he can't hear. Probably asking why he's there or telling him to go away. Probably in less polite terms. He places the note on the table in front of her, and she glares down at it. Her eyes dart back and forth across the page, reading.

*Why did you give me that note? Does Zoe really think I did something? I've never hurt anyone! You're the ones who attacked me. She already hates me just like you clearly do. Why can't you all just leave me ALONE?!*

Imogen's nose scrunches up in annoyance. She crushes

his note into a ball and tosses it to one side before picking up her things and storming out.

THAT NIGHT HE hears it again. Lying awake in the dark. The *drip. Drip. Drip.*

Down the hall. Echoing in the stairwell. Then across to his hallway... No. Echoing. Getting farther away. *Drip. Drip. Drip.* Up the stairs.

T lies frozen. Listening.

The echoing stopped. He hears it going down the hall. One floor up.

*Drip. Drip. Drip.*

And then it stops. At the end of the hall.

T lies there in the silence. Waiting for something. Anything. But there is nothing else.

THE NEXT DAY, Imogen is gone. She isn't in class. She isn't in the common room or in the dining hall at mealtimes. T sees Zoe for the first time in days, sitting in the corner with Evie, her hair lank, her face a pallid shade of grey, her eyes red-rimmed.

T wants to approach her. To say something. To comfort her or confront her, he isn't sure which. He doesn't.

Instead, he leaves the common room and makes his way back to the dorms. When he gets to the stairwell, he doesn't go down the hall to his room though. Something stops him. His legs seem to move by themselves with no input from his brain, and he starts walking up the stairs.

He heads down the corridor to Imogen's room. The girls watch him from the photographs on the wall, their eyes cold and black. He doesn't go to Imogen's room. He stops outside the blank door again.

There's a sound, quiet at first. *Drip. Drip. Drip.*

It's coming from behind the door.

T's hand shakes as he reaches for the door handle. It's unlocked. He pulls it open.

She's lying on the floor, long brown hair spread around her like a halo in a puddle of water. Her blue eyes are open, staring at the ceiling, not seeing anything.

Imogen.

T stumbles backward. He can't look away. Someone else is in the hallway then. They're saying something. T can't hear them.

T SITS OUTSIDE the matron's office. He can't get the images out of his head. First, the chaplain, now, Imogen. Both dead. Both *drowned*. They still don't know how exactly Imogen died, but T saw the puddle of water she was lying in. He has no doubt she drowned, even though that's impossible.

After T was discovered standing over Imogen's body, someone went to find a staff member. Rumour must have spread quickly because the hallway soon filled with girls, and T was ushered away by the matron.

He's glad he doesn't have his hearing aids. He can't imagine how overwhelming it all would have been if he could actually hear everything.

The door opens, and the matron steps out, a painfully

false close-lipped smile spread across her face. She holds an arm out toward T, and he walks into her office. He's been in there a few times since he started at St. Adelaide's. First, to deliver his paperwork on his first day and earlier in the term when he was running low on hearing aid batteries.

She passes him a note: "How are you feeling?"

He shrugs. He doesn't have it in him to answer.

She picks up her pen and starts writing again. "You must be pretty shaken. If you know anything about what happened, please tell us."

Shaken is an understatement. And maybe he doesn't know anything, or maybe he was just imagining the *drip, drip, drip*, and the ghost story was just a ghost story. Either way, he shakes his head.

The matron hands him a final note. "If you think of anything, come see me. Your new hearing aids should arrive very soon. Get some rest."

THAT NIGHT, T sits on his bed, reading a comic by torchlight. There's no point trying to sleep when every time he closes his eyes all he sees are bodies.

He flips through the pages of the comic, trying to immerse himself in the story. It almost works. Well enough that he can pretend he doesn't hear it at first. But he does.

*Drip. Drip. Drip.*

He stills.

*Drip. Drip. Drip.*

Getting louder. Getting closer.

Down the hall. Echoing in the stairwell. Up the stairs.

No.

Not again.

T shuts his eyes and covers his ears, but he can still hear it. The dripping. The constant dripping.

*Drip. Drip. Drip.*

Finally, it stops. The world is silent and still again.

T ISN'T THE one who finds her. He hates that he feels relieved when he hears Evie is dead, but at least he didn't have to see the body.

That doesn't stop his imagination though. His mind supplies him with images as horrifying as the real thing would have been. Evie in her crumpled school uniform or her purple pyjamas lying on the floor, her face pale, her eyes wide, her mouth open in a silent scream. Always lying in a pool of water just like Imogen and the chaplain.

He hears the news at morning prayers (now held in the assembly hall as the chapel is off limits). He skips classes the rest of the day, preferring to hide in his room under his Superman duvet. No one comes looking for him. He can't even bring himself to read; all he can do is think of everything that has happened the past few days and wish it were nothing but a nightmare.

THAT NIGHT, HE hears it again. Wrapped in his duvet, his eyes red and sore from tears. And he hopes maybe, this time, it's coming for him.

*Drip. Drip. Drip.*

Down the chapel hall, across the echoing stairwell, down the hall to his room. Closer and closer. It stops just outside his door.

He refuses to look at first, but he catches a glimpse of the handle moving out of the corner of his eye. Finally.

The door opens, and he turns to see.

Zoe.

She stands in the doorway, shaking like a leaf. Her long black hair falls limply across her face, her blue eyes are red, and her face is the palest he's ever seen. She wears the same pink nightdress as the night of the sleepover.

"T."

He can't hear her, but he can see the letter on her lips.

He slowly emerges from his duvet cocoon, getting up to stand before her.

She hands him a note. It shakes in her unsteady hands.

> *I know you're a good person, T. I know you wouldn't do this on purpose. But if you have done something, if you're the reason this is happening, please, please, make it stop. My best friends are both dead, and I'm so scared.*

T looks up when he's read it to see fresh tears spilling down Zoe's cheeks.

He shakes his head, then turns to his desk to grab a pen and some more paper. He writes, "I didn't do anything, Zoe. Please believe me. I didn't—"

He stops writing, hit all at once by a memory. Kneeling in the chapel, the stone pressed against his knees, cold through his thin pyjama trousers, his head throbbing, and his throat burning.

*Get rid of them*.

Did he do this?

Zoe watches him, fear and expectation written across her face.

"I don't know," he finally writes.

More tears fall as she reads his note. She sits heavily on the edge of the bed.

T cautiously approaches her. She reaches for the pen, and he gives it to her.

"What are we going to do?"

A part of T wants to ask what she means by "we." Does she really think he wants to help her—wants anything to do with her—after what she and her friends did to him? But...he does. He sees the scared, tearful girl sitting on his bed, and he desperately wants to help her, to comfort the girl he loves. Because he does still love her. Whether he wants to or not.

He picks up a pen and writes hesitantly. "This started in the chapel."

Zoe stands, suddenly motivated. She writes quickly, even with the tears still running down her cheeks. "Let's go back there, then. We need to stop this somehow."

T nods without hesitation. Even after everything, he can't say no to her.

The halls are silent as they slip out of T's room and make their way to the chapel. T's certain that the girls in the photos are judging him for going with Zoe again, but she takes his hand, and all he can focus on is her fingers pressed against his own.

The stairwell seems even colder than usual tonight. T jumps when he feels something damp beneath his bare feet.

He looks down and sees a puddle reflecting the moonlight through the window.

He shudders but continues walking, following Zoe's lead.

They head down the next hall. The chaplain's photo stares down at them from the walls. Zoe cringes and hurries past. A part of T is glad he's dead now.

They push open the heavy wood doors and enter the chapel together.

T's eyes dart to the spot on the floor where the chaplain's body lay just days before. He's gone. There's no sign that someone died in here.

T didn't come with a plan, but now that he's here, he walks toward the front of the chapel to the altar and drops to his knees, just like he did that night. Zoe kneels beside him, and he watches her as she gazes up at the crucifix above the altar.

Her hair falls across her face, tangled and greasy. She bites her pink lips, now looking sore and cracked. She's still beautiful. How is she still beautiful?

T turns to the crucifix himself and tries to pray, but he can't get his mind to focus on words.

That's when he hears it. Somewhere behind them, just out of view. The *drip, drip, drip.*

Zoe freezes. She hears it too.

*Drip. Drip. Drip.*

T wants to turn around, wants to look, but he's too afraid of what he will see. Instead, he keeps his eyes on the crucifix. He reaches his fingers out and takes Zoe's hand in his. She clutches at him, tightly, desperately.

*Drip. Drip. Drip.*

The dripping gets louder, closer. Then it stills, directly behind them, impossibly loud in T's deaf ears.

*Drip. Drip. Drip.*

Maybe if he doesn't look it'll go away.

He doesn't get to make that decision because Zoe turns around.

His eyes widen as she turns. He watches as her mouth opens in a scream he can't hear. Then she's choking.

Gasping, choking cuts off her scream. T watches in horror as she bends over, her hands flailing wildly as she tries to breathe.

She starts coughing, and T can't look away as the first water hits the stone floor. Then more and more, Zoe vomiting water as she chokes, unable to breathe.

*No.*

*No. No. No.*

*Make it stop!*

*Why won't it stop?*

It ends as quickly as it began. Zoe stills, no longer retching or convulsing. She falls motionless to the stone floor, landing in the puddle of water in front of her. Her fingers go limp, and T realises he's still holding her hand.

*Drip. Drip. Drip.*

T stares at the water falling around him. The tears run freely down his cheeks and hit the stone floor, mixing with the water Zoe coughed up moments ago.

*Drip. Drip. Drip.*

T stands and turns.

*Drip. Drip. Drip.*

# ABOUT THE AUTHOR

A.R. Vale/Ryan Vale is a writer, activist, and educator. He writes both short and long fiction in a variety of genres with disabled and LGBTQ+ characters at its centre. He is fascinated by death and dark fiction, which he blames, in part, on his Catholic upbringing. He can usually be found sitting in coffee shops, attending local LGBTQ+ groups, or buried under a big pile of books.

Email
ryanlvphillips@outlook.com

Twitter
@arvwrites

Website
www.valeneedstochill.wordpress.com

Instagram
@arvbooks

# SNIPPER-SNAPPER

## EULE GREY

WARNINGS: Depictions of dead cat trophies, gore, dark, and kidnapping/abduction.

CHAPTER 1.

*Snipper-snapper, snipper-snapper.*

The cat flap's been busy today, as if I didn't have enough to do. Another creature's stuck fast. Poor thing. It's dead now, and I only hope it didn't suffer unnecessarily.

Last week, we had three mice and a bird from Mister Puss. Feathers everywhere, and a flipping albatross was flying round the kitchen. I expect there's caca on the top cupboards where I can't get up to clean. Not in my thigh-length boots anyway. No, missus. Some of the bigger kills do make such a mess! It's got so I dread the noise of the cat flap.

*Snipper-snapper.*

In some ways, it reminds me of the axe at Sarah the ranger's.

*Swish-swish.*

The way she chops up a trunk is pure art, that's what. Great big muscles and a look about her like she could carry me up the stairs and away to bed if she should choose. Gawd, it makes me shudder just thinking about it.

*Snipper-snapper.*

My silly puss doesn't care about my lonesome troubles though. Not him. He's too busy being cute on his back, paws in the air, and that's how it should be. Cats aren't here to make us happy or to be convenient.

"Naughty boy. You're a cheeky little murderer. What are you?"

He likes it when I say that. For all his strength, Amour is a sucker for a tickle behind the ears.

"Cheeky little murderer! What are you? Yes, you are."

I wouldn't have him any other way, but there's no denying having a pet is a lot of work. Maybe it wouldn't be so bad if he didn't leave the bodies on my new, rose-patterned carpet. Giblets and innards do take ages to clean off, and sometimes claws get lost in the shag pile.

Our feline companions don't know or care about any of that, and why should they? We humans are too concerned about the surplus, material things in life. Puss knows what's *really* important. What's a shag pile compared to happiness and contentment? Knowing you've done your duty. Having good manners. Making the world a better place.

All things have a purpose in the world, and puss's kills are no different. According to a programme on telly, cats bring food to Mummy Alpha as a token of esteem. It's the same as taking an apple to a teacher, I suppose. No teacher in their right mind would say, *no thank you* to a dear little child. Aww. I'm just the same.

"Thank you for that delicious snack, my darling! Just what Mummy wants. I'll eat it later. Are you getting on my lap for a snuggle?"

He's grown so much. Seems like every day his shoulders have become wider, though it could be fur and not muscle tone. There's no denying if kitty gets much bigger, we'll need a special cat flap. *Think* of the questions that'll bring.

"Up you come."

My goodness, the sofa creaks from the extra weight. I shouldn't wonder if another spring has gone. "That's it, up on Mummy's legs. On you get. What's that you're saying?"

I must be mistaken, but it looks like he's pointing at the dead thing with his paw. Hah hah. Daft as a brush, I am. So funny.

"Yes, I saw, my precious fluff ball. You've brought a lovely delicacy for Mumsie's supper. Settle down now and have a snooze. I'm exhausted from wiping up lumpy blood and guts, you tearaway."

When he's gone outside, I'll get rid of the corpse. We don't discard kills while he's watching. No, misses. Imagine if I took a present to a girlfriend, and they hurled it in the bin while gagging.

I'd be the ideal girlfriend, that's what. Cook their favourite meals and remember birthdays. If she brought me something in return, I'd never, ever throw it away. Certainly not. I'd keep it next to my heart for all time. Aww. Maybe one day.

Later on, I'll go back down to the woods and have a chat with Sarah. Mummy's shy, for all her boldness, and I've been busy.

How long is it since I brought home a tiny little kitten? Time flies so fast. Puss is a big fella now, with silky fur and long whiskers that twitch when I'm talking. I'm sure he understands every word, though the cat documentary says they can only follow basic language such as food, water, and poo-poos. That it's unlikely our feline friends could have any assimilation of language.

Still, I would think he's already learnt a lot, though it's been but weeks. Scientists, they don't know everything. There's always more on heaven and earth than there are on bits of paper.

He rubs his head against my hand so lovingly when I call.

"You're a clever boy, aren't you?"

It does my heart a power of good, it really does. Later on, I'll go down to the woods and visit my Sarah. Last time I went by, she winked and asked if I like the cinema.

It's awkward. What I'd really enjoy is to invite her back here, but there's Amour to think of. Like all mummies, I have to put him first. We don't want my baby getting jealous or feeling second best. No, misses.

"And tonight, we'll watch the tigers on TV, shall we?"

It's only fair. I have my historical romances—Jane Austen is best—and Amour has his beloved cat docu-mentaries. I do try to think of his education because ours is a relationship of give and take.

Gawd knows how I'd clean up his mess in one of them nice frocks like they had in olden days. I expect the under-garments would be quite a problem, and don't even get me onto corsets.

Still, it's got me thinking. As soon as puss goes out and I've cleaned up the kill, I'll go down and visit Sarah. No, I will.

Got to clean up this mess first. The body's right in the

middle of my carpet and stretched out like he's fast asleep, dreaming of home. Poor old thing. I shall have to shift myself and sort it before rigor mortis pays a visit. There's nothing like a frozen body to turn my stomach, and then I shan't think of Sarah and touchy-feely in the all-dark.

The limbs seem to be intact with its pretty tail, neat and tidy. No gooey bits or beheaded torsos today, though there might be broken bones. Kitty does enjoy crunching the skulls, bless his furry heart.

"Mummy appreciates it, dear. I'm not as young as I was. Where're you going now, eh?"

*Snipper-snapper.*

Off out again, the big lump. My legs ache from where he's been sprawled. He does leave his mark.

Off we go again. *Snipper-snap.* The flap is a nifty contraption, considering its size. I do hope there isn't too much detritus around the edges this time. Hairy bits of skin tend to stick, and I've been a vegan for years.

"Don't go too far, my love."

I suppose he's off hunting again. It's always a worry about whether or not he'll come home. Now he's so big, I probably shouldn't let him roam free. But it would be cruel to deny him the innocent and plentiful joys of the gardens.

I've learnt to trust that Amour knows what we both need. Anyway, God watches over all creatures, whether great or small.

It's time to deal with the body before he drags in another.

"In you pop."

I never would have expected to be so blasé about poking corpses into black body liners. It's surprising how knowledgeable I've got about organs and soft tissues. It goes to show what Mummy's capable of! Maybe I should look again at that job as a caregiver? It'd be proper lovely, that would. As long as Amour didn't follow me and bother the old folks.

I don't like touching when they're still warm, can't deny. "Get in." Quite a loud thud as the body hits the floor.

Not that it's different to wiping dog dirt off the bottom of a shoe. Being a mummy is a responsible and complex role, and I complete my daily tasks with pride.

CHAPTER 2.

*Snipper-snapper.*

Pussy's loud tonight, the busy little bee.

*Snipper-snap, snipper-snap.*

Meowing loud enough to wake the dead. The floorboards do shake. I must admit it's mainly during the dark hours that the sound of the cat flap stops me falling asleep and brings nightmares about black bags, and cesspits, and what have you.

*Snipper-snapper.*

Oh, now.

*Snipper-snapper.*

It's got me all of a tremble; that it has. Whatever nasty creature he's lured in is making horrible noises. Urgh. Bloody thing. I wish it would give over and die. If the neighbours complain, the army would take Amour away. I'd have to silence them, like with him at number forty-five. He was a loud old bastard who couldn't keep his mouth shut or mind his own beeswax. Mummy can be cheeky when there's a need, tee-hee-hee.

*Snipper-snapper.*

Gawd, he's active at night, despite all those books about the challenging toddler and sleep training. It's not like I haven't tried to get him to stay asleep, but he's stuck in his ways, and it's not for me to force my will upon him. That wouldn't be right or ethical.

*Snipper-snapper.*

I'm happy with Amour. Happy.

*Snipper-snapper.*

For fuck's sake! Why doesn't he stop? That bloody noise keeps me from sleep, and then I turn into a grumpy mummy bear.

*Snipper-snapper.*

In the middle of the night, I wonder if I've done the right thing. If my fluffy-wuffy is content. Whatever will I do if he carries on bringing home the wrong kinds of dead things? The shag pile can only take so much, and my nerves are all of a tremble.

*Snipper-snapper.*

*Snip.*

The cat flap's stopped swishing. Ah. At last. Now I can breathe. Funny. It sounds like someone screaming down there. Silly old Mummy. So funny.

Here he is. Thudding up the stairs like nobody's business.

"Mummy's darling. Well done! Come under the quilt and get warm. Silly old fluffer."

I do hope he hasn't got organ seepage on his fur. Last time, I couldn't wash it from the pillowcases, and Mummy hates waste.

I'm probably wrong, but it feels like he's trying to pull me out of bed and tugging both paws at my winceyette nightie.

"What, dear? Mummy's very, very pleased! Now, shall we have some shut-eye? Mummy's fucking knackered."

He snuggles down. I love it when he sleeps right next to me, close as a sweetheart.

## CHAPTER 3.

Oh. It's caught in the cat flap. That's why we haven't had any *snipper-snapper* for so long.

Poor creature. Stuck fast, one damaged limb up front, and another bent under the torso. Unlucky, that. I can't see the tail. I expect it's dangling behind. Got itself wedged in good and proper. Hair and blood. No wonder we had all that kerfuffle during the night. *Snipper-snapper* and *snapper-snipper*.

"Oh dear. Now you can't get out. We can't have that, can we?" I do resent it, blocking Amour's entrance like that. Selfish. "Stupid mousey, aren't you? Should've run faster."

It shivers a bit when I shout, tee-hee-hee. Just about alive, then. I'm not going to get excited. Not yet. Calm down, Mummy. Mostly, they've already passed. Sometimes it takes longer. They all die in the end.

"We'll need the extra strong lubricant to free this one, my lovely. Maybe the plunger?"

Amour's beyond excited. Meowing and jumping about like a box of frogs. Proper proud of himself, the little love. I knew he'd kill the right one. We all need a soupçon of persistence and faith that our dreams can come true. Andrew Lloyd Webbed-foot knew what he was talking about.

"You're a big soldier, aren't you? What are you?"

Gawd. It's trying to scratch its way forward, but the claws have been ripped out. It's alive and kicking, all right. Grunting like the lovely tennis players in their tiny shorts. I like that. I hope it begs.

"What's that, darling? Louder, so Mummy can hear?"

Screaming. *Grr*.

I'm wary of big ears next door. Two kills in one day would be too much, even for Mummy. "Shut it up, Amour. Good and proper! Shut it up forever."

The way he whacks that creature round the head is pure poetry. Beautiful.

On with the greased lightning. I do enjoy getting my hands around those muscles.

"It'll shift now."

I'm right. Amour heaves the mousey through the cat flap, easy as you like.

*Snipper-snapper.*

*Snipper-snapper.*

That's why we're such a happy partnership. His paws can't do the teeth extraction or the taxidermy, and I can't do the lifting. A perfect team of brain and brawn, that's me and my dinkums.

"Upstairs, my darling. Into the royal box room."

This chap is ripped, not like the others. A veritable king. I suppose that's why he survived longer than they did. His arm is broken though. It'll look as good as new, if that's what Amour and I decide is best. A few broken bones won't stop the lovely things I'm going to do to him. I should say *for him* because he'd like to look his best, I'm sure.

Such a looker! Aww. Even should he wake up—and he won't—he couldn't talk or bother the neighbours. Not with all that gaffer tape, and the soundproof walls, and everything. I don't want to snip his tongue out if I don't have to. Stuffed, tongues are useful things. So pretty.

"Oh, Amour."

It's like in church, where you don't know why you whisper, but it seems right anyway.

I don't know why Amour only drags men back, but I've always understood it's proof he can read my mind.

"You beautiful, beautiful kitten. You knew what I needed, didn't you? A pretty little friend to fit on the middle shelf. Someone to keep and cherish forever. Sarah for the nice things, and men for the nasty. Everyone's happy! Love and manners make the world go round."

"Come on, Amour. Like *Cagney & Lacey*, we are."

Together, we heave him onto the embalming table we call *Sleeping Beauty*.

My surgical gloves are laid out where I left them. No pulse. The chap's definitely dead. Aww, poor old thing. What a relief.

"He's ready for us, Amour."

Mummy can play! There's no joy like that of the imagination or of a scalpel. Now I know he's dead, I can get proper intimate with my blade. "Don't you worry about appearances. Mummy's going to sort you out."

His body is lovely, despite all the damage done trying to escape. By the time he's stitched up and into the box, he'll look plenty good enough to be with the other boys. I'm sure that'll be a big relief for him.

"We can place him on the yellow shelf. Next to the one with little feet. Above the twins."

Amour bounds off. I suppose it's for the best. Mummies need their secret playtimes, just like kitties.

*Snipper-snapper.*

# ACKNOWLEDGEMENTS

Thank you NineStar Press and Elizabetta McKay

# ABOUT THE AUTHOR

Eule Grey has settled, for now, in the north UK. She's worked in education, justice, youth work, and even tried her hand at butter-spreading in a sandwich factory. Sadly, she wasn't much good at any of them!

She writes novels, novellas, poetry, and a messy combination of all three. Nothing about Eule is tidy, but she rocks a boogie on a Saturday night!

For now, Eule is she/her or they/them. Eule has not yet arrived at a pronoun that feels right.

Email
Eule8grey@gmail.com

Facebook
www.facebook.com/eule.grey

Twitter
@EuleGrey

Instagram
@eulegrey

Website
eule8grey.wixsite.com

Tiktok
@eulegrey

# THE KNOCKING BIRD

## T.S. MITCHELL

WARNINGS: Depictions of a character with obsessive-compulsive disorder, self-harm, morbid ideation, animal death, death, depression, codependency, obsession, and injury.

"I HAD HOPED we'd finally see some sunlight today," I said, wrapping the scarf around my neck more tightly. I watched over Miss Alina as she stared out the carriage window with an unusual melancholy. It was so like her to think of everything except the cold. She'd covered her lanky frame and bright green dress with the bulky gentlemen's jacket I had bought off a porter not five minutes after we stepped off the ship.

"It is quiet." Alina finally cut through the silence with a frail warble in her voice. "It seems as if home is a world away." She looked down at her clasped hands, resting on her lap. "I suppose it is."

I switched sides to be closer to her, taking both her hands into mine to keep them warm. It was clear her anxious and calculating mind was still lost in thought, mired in her homeland's war and grief. And pushing her to flee here had yet to ease any of those burdens.

"Now, now, miss." I hoped to see the life in her beautiful blue-green eyes return. "You did the right thing. You deserve some happiness for yourself." I clasped her hands tighter.

"Besides, don't you think our luck is bound to turn around soon?"

"Luck is an evil thing," Alina answered crisply. "I'm as much a servant to it as you are, Stefanie."

I supposed I shouldn't have spoken out of turn. I should have resigned myself to suffering in silence for her, as always. That was my job after all. I've been her servant since we were both adolescents, brought together by obligation—hers, to be a wealthy heiress, mine, to live up to my family's legacy of service to others.

"Ah," Alina said as the carriage jolted to a halt. "Ages of waiting, followed by a sudden stop. Our driver would make a fair executioner."

I tried not to laugh at her glum humor, knowing how much she delighted in catching me off guard. It felt like her way of letting me know she'd be fine when I was in constant doubt.

Alina could never understand what I would go through to keep her safe. It was my sole reason for being. The most fundamental truth I had come to realize was that if all my efforts only ever amounted to making Ali smile, then mine would have been a life well spent.

Alina stepped out of the carriage and onto the street slick with melted snow. She immediately turned and tapped her fist gently along the edge of the carriage door. I caught my breath, regretting I had not arrived in time to meet her hand. Regretting she had brought that old superstition along with her.

"There it is," I said quietly as I took her hand again, and we made our way toward one of the last in a long line of slowly aging estates on the New England seashore: Melody

House. "Home sweet home," I sighed. Knowing its unkempt appearance would not yet bring about that smile.

Melody House was much like all the other manors here, an elegant, sprawling home built for the daughter of a wealthy sea merchant, long since vacated. It stood with an off-center architecture, faded green plank walls, and soaring brick chimneys. Dead vines suffocated the trellises and gardens, which were very much in need of upkeep.

As we entered, Alina silently turned to the door frame and knocked three times. One, two, three. The count always slipped silently from her lips as she knocked. Sometimes in German or Serbian. Lately, in English. But always, she knocked. On tables. Doorways. Anything wooden. Anytime she entered or left a room.

At first, I thought it was a harmless superstition, the knocking on wood. She explained it to me as an old family curse. The older she got, the more inclined she was to believe that warding away evil was the only way to keep it from taking over her life completely.

I was never one to believe in such whimsical things like spirits and curses. I took the behavior for what I believed it to be—a perfectly natural way for her to cope with the helplessness of life. I only worried that if any more loss befell her, it would take control completely, and she could spiral into darkness.

Later that night, after I had lit the gas lamps, the two of us made a picnic on the floor with old sheets and blankets. I served our dinner on silverware that had been left in the pantry from the previous occupant, while Alina had been nervously appraising every shadow in the house.

"Now this reminds me of home." I laughed to try to

cheer her spirits. "Remember that picnic in the Alps?" I tried to stir up fond memories, but I could see Alina's mind was still elsewhere. "Don't worry, Ali. The movers will be in tomorrow. By the week's end, you won't even recognize the place."

"About that." Her voice became more serious. Perhaps it had been inappropriate to use her nickname. What she said next took me by complete surprise. "If it's possible, I would like the workers to finish by five, tomorrow evening. Please help them see that this is accomplished." There was a dead, apprehensive calm in her eyes.

"Why the rush?" I smiled softly. "I figured we would take things slow—"

"I'm expecting to receive a caller in the afternoon. A gentleman."

Her reply stopped my words dead cold in their tracks. I could hardly speak.

"A caller? Tomorrow? Don't you think it's a little soon—"

"Stefanie, this is why I didn't want to bring it up."

I went to speak, but she stopped me.

"I know you want life to be as it was in Austria. The two of us, always alone. But here, my name means nothing." She could tell I was uneasy as I sat beside her. "You wanted me to move to America," she said stiffly. "To do this, I must become American. Besides, I can't have come all this way just to spend the rest of my life knocking around these halls like some kind of ghost."

"Would I not be with you?" I asked with a false smile.

"I know that, Stef." She softly put down her plate, her eyes drawn to the fireplace as she sat cross-legged across from me. Anxiety crawled back into her voice. "You remember Sweetly?" Her green eyes turned cold, distant. "That summer, the day you came back from visiting your family in Germany. You found me, found what I had done."

The moment flashed into my mind, of finding her beautiful face laughing through tears as she clutched her pet bird, Sweetly. It was dead. Bleeding and crushed to death inside her shaking hands. After that incident, I vowed never to leave her side again.

"You were seventeen," I said. "You were a child. You didn't know what you were doing; I should never have—" I tried to speak up, but my words fell as they met her icy stare.

"I kill everything I love," Alina said softly. "That is the truth of it. It's my curse, the spirit that haunts me—" Her tears began to fall. "I'm not looking for love, Stef. I'm looking for a way out. If there is any advantage in life to gain by meeting this man, then I must take it." She reached out to hold my hand but pulled away at the last second to wipe her tears away. "I should turn in." Her voice cracked. "It's been a long journey. For us both."

I said goodnight and watched silently as she went upstairs. As she arrived on the first step, she turned to knock her hand gently on the newel post.

One, two, three. With three knocks, she was gone. I was left alone to repeat the moment over and over in my head.

How quickly and indelicately her sharp mind turned. How terrible it must be to believe her life's fate depended solely on the whim of those knocks.

I wished more than anything I could ease the burden from her. That she would be happy here with me and me alone. Wished she would understand that the same twists of fate that stole from her life, also gave. They'd given her me—me to be her balance, her calm and steady, purposeful guiding hand.

If only she understood the truth. If only she knew what I knew—that no man could possibly understand her like me. And above all, no amount of knocking would ever protect her happiness.

Only I would be able do that.


THE NEXT MORNING, I awoke before the sun rose to spend all my labor preparing Melody House. Furniture covered in white sheets moved in and out in a great burden of fury. I raced from room to room in manic aggression, acting as taskmaster to see this place looking its finest and lived in. My own room was of little concern as I only had a nightstand and bed to my name. The grandfather clock outside in the hallway gently ticked away.

I didn't see Alina until I had accomplished my work and had no time to rest and refresh myself. I only became aware of the lateness of the hour when Alina came down the stairs dressed in her finest deep blue dress. Pearl beads draped around her tight collar, and her auburn hair fell in gentle waves over both shoulders. She looked lovelier than I had ever seen her.

"Ali, you look—"

"Hush," Alina said to me, knowing I was about to fawn over her. She briskly paced down the stairs, gently tapping her gloved fist against the newel post. One, two, three.

"Is he here yet?" Alina asked as I stiffened and prepared

for his arrival.

THE NEXT FEW hours were a blur. Mr. Thomson arrived, driving his own automobile. I prepared dinner, listening quietly as they conversed in the drawing room. They talked of current events: anarchists, war, peace. Alina talked of her homeland and how difficult it had been to leave it. They spoke of lighter things, too, frivolous things that I never had the stomach for.

It was only when I heard Alina laugh that the dreadful truth sank in. The two of them were getting along perfectly. For this reason, I was sure I wouldn't be needed for a while. It made me feel equally delighted and drowning in emotion.

Standing outside on the front porch, I struck a match and greedily inhaled some smoke from a dime-store cigarette. My hands trembled ever so slightly. And my muscles ached from helping the movers pack in every heirloom, trunk, and livery that would make this drafty old place look like a proper home.

My reward? A stranger soaking in her company, all her grace and charm, perhaps even the rarity of her smile. While I waited outside in the unfeeling cold.

I held my arms crossed tightly over my chest and watched over the sad gray landscape, the setting sun hidden behind cloudy skies. Something had changed in me, was changing. I had always loved Alina. That much I knew long before this day. But what I had never confronted was the dark shadow of that love. The cruel pettiness of it. How it made me hate that man in there. Hate myself. Hate every-thing that stood in the way of us being together for now and all time.

As I gazed at the gentleman's garish black automobile, I couldn't help but feel that hate turn into an all-consuming greed. How easy would it be, I wondered, for this love to turn to hate and, in turn, to violence?

I calculated how much of a simple domino fall it would be for me to walk over to his vehicle and sabotage it. Wondered if doing so would risk inadvertently destroying my love by keeping too tight a grip on it, just as she had done with her beloved pet bird. I found myself shocked at how easy it would be for me to do such a cruel, monstrous thing.

Then I asked myself what Alina would do if only her feelings happened to be the same?

Soon, I was back in the study. Time passed as if I'd blacked out, with no memory of how I had gotten here, wait-ing awkwardly between the two of them for the tea kettle to sound.

"You smell of smoke," Thomson said as he huffed a ci-gar in my face, then to Alina, "You let your servant smoke?"

"Slavery over a person has been done away with in America, has it not?" Alina laughed. "No, Mr. Thomson, I don't care if Steff does as she pleases. She's more than my servant. She's a friend of the most important kind."

"'Steff'?" he asked.

"Her nickname." Alina laughed with a smile. I indulged in the sweetness of that smile for a moment, though feeling betrayed, as if she'd said a private, intimate thing before a cruel and unfeeling crowd at my expense.

Before I could die from embarrassment, the tea kettle

called. I stood to leave, but Alina beat me to the punch, placing a hand on my shoulder.

"Stay, I'll fetch the kettle. Take a break; you'll find Tom an excellent conversationalist."

"'Tom'?" I asked, trying to hide my disgust.

"His nickname." Alina laughed with all the charm expected of an heiress. Before I could protest, she left for the kitchen, and I was alone with the man.

"Your friendship with Miss Alina astounds me. My father never made friends with his servants. Surely, some days, you two girls must be at each other's throats?" He chuckled.

"As you say, Mr. Thomson." I nodded politely.

"There is one thing I wanted to ask you about though. If you'd be so kind? About Alina." He crossed his arms and looked at me with deep concern. Again, I reluctantly nodded, hating to hear him say her name so informally. "She's quite charming. Quite clever. Well educated. But I couldn't help but notice—"

"The knocking," I said quietly and turned away. "It's just a funny quirk, sir. Nothing unusual. You must remember—before I was employed in her home, she had quite a lonely adolescence, devoting all her time to study."

I could see he wasn't satisfied with my answer. I began again. "There's an old saying in our country, much like you Americans have. 'Knock on wood.' Avert some catastrophe or wish for the best with the knocking on wood?" I softly rapped on the table twice. "Alina's always taken it to an extreme, of course. She believes doing it religiously will help ward off some horrible catastrophe caused by evil spirits."

"Has it?" he asked, sipping his whiskey.

I quietly flattened out my skirt and nodded in a way that indicated no definitive answer.

"Should she not have help for it, then? This business about spirits..." He shook his head. "She lost her whole family, for heaven's sake. Shouldn't she understand how meaningless that is?"

"Meaningless to you, sir." I stood from my chair. "But not to her." I curtseyed. "Now if you'll excuse me, my assistance is likely required in the kitchen."

The rest of the evening dragged on, and I was grateful to hear the knocks that signaled his departure.

"I do hope he gets home safely," Alina said with the soft lull of worry. She fell to the sofa and stretched out with a yawn. "What did you think?"

"Of Thomson?" I asked, and when she nodded: "He seemed a kind man." I shrugged. "If kindness is all that you need."

"You believe he thinks of me as a charity case." Alina sighed. "You always see the worst in people." Alina crossed her arms and sat back. "I know what you're thinking, Steff. That I'm just seeing what I want to see."

Suddenly her hand was on mine, softly resting between my fingers. She appeared so run down; how exhausting it had been for her to put on a show all evening.

"I know you don't wish to be rid of me," she said, "but I must act. Get married. Start a family. I must for both our sakes. If I don't begin now, I fear I never will."

Us, I wondered. Us both. I bit my tongue and refrained from asking if she thought a man, even one as kind as Thomson, would ever allow a servant such as me to be close to her ever again if he knew the true depths of my passion for her.

I wanted to say something. I wanted to fight for us. For me. But guilt kept my words in, and fear of rejection kept my mouth shut. As always, I held in my feelings, alone. Happy as ever just to sit silently in her cage, even if I spent my nights quietly weeping.

The next day, she saw another caller. And the day after that. But her mind kept coming back to Thomson. She kept circling around his every word and his apparent kindness. And the fact that he hadn't called back was becoming more and more alarming, only making him all the more fascinating to her.

Every few nights after nightfall, I would scrub her back in the bathtub. It always took her mind off worrying. The physical ache of being so near to her was just another emotional burden for me and me alone. Or, at least, that's what I had thought.

"I know what you would have me do," Alina said quietly as I carefully bathed her snowy-white back, marked with scars and stretch marks from her adolescent growing pains. "But I've made my decision. If he returns and asks it of me, I will court Mr. Thomson."

I said nothing. We had practically grown up together. Been friends together. Indulged in each other's touch. I never expected her to share this wicked, petty love of mine. Never asked it of her. But the thought of losing her, even to the happiness I desired for her, caused that vengeful, jealous darkness to crawl forth, though I took great effort to suppress it.

"As you say, miss." I continued scrubbing. She reached behind her head and grabbed me by the wrist, stopping me.

"If I could, I would not have it be this way. I would feel

the happiness that you want for me."

"What do you feel now?" I asked as she held my wrist.

"I feel nothing. I haven't felt anything in years. I exist, so I must continue to exist. But that isn't the story I want." Her fingers ran up and down my wrist. "I've seen how everything I want ends, Steff. Over and over in my head. We are too alike, you and I. We can only harm each other."

She didn't let go of my wrist. Instead, she started kissing it intensely. I dropped the brush and found my hand helpless. She tilted her head back up to look at me. Tears fell from her pearlescent green eyes. "I see the harm, but I want it anyway." Ali kissed me tightly as I sank into her grasp, feeling the goosebumps along her neck. She slowly led my hand down along her body and into the water as we kissed.

This was not the first time she had lost herself in the passion of emotion, and I was always grateful for it. But later, as she knocked on the bedside table before wrapping herself under the covers with me, I had a horrible feeling, which her rhythmic tapping couldn't dispel.

I held her tightly in my arms, closing my eyes, hating myself for wanting her happiness so badly that I would do anything for it. Even should it destroy me. Even should I never again be able to clean the blood from my hands.

When I awoke the next morning, she was missing from my arms. I still felt the warmth of her in the sheets, but her body was gone. I quickly dressed and made my way through the house, only to find her in the kitchen with the telephone dangling loosely from her hands.

"Thomson," Alina said, eyes grim with a hollow expression. "He's dead."

FROM THAT DAY onward, the shutters of Melody House remained closed, the curtains drawn. The knife cupboards were locked for her protection. Alina was once again haunted by the idea she had been responsible for death. His automobile brakes had failed, and he'd perished in a collision on his way home from Melody House. To her, it was proof of her curse.

The knocking became incessant. *One, two, three. One, two, three. One, two, three.* Upon every word, every decision, the woman I loved would knock on wood, look both ways, toss salt over her shoulder. Anything and everything to keep the harm at bay.

Every day, she grew closer to me in those shadows. And the closer she was, the more I felt the weight of having failed her. The more I wanted my bright, smiling Alina back. And the more I wanted it, the more I felt a raw, nerve-rending guilt. The guilt of death. I had gotten my wish to be alone with my forbidden love; it had come to pass, only I had no idea the cost.

Then came the last day of March. The cold had turned to rain, and the rain wouldn't stop. I woke up to the sound of it, and she was again missing from the bed. I searched everywhere for her. Until I heard a creak in the ceiling above me, and my dread turned to panic.

I flew up to the hidden door leading to the attic, climbing as fast as I could through the musty darkness. Horror struck deep in my heart when I saw the open window, the attic floor wet with pouring rain. I climbed up and out, into the storm, and onto the roof.

Alina was there, standing alone on the roof's edge. Soaking wet in her nightgown, she turned toward me with nothing in her dull green eyes. She stood on the rain-slick edge of Melody House and stared hopelessly at the ground below.

"Alina!" I shouted.

"Get away from me!" she screamed and turned around, holding herself in her arms. "I'm cursed. I'll only hurt you."

"Ali, stop—" I pleaded with her, moving closer in the driving rain. I had to do it. I had to do something. I had to protect her. No matter what. I had to speak. "I killed Thomson."

There was silence, her eyes still lifeless as I stepped closer, my feet nearly slipping with every cautious step.

"There is no curse, no spirits. Just me." I let my own tears fall, thinking of what I had done. "I was jealous. Jealous you would marry him. I sabotaged his automobile. I killed him, Alina. It was me."

I could see Alina working it out, see her grappling with the truth that I would do anything to be with her, always. "You have to forgive yourself, Ali. Bad things happen. You can't always control it. The blood is on my hands. Mine and mine alone."

As I stepped closer, she launched forward, attacking me. I grabbed hold of her as tightly as I could.

"How could you?!" She hit and flailed with all her strength as I pulled her toward me. We spun in place until I had her farther from the roof's edge and away from danger. "Why? Why did you do it?!"

"Don't make me say why; you already know. I love you."

"No. No. You're a murderer. You're a monster who

made me feel things I did not want to feel. You're a—" Her eyes returned to life. "What are we supposed to do?"

We held each other tightly.

"Be rid of me. Be rid of this curse," I told her. "Once and for all. Open up the shutters. Leave. Lock me away somewhere, and be happy again. Just ask it of me, and I will go." I could feel her head shaking.

"I can't—"

I closed my eyes and let the rain wash over my face. My long nightgown soaked heavier and heavier as I stood there on the wet-slick roof. Her hands caressed my cheek, the tender passion of her soft lips against mine. I opened my eyes to see life fully returning to her beautiful green eyes for the first time in years.

"I feel hate," she cried. "A hate for you I have never wanted for a love I can never truly have. I hate you for it."

At that moment, I could see what Alina had to do to be free.

"I know why," I said helplessly through tears, remembering the bird she once loved so much she removed it from its cage but wouldn't let fly away. "You love me." I now understood the depths of her curse. The power of her love. How tightly she held on to it. And how strongly she pushed it away.

Alina had crushed the bird in her hands until it was dead.

She pushed me away with a single forceful blow. My leg slipped as I tumbled backward, right off the edge. I heard her screaming as I fell, felt a crack of pain as my leg broke when I hit the eaves, just before the moment I tumbled off the house.

I fell until I smashed, headfirst, into the ground with a thud.

WHEN MORNING CAME for me, most of the pain had subsided. The energy of my passions had faded. I felt all at once quite normal, perhaps numb from all the pain, I believed. All I felt was the urge to rise. To find Ali.

The sun filtered in through the windows, along with the birdsong from outside and the steady ticking of the grandfather clock in the hallway. All these little reminders of the everyday routineness of life flooded my senses with relief.

I tried to recall what had happened. How I had gotten here. What had happened to me that night. I wondered whether Alina truly knew I would fall over the edge if she pushed me away or if she had actually meant to harm me for her own sake. Either way, I had to find her. I had to make things right between us again.

I rose from my bedsheets and looked myself over. I stood, half expecting my leg to give out, but instead, it held. There was no blood. Nothing sore, nothing bruised. I was elated but also felt an uncommon sense of déjà vu, as if, all at once, I had become aware of a great amount of time passing without me.

Perhaps it was my having been unconscious. Or perhaps my mind had protected me from a lengthy recovery. I looked around my room, and slowly, the servant in me began to awaken.

My room was filthy. Dust and cobwebs covered the nightstand as if it had been untouched for years. I knew I had long neglected caring for myself in my obsession with Alina, but had I truly lost myself so much to have not noticed?

No. Something was wrong. Now, the sunlight felt cold, the ticking of the clock like an enemy, the birdsong a desperate warning to escape. I rushed to the door to open it but found it a struggle. It was as if my hands were somehow still slick-wet with rain, and it took all my effort to turn the rusted doorknob.

In the hallway, the dust stopped, the walls completely clean. I wandered from room to room, dressed only in my long white nightgown. All the furniture was, once again, covered in sheets, as if it were still, somehow, the morning after we had arrived. It felt as if all my difficult work had been undone, and when I saw a trunk at the top of the stairwell, my heart sank.

She was moving away. Alina was leaving me. I rushed toward the stairwell.

"Alina!" I yelled down to the foyer.

She was dressed all in black and talking to a man in the doorway.

"Alina!" I yelled again, only to be met with no answer. I carefully made my way down the steps, then heard the sound of footsteps following behind me. There was someone else in the house, I realized, as I turned around.

A child. A little girl.

She ran down the staircase past me and into Alina's arms.

"Mommy, the door opened again!" she said with a playful chime.

"Now, now." Alina turned, her face lit with happiness.

Older. Wiser. "What have I told you?" She lifted the child up and walked her around the room. "No more superstitions. We leave that room alone. It's just an old door, bound to open from time to time."

I sank into myself, collapsed into a huddle as I sat on the stairs, shaking as I realized the implications. This child, at least seven years of age. My love, years older, and I couldn't remember a day of it. Only remembering my love. My fall. My murder.

I looked down at my hands, desperately wondering how I could feel so many emotions, so much anguish, if I were no longer alive?

How many days? How many days had it been since my fall, and why had I not remembered any of them? All I could do was watch Alina standing there. The years had only made her more beautiful.

Years I had forgotten, I realized, as the truth slowly sank in. I was trapped. Trapped as I had always been. The more time I spent there, with Alina and her daughter in the foyer, the more the déjà vu made sense. The more I realized the truth of my afterlife, trapped here in Melody House, a hollow echo of my former life. Rising. Waking. Watching over her. Forgetting. Slowly fading into nothing every day as time went on without me.

Rising. Waking. Waiting. Waiting for Alina to just love me back.

She put her daughter down. "Run along now." Alina smiled. "It's time to say goodbye to the house."

"I don't want to!" the little girl cried.

Alina gently took her by the shoulders. "Now, dear, we mustn't fuss. Your mother had to move from her own country, say goodbye to everything she loved." She gently rubbed her daughter's shoulders. "Still, luck has been kind to us," Alina said wistfully. "So run along now. We mustn't keep our new home waiting!"

I rushed down to be close to her. She really was leaving Melody House for good. Leaving me. I watched Alina as she comforted her daughter, sending her away.

"I'd just like a moment alone, if I could," she said. "Say your goodbyes, dear."

The child sadly waved and was taken away to the carriage waiting outside. Now, Alina was alone again in the foyer, looking herself over in the mirror.

Alone except for me.

She was happy now. Finally happy. No longer knocking on wood at every turn, afraid of the shadows. She had locked them up somewhere, just as I told her to. She had sealed the memory of me away in a locked room.

I stood as close as I could to her. Hoping perhaps she would see something, any sign of me. I felt fainter and fainter, the more her green eyes stared at my reflection and saw nothing.

I wanted to tell her, tell her everything. That I didn't really kill Thomson. That his death really was just a tragic coincidence, not her curse. That I would have told her anything in order for her to stop blaming herself. That I didn't even blame her for killing me.

But more than anything, I wanted to apologize. To apologize for loving her more than I could ever love myself.

Those words were frozen in silence, in my mind. I realized how little respect I had for my love. How I had kept it for Alina alone and never myself. How I had underestimated its power. My feet locked in fear. Helpless. A ghost in life and a ghost in death.

I looked down at my hands. I truly was beginning to fade away, letting myself believe I deserved this. But then I looked up at her face, the smile gone.

That's when I felt it return. The shadow of my love. That powerful darkness in me returned to the surface. At first, very slowly. Then faster. Faster. Some furious desire always there had begun to fester and boil, simmer and rage. It was something cruel, something beautiful. Something I wanted for myself and myself alone. And I had the power to unleash it.

So what if Alina couldn't hear my voice? Maybe she never could. My fist clenched. My will strengthened. I could go with her. I knew I could. My will wasn't bound to these walls. My strength wasn't doomed to waste away here. I could be with her, always. Walking in her shadow. Basking in the shade of her light. I could fly right alongside her; all I asked was that she let me in. Open the cage.

As Alina went to step outside, she raised her hand to knock alongside the edge of the door frame. She stopped herself. "No more," Alina whispered to herself, fighting her every compulsion to knock three times.

That was it. I finally realized how. How I could do it. How I could be with her forever! I smiled as I ran to the banister. Smiled even against the pain of my entire being, my very soul fighting against being bound to this house.

I grimaced wildly, gleeful in my pain as I ran, no longer heavy from a rain-soaked nightgown, but instead, carrying the weight of my wicked, reckless, audacious love. To ask of Ali, one simple question.

The last question I would ever ask.

I grabbed ahold of the banister like a lifeline and pulled myself back up, even as my body was quickly fading. I turned to see Alina still standing there, fist at the ready, clenched in indecision, fighting her instinct to knock. I curled my own fist and knew exactly what to do with all the strength my passion could summon.

*Knock, knock, knock.*

Alina's face snapped around at the sound. Three familiar knocks, from out of nowhere. At that moment, time stood still. She looked right at me and yet, not through me, invisible as I might be. Fear was in her eyes, knowing the sound intimately.

*Don't leave me*, I silently begged. *I'm not just any ghost. I'm your ghost. Take me with you. Take me with you in your heart, and I will haunt your every step.*

Alina looked around anxiously, a cold sweat on her brow, unsure of the ramifications of leaving my knocks unanswered.

I was unsure as she was what would happen if she answered back. Unsure that if she rebuked me I would ever even wake again. Unsure I would not become a vengeful and unreasonable spirit if I were allowed to follow her. But all I knew for certain was that if I did not act for myself now, I would never again get the chance.

Alina took a resigned breath. "At least once more, then." She made her decision and gently rapped three times against the edge of the door: One, two, three.

"For my spirit," Ali answered.

With every knock, I could feel myself grow more powerful, could feel everything again. I looked down at my hands, once again whole and full of life. I manifested myself with all my strength and ran toward her with weightless abandon as I reached out to embrace her.

It was then I realized a new truth: Ali had never been the source of my love. I was. And it wasn't all wicked. It was powerful. Beautiful. Strong. And it deserved to be free. I grabbed onto Alina and wouldn't let go as we stepped out the door of Melody House for the last time.

I smiled, feeling the warmth of the sunlight on my face. Or maybe it was Alina's face? It was a little hard to tell. We were just so close together. But then again, maybe I was always meant to be her shadow. The chill down her spine. The knock that answered her call. Her good luck, and her curse. Together forever, in sickness and in death. And I wouldn't let anything ever tear us apart again.

For better, or for worse.

# ACKNOWLEDGEMENTS

Special thanks to my family for their support, R.B. Thorne, Elizabetta McKay, and everyone at NineStar Press!

# ABOUT THE AUTHOR

T.S. Mitchell is a nonbinary author of queer fiction from the Sunshine State! When they aren't obsessing over fictional people, you can find them hopelessly adrift in attempting to craft their own. T.S. is particularly interested in making intricate and detailed narratives about beautiful, twisted, intense love stories.

They also like to write about robots, mermaids, fairies, ghosts, demons, systems of oppression, gender stereotypes, depression, anxiety, yearning, and pretty much anything else that could make or break their characters' happiness!

## Email
epcotservo@gmail.com

## Twitter
@epcotservo

## Website
www.sites.google.com/view/tsmportfolio/home

# BRIDE OF BRINE

E.E.W. CHRISTMAN

WARNINGS: Depictions of death/dying.

SYLVIE CRAVED STILLNESS. Growing up, she remem-bered so much movement. The whipping wind, the crashing waves, the rising tides—the world never slowed by the sea. The desert had a calming stagnation. The warm air almost seemed to stop entirely. Even the movement of the sun was an afterthought, as if the Earth couldn't be bothered to ro-tate. Sylvie loved the peace of the motionless, red earth. She loved the silence most of all. Sweet, blissful silence, a void of sound she could wrap herself in. She'd been here so long, sometimes she even forgot what sound the ocean made. She barely dreamed of it anymore, was rarely haunted by the song of high tide or the smell of salt. She looked out across the empty wastes from her back door, seeing nothing and thankful for it.

However, Sylvie had learned long ago that any peace could be broken, and all calm was temporary. All it took to turn a placid ocean into a roiling sea was a little bit of hot air. And all it took to erase her quiet arid paradise was the vibration of her phone in her pocket.

One email. Like a sudden storm after years of tranquil

waters. Sylvie knew she was ruined before even reading it. She saw the name and her stomach sank like a lost ship; she knew it was over:

*Dad.* The desert, unmoving, silent, and perfect, already seemed like a distant dream. The day she'd left was the last time they'd spoken. Sylvie remembered the harbor, the lighthouse on the horizon, and the nearly vacant bus stop. Even from here, she heard the water calling to her. Waves rolling in, rolling out, an undulating voice in the distance, beckoning, promising, threatening her. She had thought he'd come to say goodbye. But Dad wasn't good at goodbyes. He'd told her in a flat tone that if she left, she wouldn't be welcome to return. It was a matter of fact, spoken without the faintest hint of emotion. Her father hadn't banished her. It hadn't been an ultimatum. Not to him. It was merely the nature of things, as immutable as the tides.

The last thing Sylvie ever expected was for him to beg her to return.

UNDER NORMAL CIRCUMSTANCES, Sylvie loved long drives. The night she'd left the sea behind and drove gloriously inland, the long stretches of lonely highway had been such a quiet comfort. Her only company had been the illuminated signs of the truck stops and chain restaurants she passed, the yellow orbs above the empty four-lane highway, and the old *Clan of Xymox* cassette that had gotten stuck in the tape deck a decade prior. She could only listen to one side on repeat. She hadn't minded. The only thing she cared about was *beyond* the highway. The long empty stretches of land that waited there, oceanless.

This time, the thing that waited for her wasn't the desert, but the all-too-familiar sea of her childhood. Sylvie swore she could feel the moisture accumulating in the air as she drove farther northeast. As if even the wind was whispering a dreadful "welcome home." She didn't even have the dark crooning of Ronny Moorings for company this time.

She stopped for lunch in a strip mall that hugged the space between the highway and a flat little town in Virginia. The kind of place that had every chain lined up one by one, their cartoonish mascots all smiling as you drove by, each trying to entice with the promise of familiarity. Sylvie stayed too long, pretending to fret over the choice, then spent too long ordering, too long in her car dipping her fries in a milkshake, and much, much too long making a new Clan of Xymox playlist on her phone.

She at least deserved good tunes, after all. A soundtrack for her misery that she could enjoy.

Sylvie slept at a roadside motel and dreamed of murky shadows and the voice that called from within. A figure floated in the darkness, familiar and yet unidentifiable. A hand reached from the depths, grasping for a prone ankle, calling her name in salty undertones—

Sylvie woke up. The cheap sheets stuck to her body, sticky with sweat. The sun wasn't even up yet.

She needed to hurry.

SHE SMELLED IT before she could see it. The air was thick with brine. Her gut twisted at the familiar stench. The air seemed to hum—a thousand murmuring voices whispering to her, drowning out poor Ronny. Sylvie pulled off the highway onto the familiar backroads of her childhood, lined with narrow white cedars. Even the potholes seemed unchanged. Perhaps they weren't, besides being a bit bigger from years without maintenance. The smell was suffocating, the hum maddening. How had she managed for so long, trapped in this atmosphere of unceasing sound and movement?

Even from here, the infernal thundering of the cresting surf called to her. And something just beneath the surface, a song, a promise, a threat...

Then, she rounded a bend. The trees broke. Her small hometown spread out before her, a smattering of houses with chipped paint and small, unkempt lawns stretching down the hill. The familiar steeple of the church rose from the tiny homes, the white of its paneling faded and one broken shutter flapping in the wind. *Thwack thwack thwack*. A depressing war drum. Beyond that sat the harbor, with its little dock and tiny fleet of fishing boats. It was late in the day, so most of them were docked. The weather looked bad anyway.

And the sea. Its song grew louder. Sylvie watched the gray water seethe as she drove into town. Little had changed, except for more businesses and homes emptied as people drifted away to brighter prospects in other, bigger towns. Few people were out, save for the few preparing for a storm, shuttering their windows and such. The scent of the impending rain fermented under the salty aroma of the ocean waves. Sylvie hurried through town, past the main square with their single grocer and the world's tiniest McDonald's, the only major chain in town. She went beyond the residential area, beyond the park with the dilapidated swings and wobbly merry-go-round. Up another hill, then right to the cliffs.

At the top was home. A two-story farmhouse positioned at a craggy peak overlooking the town below. The wood was unpainted; what was the point when the salt would strip it away in a matter of weeks? The barn had been unused for decades until Philip fixed it up and moved into it. One of his projects stood in front of the wide barn doors: an eruption of metal spires reshaped with fire. It was unlike any of Philip's other sculptures. He remade reality in bronze. Enormous fish and metal ships littered the yard. The things their family dealt with every day, recast into art. But this was something *un*real. A fabrication of nightmares cast in dark alloy. At first, it looked too abstract to make sense of. But the closer Sylvie got to the house, the more she could make out. Hands in the metal reached plaintively toward the sky. Closer still, and she could see half-formed faces, frozen in screams. It looked as if Philip had trapped real people in his sculpture. It was a far cry from the enormous trouts and schooners she remembered him making in their youth.

The more she looked at it, the more she knew: *She* had called to him in Sylvie's absence. Lured him with her briny song, twisted his mind to her will with wordless promises whispered in the night. But unlike Sylvie, Philip hadn't fled. She just hoped there was still time.

Dad came out at the sound of her car hitting the gravel. Sylvie was surprised by his gaunt face and frail frame. It had been a decade since they'd seen each other; she knew he'd passed from middle-aged into elderly. She knew logically that her father was no longer a young fisherman but, instead, an old, salty dog. And yet, when she thought of him, it was always as she'd left him: tall, imposing, skin leathery from a lifetime spent under the sun, riding the waves. He'd become shrunken and shriveled in his old age. But as Sylvie parked and got out of the car, she saw his expression, his eyes, the dour curve of his mouth. The changes were superficial. Her father seemed unchanged, in any way that mattered, save for the absence of his loyal, favorite child.

He said nothing as he waved Sylvie inside as if there hadn't been a decade-long silence between them. As if she'd never left. They sat at the same canary-yellow Formica table in the kitchen, and Dad poured them coffee from the same percolator he'd had for at least as long as Sylvie could remember. She took the proffered tin cup and sipped. The stale flavor of the old coffee Dad always bought was a bittersweet nostalgia. She recalled the first time he'd taken her out on the boat before dawn. She'd been nine. He'd given her the tiniest drink from his thermos. That had made Sylvie feel so special, so grown-up. *Just like Dad.*

Sylvie stared at the steam rising from the bad cup of coffee. What happened now? Were they supposed to start talking about why she left? Should they skip that particular bushel of trauma and ignore the decade of no contact and just talk about Philip? She wasn't sure what the protocol was for reconnecting with your estranged father due to a familial emergency.

Dad saved Sylvie the trouble. He downed the astringent brew, stood slowly once more, and reached for his hat. "I suppose you'll want to see it."

So that was how it was done. No preamble, no discourse. Just down to business. Sylvie nodded and followed her father back outside, leaving her unfinished coffee on the table. After all, they weren't *really* reconnecting. He'd only reached out because he was desperate. What was the point of small talk when they both knew she'd only been invited home to find Philip?

They got into Dad's pickup and headed for the beach.

THE FISH FOLK of Sylvie's town told stories of the creatures beneath the waves. Not the silver-blue mackerel or yellow cod they caught and sold every day, but unseen things. Shadows in the waves that became monstrous on wagging tongues, loosened by beer at the bar each night. No one said the word *mermaid* because mermaid was too feminine, too sultry, too beautiful-sounding to capture the terror of an unseen thing. They chose other words in its stead: merfolk, water women, brides of brine. None of them were willing to admit the terrible horror that was found in something so beautiful and so wicked. They could not imagine a lovely face filled with awful power.

THE DRIVE TO the beach was wretchedly silent. Sylvie turned the knob on the radio, and Dad silently switched it back off. This was the closest they'd come to conversing. Sylvie settled on staring out the dirty windshield. Clouds gathered on the horizon, dark and rotund, ready to unleash a storm on the small fishing town. By the time they reached the small strip of sand that wasn't dominated by rocks, the wind had picked up. Dad gripped his cap to keep it from flying off his head, and Sylvie, now accustomed to the warm silence of the desert, found herself sinking deeper into her coat.

Dad pointed to the wreckage as if Sylvie had been away so long she needed help identifying the trawler she'd worked on her entire childhood. The *Matilda* was broken down the middle, her forty-foot hull split like a ripped seam. Gurdies and taglines littered the ground; part of the net was caught in the mast. Some gulls had made a nest up there. They screeched in annoyance as she approached before flying off to watch her from the nearby rocks. Sylvie inspected the damage, feeling the critical eyes of her father on her back as she bent to pick over the debris. *Just like old times*, she thought sourly.

The barnacles that had been living on the bottom of the *Matilda* had dried out and died in the sun. Crouching over their sessile corpses, she looked at her family's livelihood, split open like an egg. The place where the boat had broken apart was perfectly straight, as if an enormous knife had sliced the trawler in half like warm butter. An impossibility. Sylvie climbed deeper into the wreckage, hunching in what had once been the cabin. The radio's wiry guts spilled out of the console, and her dad's collection of sea charts and maps lay scattered across every surface.

She plucked a shell from the chaos. A pale calico clam traced with fine mulberry lines. When she was little, Sylvie had loved scavenging the beach for such treasures. Sometimes, she would leave gifts for the sea as well. It hadn't felt like littering (although, of course, it had been). It had seemed logical enough, like the take-a-penny, leave-a-penny tray. Her heart still, she pried the clam open. Inside was a child's plastic ring. The kind bought for two quarters out of a gas station vending machine. Once red, it was now a dull pink, the false-jewel centerpiece almost completely worn away.

Sylvie was sweating as she reached into her coat pockets, fumbling for something small enough to jam into the clamshell. She found two pennies, a nickel, and a quarter. It would have to suffice. She stuffed them into the clam and closed it once more before crawling out from *Matilda*'s remains. Her father watched silently as his daughter slid on her belly across the sand, walked to the sea, and threw the seashell into the waves.

After a minute had passed, he finally spoke. "What now?"

Sylvie shrugged, although her heart was racing. Even now, she didn't like to show him any weakness lest he think any less of her.

"We wait."

SYLVIE HAD FORGOTTEN how gray this place was. Gray skies, gray harbor, gray water, gray rocks along the shore. Not a gleaming, metallic color, but a dull hue. A lack of anything, even the starkness of black or white. This town was *lacking* incarnate. She couldn't even appreciate the sunset over the Atlantic as the heathery jowls of cloud cover swallowed up the entire sky. The only way to tell it was getting later was by the shifting of temperature and tides. Sylvie's coat was inadequate. She thought about waiting in the truck but imagined the way her father's face would grimace at her lack of stoicism. The wind was nothing compared to those endlessly disappointed eyes.

They spent the first half hour in complete silence. Near-silence, at least. It was impossible to ignore the sea. Reaching, recoiling, like a tentative lover's hand. All the while filling her ears with the ceaseless thrum of its infernal movement. Coming, going, dragging debris from the *Matilda* back into the dark surf. As if saying, "You're next."

Dad hung back by the truck, opened the driver's side door as if to leave, then closed it again, realizing that would be indicative of *his* lack of stoicism. He leaned against the hood and carefully rolled a cigarette from a pouch in his jacket pocket. His eyes, sharp and wrinkled, were laser-focused on the pinched tobacco between his fingers. To Sylvie's surprise, he lit it with ease, even with the wind whipping all around them.

When he finished his cigarette and began rolling a second, he finally spoke. "Your grandma could hear the ocean too. Said it spoke to her in her dreams. Said she saw brides of brine in the waves at night." He sighed, lit the second cigarette, and exhaled a large plume of smoke. "Never did believe her till she disappeared."

He said it with reverence. As if being swallowed up by the sea was the greatest honor one could ever hope to receive. He wouldn't look at Sylvie as he continued.

"She never shunned the gift."

Sylvie bit her lip. He was predictably stubborn, yet she couldn't help growing angry at him. He had so much judgment for a man who had never heard the singing waves. He'd never seen the blue-black hand beckon from the water. He'd never felt drawn to a place and a creature that would squeeze the life from your lungs. He'd never heard the word-less song of a siren, more beautiful and terrible than any-thing she'd ever witnessed.

Grandma had. Sylvie had grown up on the stories. And when gifts began to fill the clamshells she collected, ones she hadn't left, she suddenly found herself trapped in a story of her own. The gifts led to friendship, and as she grew older, friendship became more. Something dark and amorphous, terrifying and sublime. Late night walks on the beach, feel-ing the eyes beneath the waves watching her hungrily. Salty kisses under a full moon. Cold hands touching and grabbing and tugging, a longing that could never be fully realized. Beautiful and horrible, a gut-twisting, elating kind of love. Sylvie used to imagine Grandmother's disappearance as a horror story, a kind of cautionary fable. But the older she got, the more she wondered if Grandma had walked into the waves willingly.

Leaving had taken everything Sylvie had. The only way to forget the song was to move to a place with no song at all. A silent earth. A quiet house on empty sand. Sylvie hadn't wanted to sacrifice herself for love.

"You never understood," Sylvie said loudly enough to be heard over the whipping winds. "And you never will. Just don't forget. I'm here for Phil. *Not* you."

The rest of the waiting was spent without talking. Sylvie was fine with that. The longer she stood by the sea, the more her heart began to thrum in her chest. Panicked, excited, ea-ger, terrified. The smell was intoxicating, the roar of the waves growing closer, becoming a constant trill in her head. Before long, there was nothing but her chilled body and the noisy, frothing ocean.

The sea-slick body rose out of the water just as the rain began to fall, her skin the grays and blues of a storm, her long black hair clinging to her neck and chest. Sylvie felt dizzy—with fear or desire, she could not tell. The two feelings became indistinguishable. Sylvie couldn't help smiling back at the woman in the waves, who raised a long hand and beckoned her forward. As if she'd never left at all. As if they were still silly kids dreaming of an impossible future.

The woman of the waves opened her mouth, and a voice rose from the chorus of the tide. There were no words. After all, she didn't need them; Sylvie knew what the song was about—love, death, the sea. Her voice, a beautiful promise, filled Sylvie's head. She felt drunk on it as she stepped forward, the icy water immediately seeping into her shoes. She barely noticed the cold, was vaguely aware of shouting, of a hand trying to pull her back as the water reached her waist. Sylvie pulled away, the sensations disappearing even as the water reached her neck. There was only *her*. The bride of brine (*her* bride of brine) and her intoxicating song.

Hands grabbed her waist and pulled her close. Sylvie sighed, saltwater filling her mouth. She didn't care. She ran her fingers through the black cloud of hair hanging around them, pressed her lips against her, said *I missed you* in a cloud of air bubbles that floated upward. Even as they kissed, the song continued, carried by the water itself. It swallowed them whole in a cacophony of lust. The currents (or maybe the tugging hands of her lost love) dragged her down into the ever-churning sea. Noisily. Hungrily. Eagerly.

WHEN PHILIP WASHED up on shore, he had no memory of the past week. He'd been hounded by nightmares for the better part of a month, he recalled. Dreams filled with hands reaching for him from the dark. He'd taken the *Matilda* out late (he could no longer remember why), and then there was nothing. An enormous hole where memories should have been. He woke up in a hospital bed with his father crouching over him like a shrunken, maritime gargoyle. Dad cried then, a rarity Philip hadn't witnessed since mother died.

When they went home, Dad was a changed man. He stared at the sea but no longer wished to sail its waves. He mentioned Sylvie. Another rarity. But when Philip asked about her or about what had happened to him for that forgotten week, Dad would go quiet and fumble for his tobacco. His only coherent response was "I didn't know. How could I know?"

Philip replaced the *Matilda*. He named the new trawler *Sylvia* in honor of the sister who had disappeared. Dad had all but retired, something Philip swore would never happen, so the fishing business fell to him. He didn't mind. He liked the time alone on the sea, with nothing but the net and the line for company.

Sometimes, though, early in the morning when the world was still and empty, Philip would miss his father's company. And he missed Sylvie. He missed their phone calls and her descriptions of the desert she loved so much. In those moments, he'd play the music he remembered she'd liked. Gothy, dancy stuff that Philip had never enjoyed. He'd smile at the memory of him pounding on her bedroom door to turn it down.

Once, he thought he saw figures beneath the waves.

Two intertwined bodies darting through the water, fishlike, scaly skin glinting in the dawn. But when he bent over the bow to get a better look, they were gone. Like a trick of the light on the water. Like there was nothing there at all.

# About the Author

E.E.W. Christman is a horror and fantasy writer working in the Seattle area. Their work has appeared in a number of anthologies and magazines, including TheNoSleep Podcast, Lavender Bones, Limeoncello Magazine, Uncanny Magazine, PULP Magazine, Exploits, American Gothic Horror (Flame Tree Press), Supernatural Horror Stories (Flame Tree Press), It Calls From the Forest Volume 1 (Eerie River) and others. Their full publication history can be found on their website: www.eewchristmanwrites.com. They are an active HWA member.

### Email
e.e.w.christman@gmail.com

### Twitter
@eew_christman

### Instagram
@izzybuzzkill

# HAUNT

## ALEX SILVER

WARNINGS: Discussion of family transphobia, depictions of grieving for the loss of a loved one, alcoholism in a secondary character, and arson.

THE RINGING ISN'T a real sound, echoing in my ears. It's the reverberating silence when the power cuts out, and we're alone in the old house that used to be a home. Once, the high ceilings sang with children's laughter. My laughter. Mine and Levi's. The tall windows let in summer sunshine, and the door was open to anyone who needed shelter.

Now, that's ancient history. Dated furniture molders under moth-eaten dustcloths. Every surface is piled high with the detritus of a lifetime and the evidence of my father's precipitous decline in health over his final years. Flaking paint covers the walls. Water damage from a longstanding leak in the roof traces brown furrows in what used to be cheery pale yellow. The pretty facade, ravaged by time and neglect, is like looking in a mirror. Lucky for me, I have decades of practice not looking.

Still, the absence of sound burrows into my eardrums and won't stop. I get up from the sagging mattress, redolent with disuse. We brought clean bedding, at least. The bed squeaks under my weight as I stand. The floor creaks under me. I used to have the squeaky floorboards memorized.

Bert doesn't get up, but his hand finds my wrist, tries to pull me back down beside him. "Come back to bed, love."

I shake him off. "Just checking something."

I pad along the once familiar path to the kitchen. The silence is worse here. No buzzing hum from the fridge's motor, keeping our food cool. No bustle of my mother presiding over the stove. No chatter of family gossip or rehashing of the family secrets. No more acrimonious words yelled over the dinner table. No stomping feet on the stairs or slamming doors. Nothing but the all-encompassing silence lingers here.

I didn't think I'd miss the noise, but I do. Even the midnight clink of ice in my father's nightcap after a late shift at the hospital, where he worked a second job as a janitor. The snap and fizz of my brother opening a fresh can of beer after Mom was asleep hasn't graced these walls in years. And come morning, not even the steady drip of coffee into the carafe will break the silence of the dead.

The kitchen hasn't been the heart of this house in a long time. The steady pulse that once drove the family who lived here has long since stopped. Shrouded in predawn stillness, the house feels like something long dead. I used to think Bert and I could bring it back to life, but more and more, it feels as though we're just maggots. Parasites under the skin, giving the place a semblance of the life it once held.

This isn't a home, and with the way the old place is falling down around us, I don't know if it will remain much of a house for long. Bert says it's just the grief talking. I'm not so sure. This place isn't fit for the living when all I can see within its walls are the ghosts of its dead. My dead.

The ringing fades as I run my fingers over the filthy

countertops. I don't know how it got so run down. We have plans to start cleaning in the morning, but I can't sleep while the house is rotting around us. I prop up my phone to light my work. The power company was supposed to turn the electric back on after we paid the bills last week, but it hasn't happened yet. Something about a recent storm and a tree falling on the line. We're too far from town to be a priority.

I dig under the sink for cleaning products. I can almost hear Grandma's voice telling me to wear gloves or I'll ruin my hands. It used to make me want to scrub them in bleach out of sheer pigheadedness. As though ruined hands might make her stop seeing a girl when she looked at me. Now it just makes me sad.

"What man wants a wife with callouses?" she'd ask, cupping my cheek in her wrinkled, work-rough palm. Even when I didn't understand why, I hated when she said those things. Her thoughtless words burrowed into my skull and made me feel less. Made it seem like the marks of her hard work to provide and care for her family made her less. As though her worth and my worth had an intrinsic link to our value to a man.

I wish she had seen her own strength. And I wish she could have seen past all the societal assumptions of who I should grow up to be through to the real me. Those tangled truisms of hers, so often repeated, seemed like unbreakable laws. Laws my parents hoped would bind me to the life of their choosing.

They made it so much harder to embrace myself as a man. Until I shook free of them, it was all but impossible to understand my worth isn't about what I can give to others. Their expectations used to ring in my ears, but now they're gone, and their voices are as silent as this old dead house.

I don't find the cleaning products where they used to be. So I have to go out to Bert's shiny new Jeep for the bag of supplies we picked up on the way through town. The scope of work required to fix the old place is daunting. Bert joked it looks more like a family curse than an inheritance when I showed him the pictures. He tried to convince me to just hire someone to tear it down and sell the land. The farmer who owns the surrounding acreage would probably buy it, but this house and I are all that's left, the only ones who can share the memories.

I scrub the counters until the gray grit gives way to the pink flecked white Formica underneath years of neglect. Pink, like the prom dress Mom surprised me with when I told her I didn't want to go and she thought it was because I didn't own anything nice enough. Pink like the anger tinting her cheeks when I told her I'd rather go in my brother's old suit, even if it was at least two sizes too large for me. Better swimming in a dated suit that gave me space to breathe for the first time in years than strangling in the expensive gown in my size she blew her budget on. I'm not crying; it's just sweat dripping onto the grease-stained stove top. This is more work than I thought it would be. Harder work. No one has lived here since Mom died and Dad ended up at the long-term care home with his cirrhosis and his bad temper. Two years sitting empty left their toll. The paperwork I got from the lawyer said a neighbor was supposed to drop in and look after the place after Dad moved into the home. I guess no one gave her the memo. Didn't stop her from taking the monthly checks for her housekeeping services.

I shouldn't shoulder the guilt over not being here to

oversee things. Not when I wasn't welcome. Sometimes, I think the family ended when my brother came home from his first tour of duty in a casket. Dad got drunk, and Mom got silent, and I got gone. Left after my graduation and didn't look back. I might have gone away, regardless.

This old house reminds me of being a teenager, small, scared, and alone. Those years when it seemed like I was holding my breath waiting for the chance to become.

I'm not waiting now. I've made a life with Bert far from here. So I scrub the counters, the stove top, and the years of accumulated grease from the oven. I wipe the windows and clean out the fridge, thankful at least someone removed all the food before unplugging it years ago. I scrub every inch of the kitchen as though enough elbow grease might some-how replace the irreplaceable. Restart a pulse long since still.

It's a shock when Bert wraps his arms around me from behind as I'm sweeping. I jump at his touch, fumbling and then clutching the broom to my chest. He chuckles, a low, happy rumble so out of place here it shocks me almost as much as my not hearing him approach. It jars me out of my melancholy and almost makes me smile too. Almost.

"Sh. Relax, it's just me." He props his chin on my shoul-der and murmurs near my ear. "Didn't mean to startle you."

I tip my head back to look at him. "Hey. Guess this place has me on edge."

"Hey, yourself. How long have you been up?"

I don't know for sure, but the grimy windows are aglow with the first light of dawn now. Hours. "Doesn't matter; I couldn't sleep. There's so much to do before we can leave."

Bert tightens his arms around me, and the warmth of

his body makes me more aware of the chill air. I'm cold, so I turn in his arms and burrow into his embrace, tucking his fuzzy bathrobe around me and getting another chuckle out of him.

"You know I packed your robe, too, if you're cold." Bert teases, knowing it's not really the robe I want. It's being close to him.

"Yours is better," I reply, the words familiar between us, part of a routine.

"It's exactly the same." Bert makes no move to pull away or refuse me access as I link my fingers behind his back, the robe soft and warm around us.

"Nope. Sharing is better," I insist.

"Whatever you say, Kev." Bert kisses the top of my head. He holds me for a while, and the steady beat of his heart fills the silent spaces from last night. I'm not sure how long we stand there. His presence makes this easier.

"You want to come back to bed for a little while before we tackle the rest of this?" Bert gestures at the ruins of the house.

"No. Can we go somewhere for breakfast?" I pull my arms out from under his robe. He tucks it closed again.

"Sure. Where did you have in mind?"

I shake my head. "Anywhere." *I mean* anywhere other than here, some place without all the memories to haunt it.

"Sure, go get dressed, and I'll see if I can search our options. Here, hang this upstairs?" Bert shrugs out of his robe and hands it to me. He pulls out his phone and turns his attention to it, expecting me to go.

I don't want to leave him to venture back up the stairs into the silence of my old room, but I go. Each step away from him drives the chill of this place deeper. I hurry my steps, all but sprinting from the stairs to my suitcase. I throw on the first warm things I find and jog back to my husband. He smiles at me.

"Ready?" Bert's already wearing his light fall jacket. He's got his keys in one hand and his phone in the other.

"Yep. Where are we going?" I already have my shoes on. The floors are too filthy to risk walking barefoot, even though it goes against years of habit not to kick them off by the door. I pull on my jacket, and we leave.

"No signal out here, but I seem to recall passing a diner by the gas station we stopped at yesterday. That should do the trick." Bert takes my hand as we walk across grass icy in the morning light.

It's still early fall, too soon for snow, but that doesn't stop the grass from crunching underfoot. My breath frosts the air as we get into the Jeep. Bert leans over the console to kiss me before he puts the car into gear. It's nice. A needed affection. A reminder he's here with me, even if he didn't want to be.

We get to the end of the long, tree-lined drive before the engine stalls. Bert tries to restart it, but the car stutters and stops again. And again, when he gives the key another twist.

We pop the hood and get out to look. Bert isn't a car guy. He likes the aesthetic of the Jeep, even though I told him it wasn't the most reliable cold-weather vehicle. I'm not really a car person either, but my brother was. From the time he got his learner's permit at fifteen until his death, he always seemed happiest when he was elbows deep in an engine.

I was eleven when he got an old clunker and a hand-me-down set of tools from our uncle to fix it with. My child's logic thought if I just copied him, I might matter to my family the same as him. They'd see me as more than a future wife and mother.

I convinced myself if I was enough like him, then my family might see me under the frilly dresses my parents delighted in making me wear. If I could just be like Levi, they might offer me a future as bright and shiny as his. So I copied him. I didn't love cars, but I picked up a thing or two hanging around, pestering him as often as he'd allow.

The Jeep has a blown spark plug. Weird, since I'm pretty sure we'd have heard it break yesterday on the drive here. Must have just happened. Which means we should be able to start it up and get it to a shop, but breakfast is probably out. At least until we get the car to a garage.

"That's going to need a mechanic." I gesture to the broken plug.

Bert gives me a look. "If you say so. Do I need to get a tow or can we drive it there?"

"Should be able to drive it." I poke around to see if there's anything else obviously amiss, but the engine seems fine. I shrug and close the hood. "Might be good to call ahead and make sure they can take it today, if you can get enough signal."

"On it." Bert gets back into the vehicle and pulls out his phone to find a garage. I'm not ready to get back in the car. Something about this feels wrong. I need fresh air. There should be nothing but open air behind me. A few more feet of driveway and then the empty rural road. I step back, right into a wall of ice where the edge of the property ought to be.

The cold is so intense it steals the breath from my lungs and anchors my feet to the ground. I try to inhale or cry out for help, but the air catches in my throat. I'm frozen. Cold and unable to move. My vision tunnels. My head swims like I'm buzzed without drinking a drop.

The world tilts and spins around me, and all I can think about is getting back to Bert. He catches my eye through the windshield, watching me, oblivious to whatever unseen force is trapping me here. I stop trying to step back and put all my strength into getting to him.

I jolt away from the icy barrier holding me in place, only to stumble and catch myself against the car's hood. Bert looks concerned as I remain braced, trying to catch my breath.

"Kev, what's wrong?" He opens the door and comes to stand beside me.

"Nothing." I try to wave him off. "Just a dizzy spell. Must be hungrier than I thought. I'm fine." Bert's concerned gaze bores into me. "Really," I insist. "The sooner we take the car in, the sooner we can grab a bite to eat."

My loving husband purses his lips. He seems poised to question me more or argue I'm not fine, but he thinks better of it. "Well, the internet isn't coming in any better here than it was inside the house. We'll just have to hope we get a signal on the way into town. Or else the folks at the gas station might be able to point us to a garage."

We both get back in the car. The engine won't start, and I suspect we aren't bringing the car anywhere any time soon. After several more attempts, the car splutters to life.

"Yes!" Bert pounds the steering wheel in triumph. The engine grumbles loudly as we idle; the lights on the dash dim and surge.

"Go, before we stall again," I urge, patting his thigh.

Bert puts the car in gear and hits the gas. We make it to the property line before the engine cuts out and the car stops. Not a slow roll to a standstill as if we'd run out of power either. No, this is an instantaneous loss of momentum that shouldn't be possible. Even if we *were* barely rolling. It's a lurch as though we've slammed into an invisible barrier.

My stomach drops at the confirmation we're stuck here. Trapped, just like in my childhood nightmares. Stuck in a life that could never fit.

Bert was right; we should never have come here. Back to a home that never really existed. Back to a place that can't accept me as I am. The whispers of remembered conversations, telling me who I ought to be, who I could never be, swell inside my head until I want to scream them into silence. But I know I can't out scream the voices of the past. Not when they only exist in my head.

I scramble out of the car and stride across the lawn. It's possible whatever is keeping us here is only at the end of the driveway. I pause at the low stone wall demarcating the property line. I reach out ahead, desperate for the barrier to be a silly fantasy. Not real. It can't be real.

My hand plunges into the ice of an invisible wall again. The cold burns my bare fingers, pain pulsing along my arm. I can't seem to pull back, but as I watch, the tips of my fingers turn a bright red. They start to tinge blue. I need to pull away before the cold destroys my unprotected flesh. But I can't seem to make my hand obey me.

Bert pulls me away from the barrier. His familiar voice is nothing but a roaring in my ears as I stare at my fingers. I half expect to see nothing but necrotic flesh where healthy skin used to be.

As he pulls me back, I stare at my hand, seeing wrong-ness. Not frostbite, but chipped polish from a manicure I got when I was powerless. My teenage self felt like I didn't have any choice but to agree to something that made my insides twist with wrongness. I blink, and the French tips fade back into my usual neatly trimmed nails. No polish. My hand is fine. I'm *not* fine.

"Kevin?" Bert turns me to face him, holding me by both shoulders. The jostling tears my attention away from the searing pins and needles of my hand returning to a normal temperature.

"This is going to sound crazy, but I don't think the house is going to let us leave."

"What?"

"That's the property line, and I can't cross it." I point at the barrier.

Bert gives me an incredulous look. "What are you talk-ing about?"

"Try to step over the wall." I gesture—seeing is believ-ing, right?

Bert glances from me to the wall. He purses his lips like he does when he thinks I'm being foolish but doesn't want to start a fight. He takes a step toward the wall. I want to grab him, stop him before he experiences the searing cold for himself. But we can't come up with a way out of this until he accepts there's a problem to solve.

Bert steps over the low wall, turns, and gives me an ex-pectant look. "Well?"

"But..." I shake my head. Could I have imagined the bar-rier?

"Come on. If we follow the road, we're bound to get a phone signal eventually. Or the neighbors must have a land-line to call for a tow." He offers me his hand. I hesitate, unwilling to experience more of the burning cold. Bert reaches through the barrier for me. I take his hand, trusting him to pull me through.

This time, I scream when the cold engulfs me. Bert stops pulling when he has my arm elbow-deep in the barrier.

"Kevin? What the hell is going on here?"

I just shake my head, unable to answer through the pain. He steps back over the wall and pulls me away from it. I sit heavily on the ground, shivering like I might break into pieces.

"Your arm looks burned," Bert says, staring at it like something impossible.

It *is* impossible. I'm too numb with the realization that he can leave, and I'll be all alone here. Trapped with my ghosts.

"New plan," Bert continues. "Let's get you back inside to warm up while I go for help."

I hate that plan. I don't want him to leave. Bert hauls me to my feet, and I hobble back up the long drive to the house. I'm cold and exhausted from cleaning all night, and all I want to do is go to bed so I can wake up from this nightmare.

"Stay with me?" I ask as Bert guides me to the recliner where my father drank away the last few healthy years of his life. I don't want to sit in it, but it's the most intact piece of furniture left.

Bert shakes his head. "One of us has to go for help. We need food and water."

I grimace. He's right. The house has a deep well, but the water requires a pump to access it. An electric pump. My folks had a generator for emergencies, but there's no fuel left. At least there's still a woodstove in the living room for extra heat and a cord of dusty wood stacked inside the shed.

Wood Dad didn't have the strength to carry inside by the end of his illness. I don't want to think of him wasting away, trapped and alone. It's not my fault. It's not.

Even if the last time we spoke, we fought. I don't want to be stuck here. I can't stay here. But I can't leave either. The barrier is seeing to that.

"Your hands are like ice, and you're clearly not well. I told you to pack a warmer jacket." Bert tsks. "Stay here, rest." Bert takes my hands between his and tries to chafe some warmth into them. "We'll figure this out." He brushes his lips against my temple.

"I guess I'll start a fire." I gesture toward the squat iron stove.

Bert nods. "Just be sure the chimney bits are clear. I still say we should tear the place down, but I'd rather not burn it while you're inside." He flashes one of his teasing smiles, but the attempt at humor falls flat.

"I'll check the vents. I'm sure it's fine." Though now that he's mentioned the possibility it's not, I'm less certain. Still, the cold seems to have sunk into my bones, and I need the fire to breathe warmth back into me. "Go. The sooner you leave, the sooner you'll be back."

"Yeah. Guess I'll try the car once more before giving up on it."

"Good idea. Drive it straight to a garage if it starts," I suggest.

Bert gathers me in his arms for a quick kiss goodbye. His embrace blocks out some of the cold. Until I realize if the house is keeping me here, Bert's car might start just fine without me in it. And there's nothing stopping him from leaving and never coming back. That's what I did when I left. Never even looked back until I got the inheritance papers from the lawyer.

Bert turns in the doorway, almost like he can read my thoughts. It makes me shiver. "I'll be back as soon as I can, Kev."

I nod. No sense arguing. Either he'll come back, or he won't. And, of course, he *will* come back. This place and the ghosts of the past are messing with my head. It would be easier if they'd only stop whispering in my head, subvocal reminders of things that no longer matter.

I grab a fresh garbage bag from the stash of cleaning supplies and open the grate on the woodstove. It's as big a mess as everything else here. Dad never did raise a hand to keep the house tidy. That wasn't his job, he'd say. I get to work shoveling out the accumulated ash and a bit of partially burned wood.

The distant rumbling purr of Bert's motor starting makes my hands tremble. The engine sounds fine from here. From inside, I can discern no sign of the busted spark plug. The engine revs, then the tires crunch over the last of the gravel drive and onto the asphalt of the road, and the car sounds fade into the distance. Bert is gone, and I'm alone with my memories.

There's something in the ashes; I cut my fingers on a shard of broken glass while trying to pull it out. It's a badly charred picture frame. One I recognize from my parents' bedroom. It used to be a pretty thing, filigree metal and wood evoking tree branches to shape the word family. He must not have let the fire burn for long after throwing this in. There's still some charred photo paper pinned under the broken pane of glass.

I recognize the photo from what little remains. Mom took a picture of the four of us every holiday season to add to the front of the stack. This frame held over a decade's worth of family photos. And now they're reduced to fragments and ash.

The bit peeking up at me is a version of me I hate to see. A little boy with long curly hair in bows, a green satin dress to match his brother's tie, and a smile so sad it makes me want to cry. I hated that dress. Loathed the picture. I was twelve, and it was the last year I let Mom badger me into a dress. It's jarring to see it there, surrounded in ruin. Eerie that the only part of the photo family to remain is a little girl who never really existed.

I use the dustpan to flip the remains of the frame, broken glass and all, into the trash. The picture was a lie. It was always a lie, and it can't change who I am. But when I catch my reflection in the broken glass, all I can see is her long hair framing my face. I blink, and my hair is short again. As short as I've kept it since I left home and didn't have to justify my appearance to anyone.

I run my fingers through my hair to be sure, leaving ashy streaks that make me grimace. I need a shower. But we won't have water for bathing until there's power.

It's still freezing in here, so I finish cleaning the belly of the stove and inspect it as best I can. I recall a time when I hung on Dad's every word as he passed on the manly secrets of fire to my brother. There's a draught through the flue, so I'm pretty sure it's open enough not to fill the house with smoke or carbon monoxide. I find the kindling in the bin where Dad kept it and get a fire started with the matches he kept on the shelf above the kindling. Dad always was a creature of habit. Too bad he let his habits kill him.

Once I get it burning, the heat of the fire makes the house bearable. I sit with my back to the iron stove, soaking in the first warmth I've felt outside of Bert's arms since we got here.

It's a mistake. The sweet tang of woodsmoke reminds me of cozy winters with my family before I realized I was too different to ever fit here. It's as warm as my mother's hugs and my father's approval, back before I got too old to harbor anything but antipathy for the things that could earn it.

I can't sit there with the heat burning into me as deep as the cold outside. I'm restless, so I pace around the house, glancing up the long drive for any sign of Bert. He's not there, and no amount of staring at nothing will get him here any faster. I go back to clearing away years of neglect from the living room.

The piles of trash and empty bottles by Dad's favorite chair are a depressing portrait of how he spent his final years after Mom died and before the care home. I try not to think about it. Try not to see the flashes of the past every time something triggers a memory. I don't want to remember. I thought this might be cathartic, but wading through the past tugs at long-buried parts of my psyche. The memories hang over me like a threat, holding me captive until I'm choking on the ghosts of my childhood. I'm afraid they won't let go until I'm as dead as they are.

I fill several bags of trash before the floor is clear enough to sweep. It's depressing how much work remains, but I feel lighter after cleaning out all the accumulated junk of a lifetime from downstairs.

I don't know if I can face cleaning out the garage where I spent so much time with my brother. The bathroom where I cut my own hair in front of Mom's vanity and told her who I am. Where she ignored me and pretended nothing had changed. The bedroom with the pink walls I hated makes me claustrophobic.

I want to search for a memory that doesn't hurt, but everything seems to have sharp edges. The longer I'm here, the more it seems like the past is a pile of broken glass and holding onto it will only tear me to ribbons.

It gets late, and Bert isn't back. I keep cleaning until it's too dark to see. Then I work some more by the light of my phone until its battery dies. Not as though it was good for anything else with no signal.

It's too dark to see what I'm doing inside, but the sky is bright with moonlight. Brighter than it ever seems in the city. Enough to see the driveway. I walk along the gravel to the end. And run into the same wall of ice I hit before. Whatever this place wants with me, it isn't ready to release me. I go back to the house and continue dismantling the memories.

I haul the bags of trash out onto the empty front porch. When that's done, I drag the broken furniture out too. Everything I can carry on my own follows—chairs, tables, cabinets and shelves, rugs, the ancient console television. All of it is so much worn out and dated detritus of the past. I leave it heaped outside to load into the dumpster that's supposed to arrive sometime this week. Dad's recliner pinches my fingers as I force it through the front door, and I drop it where I stand, kicking it and cursing.

I hate the stupid chair. Hate everything about it. Tears burn my eyes, and I don't stop spitting vitriol until I'm curled up in the chair, sobbing and wishing things could have been different.

That's where Bert finds me when he gets back hours later. I'm sure it must be after midnight, but it's only nine, according to his phone. I forgot how early the moon can rise in October, how bright it shines with no city lights to dim its glow.

The Jeep's broken spark plug is still stuck in the engine block. The shop couldn't get to it today. Bert spent most of the day waiting in case they had a gap in the schedule to squeeze us in, but it never happened.

The shop let him pay for a rental car while they fix his since they're keeping the Jeep overnight. It was after six by then, so he had to go two towns over to find an open grocery store. I don't miss that part of small-town life. There's a lot I don't miss. The stillness of nature and the bright moon hanging low in the sky as my husband takes my hand and leads me inside, though—that I've missed.

Bert thought to buy wet wipes to clean up with, and I'm grateful to be able to swab away some of the grime from my skin before we eat. He offers me a fully charged battery pack for my dead phone, courtesy of the garage lobby where he spent his day. He got us a lukewarm rotisserie chicken for dinner. I'm sure it was hot when he bought it, but not so much anymore. I'm not complaining. He came back to me.

By the time we finish eating, I'm exhausted. Bert puts

away the rest of the groceries he picked up, nothing requiring refrigeration, while I adjust the woodstove's damper down for the night. Then we head up to bed. Lying there in the dark, the doubts and memories creep in on me again.

I can hear all the critical voices that used to drag me down. People calling me things I never was. I don't want to listen. I left those voices behind, but being alone with them all day makes them harder to ignore.

Bert seems to notice my mood. He takes my hand under the covers, offering comfort. "How are you doing, love? This has got to be hard on you."

"Yeah. Didn't think I'd feel this much. Not that I miss them, I barely knew them anymore. I miss the possibility. The potential we could have been a family again." I shift closer to him in the too-small bed.

"I'm sorry." Bert wraps his arms around me. "I'll listen if you want to talk about it."

I shake my head, too tired to talk through all the emotions tangled up inside of me. Mostly I'm afraid I'll be trapped here forever, that the past will never let me leave.

I didn't think I'd want to be physical with Bert tonight. Not here. But when he spoons up against me under the covers, I'm struck by my need for him. I need to know he sees me, the real me, and that he wants me as I am.

I grind my ass against his groin.

Bert freezes. "You sure?"

"Yeah. Want you to love me." I grind more insistently. Bert pushes forward to meet me. He kisses along my neck, lips brushing over my stubbled jaw.

"I always love you," Bert whispers near my ear. "Love kissing you." He rubs his fingers over my cheek. I crane my head to capture his lips with mine. It's worth risking beard burn to connect with the man I love. Bert seems to agree, even though neither of us has had a chance to shave or wash since we left our cozy condo to fix up this place. I roll around to face him, savoring the sensation of his dick hardening against me when I rock my hips into him.

I moan, empowered at the effect I have on him. Growing up in this room, I was so certain no one could ever love me the way he does. I bought into the lie that if I tried to break the facade of who I had to be, it would mean I'd have to give up any chance at romantic love.

But Bert reminds me every day that the voice in my head telling me I have to be good enough to be worthy of love is wrong. I am lovable. I am loved. And Bert makes love to me there in the dark bedroom where I used to cry myself to sleep thinking I'd never get to be open about who I am.

I'm too comfortable in my lover's arms to worry about the once familiar sounds of this old room. The creaking of the house settling around us, the crack of a log succumbing to the fire in the stove below us. The rattling of bare tree limbs outside the window and the soughing of the icy wind.

Branches tap on the window, sounding almost like the clink of a bottle being set down or my dad's alcohol-roughened laughter. He's not here. He's dead, and the noise is just in my memories now. None of it matters as Bert holds me closer.


WHEN I WAKE up, it's still dark outside, but the first blush of dawn on the horizon reminds me of countless other dawns I met within these four walls. I get up and brace my-self to face the rest of the work. I'm already shivering from the chill in the air. The fire must have burned out overnight. I'll have to build it back up when I go downstairs.

Yesterday's certainty I was trapped here by some un-seen force seems like a silly flight of fancy after a good night's rest. Still, the memories of home I held on to in my heart when we planned this trip are nothing like the realities of being here. It seems far too much like being held captive to want to linger any longer than it takes to clean out the house and get it ready to sell.

The steady progress I made yesterday leaves me hope-ful that together Bert and I can finish our task by the end of the week. We can leave this place behind for good. I consider waking him, but he looks so peaceful sleeping in a bed I never dreamed I'd share with a man who loves me. I let him rest. He's never been a morning person. Bert will be happier to get to work if I can press a warm cup of coffee into his hands when I wake him.

If only the electric company would get the power re-stored, I could do that easily. As the situation stands, I can heat some bottled water on the woodstove. I'll wake him with a hot mug of the instant coffee he picked up at the gro-cery store. I might even make some toast to go with it. Not exactly a gourmet brunch like we'd have at home, but better than nothing.

After a moment's hesitation, I pull on Bert's robe, leav-ing my identical one on the hook where he placed it beside his when we arrived here. He'll grumble about it, but I think he secretly appreciates the comfort I take in his scent and wrapping myself in something of his like a claim.

When I reach the bottom of the stairs, I expect to see the living room cleared of the detritus of my father's final years. The floors should be bare and ready for whatever the new owner wants to make of them.

What I find instead is the same familiar outline of furniture that hasn't been so much as rearranged since Levi died. As if turning our home into a monument to his life might erase his death. I know I dragged it all outside last night. I still have the scrape on my knuckles from barking them against the jamb while I wrestled with Dad's chair in the doorway. And yet, here it all is, every item of furniture back where it sat when we first arrived to survey the mess.

The scene in front of me is so impossible that I close my eyes. I stand there, wrapped in Bert's robe like armor, willing the mess to be gone. I know I cleaned this room already. It should look the way it did last night when I let Bert lead me up to bed.

When I peek at the room again, the garbage and old bottles are still heaped around Dad's favorite recliner. I walk to the chair, stunned with disbelief. Surely, I didn't imagine cleaning out all this old junk?

It's as if while we slept, the room reset to the exact way we found it when we opened the doors with the keys the estate agent gave us. Like I never laid a hand on it. I press on my scraped knuckles; the sting reminds me I'm here, and this is real. I really cut myself last night, and the chair that caused the injury is still sitting just where it was before I moved it.

Part of me wonders if Bert might be playing some absurd prank. But I cannot fathom a reason he'd go to the trouble when he'd only have to help me clear away the mess a second time.

I must have dreamed it. Yesterday was a long day, and I must have curled up in the chair, remembering better times. Before Levi died and Dad crawled all the way into the bottle. Before Mom was so checked out she couldn't even pretend to care about the kid she still had. Just before.

I must have dreamed about cleaning the living room. It's the only answer that makes sense. I've been thinking about nothing else aside from the daunting task of how to tackle each room. Those thoughts and plans must have bled into my dreams. Sometimes they can feel so real.

Mystery solved, I go to the stove and reach for the door, wary the metal might still be warm from last night's dying embers. The stove is as cold as ice to my touch. It must have gone out as soon as we retired to our bed.

Except, when I open it, the ash is far too thick to be just from the logs I burned yesterday. The broken glass covering the charred picture it protected glints up at me from the belly of the stove.

A hand on my shoulder makes me scream, jumping back.

Bert laughs. "Relax, Kev, it's just me." He pulls me into a good morning kiss. "You're so jumpy since we arrived."

"Sorry. I guess I'm on edge. There's something strange about this place."

"I won't argue with you there. I did suggest we should hire a company to take care of the mess. Or sell it as is." He bops me on the nose.

The gesture makes me irrationally angry with him. As if I'm some kid he told not to run on a slippery pool deck whining to him now that I've skinned my knee after ignoring his wisdom. It's infuriating, even if he is right.

This is *my* family's home. *My* last chance to find—what? Absolution? Acceptance? Maybe it's a chance to say good-bye. But is it a farewell to the family that shaped me, or the girl I never was?

I don't quite know what I came here to find, but it wasn't Bert's snobbish assumption that he knows best. It wasn't to have him belittle me as if I were some silly creature ruled by my emotions and easily dismissed by men who know better.

I pull away from him and tug his robe tighter, taking less comfort in the gesture than usual.

"Don't be surly with me. You know it's the truth." Bert wraps his arms around me, hugging me from behind.

I normally crave his affection, but I *am* surly toward him right now. I want to shrug him off, but that will only prove him right. Ugh. As he kisses behind my ear, I go pliant in his arms.

"I didn't mean to upset you, Kev. I know you're going through a lot right now. It's hard to say goodbye, even if they don't deserve your grief."

Do they? I don't know. The bitter old man who drank himself to death here might not need me to mourn him. He might have given up any claim he had on me when he let me walk out of his life without even trying to see if I was all right. But he wasn't always that man.

Dad wasn't always drowning too deep in his own grief to notice mine. Mom wasn't always so afraid to lose another piece of herself that she locked her heart away from any-thing that might matter enough to be upset over losing.

I might not have known my parents these last years, but

as long as they were alive, there was always a chance they might return to me. Become a part of my life again. Get to know the man they raised, even if they expected a woman in his place. We could have reconciled, and now we can't. This grief is like all the eulogies spoken over my brother's grave by people who barely knew him. I'm not mourning the person as much as I'm mourning the potential I lost along with them.

I don't want to be here. But I have to lay these memories and the hope that things could have been different to rest. Bury it and mourn.

"Kev?" Bert turns me to face him, and I let him.

"Yeah." I clear my throat. "You're right. It's hard to say goodbye."

"Come on; let's see if we can put together a decent breakfast without modern technology." Bert tries to put a cheery face on it.

"The horror," I say dryly, but I let him pull me into the kitchen. I stumble at the threshold, not nearly as shocked as I perhaps should be to find the counters that I scrubbed for hours on our first sleepless night here are back to being coated in a thick patina of dust and grime.

Those hours of scrubbing seem to have happened a lifetime ago. To some other version of me. Perhaps that's what's happening here. Hysterical laughter bubbles up in me at the sight, but I don't let it spill from my lips because if I do, I know it will soon turn to sobs. And I don't think I can explain my hysterics to Bert.

The sense of being trapped here settles over me again. I push back the despair that I'll never make a dent in the work to be done here, no matter how hard I toil. I still have to try.

The burden settles over me, and it all seems so inevitable.

Maybe it is. Maybe I can scrub this kitchen a thousand-thousand times only to wake and find all my hard work erased. For all I know, there are infinite versions of this decaying house. Each one as filthy as the last and I won't be able to leave until I've cleaned them all. Until I find one that isn't crumbling into disrepair. One that doesn't mirror how the family who lived here fell apart.

I want to fall on the floor and weep at the pointlessness of it all. If I do, I'm not sure I'll ever get back up. And there's Bert to consider. So I square my shoulders, face the impossibility of my situation head-on, and grab a trash bag and a pair of thick rubber gloves. Time to clean the woodstove again. It's too cold, and a fire in the stove will be just the thing to fill our bellies with something warm and keep the worst of the chill at bay. Everything will look more manageable with coffee in hand. Even if it is the cheapest instant crap mixed with powdered nondairy creamer.

THE SECOND DAY passes similarly to the first. Bert and I work in the kitchen together after breakfast, scrubbing away years of accumulated grime. Bert doesn't seem to remember I've already done this job before, on that first sleepless night.

He doesn't comment about having to help me drag furniture out to the property line. I embrace the desperate hope that if we move it far enough from the house, whatever power put it back won't be able to reach it. Except I wasn't imagining things yesterday. I still can't cross the property line to bring the bags of trash and ruined furniture those last few feet to the edge of the road. If Bert notices, he says nothing, agreeably piling everything at the side of the long gravel drive as far as I can take it.

We've restored my work from the previous day and are about to work on the garage, Levi's former domain, when Bert gets a call. I side-eye him, recalling the complete lack of phone service yesterday. He answers like nothing is odd about suddenly getting a call when it should be impossible.

"The car is ready. You okay to stay here while I go pick it up?" He sticks his phone back in his pocket.

"Yeah. No problem. Go ahead." I nod, knowing in my bones I couldn't go with him if I wanted to. The same force that held me here yesterday would do likewise today. Even if I'd sound beyond foolish to say as much aloud, I know it to be true. I'm trapped here. Trapped as I was when I was a child. With the walls closing in and no way to see a happy future if I didn't get out and go as far from here as my ambitions could carry me. "I'll get started on the upstairs."

Bert kisses me goodbye and leaves to trade in the loaner for his Jeep. I consider going upstairs to pack up the more intimate traces of my life here. I could scrub away every scrap of evidence of the child I used to be. Throw out every keepsake and memento. Every childish treasure. Then move on to Levi's room and the garage and do the same for him.

I could uproot every trace of the family that no longer lives here. I should. That's the entire purpose of this final visit. Part of me wants to. And part of me knows it won't be enough to root out all the memories. Silence the voices of the past. It won't be enough to keep the progress we've made downstairs. Nothing will ever be enough. Part of me will always be trapped here in this house, always cold and alone.

Shivering, I go to the woodstove and stack more logs into the guttering fire. The heat pours off the iron belly of the stove. Its warmth is a comfort against the bleakness of the unending toil that stretches ahead of me. I sit on the floor with my back to the wall of heat, letting it suffuse my body as I survey what remains on the ground floor.

I used to sit like this with my parents and Levi on the long cold winter nights. Storms knock out the power here frequently enough that we often relied on this stove to heat the house in the bitter cold of a blizzard. There were nights when, with a child's fancy, I thought the fire glowing within the stove's belly might be the last point of heat and light amid the desolation of winter. Muffled under a thick layer of snow, it was easy to imagine we were the only ones left in the world.

Our little family, sustained by our little fire, tucked away from civilization. The bonds of family held us together. When I was small, those close ties were a comforting thought. As I grew, their love felt more and more like a cage. After Levi, those frigid nights gathered around the fire only meant forced proximity to my silently mourning parents and their unpredictable moods.

I can't sit there anymore. The heat might eat me alive if I rest here for another moment. Doubtless, it could devour me as surely as it devoured the family photo my father fed to it. My fingers and toes are warm enough to get back to cleaning.

Bert and I cleaned out the downstairs before he left, so I climb the stairs to my parents' bedroom next. The mess isn't as comprehensive here. Mom always kept her space neat and tidy. Everything in its place and a place for everything. Knowing Dad, he wouldn't have been able to bear changing anything in their room after she passed.

Sure enough, her clothing is still hanging next to his in the closet. Her makeup, crusted in a layer of thick dust, remains where she left it on the bathroom counter. A bottle of her favorite perfume sits out with the cap next to it. That is conspicuously clean-looking. Almost like she'll be along at any moment to use it. Or like he might have sprayed it sometimes, just to smell her.

On a whim, I depress the top of the bottle, and the sickly-sweet floral fragrance reminds me of her. The visceral reminder of Mom makes my heart ache for Dad in a way nothing else has since I heard they're both dead. Whatever else they were, the two of them loved each other.

I can't imagine my dad living without my mom. No wonder the house is a disaster area without her to keep it running. She held him together. He could have learned. Should have helped. Just as quick as the pang of sorrow hit, it turns to anger at him for making this place a cage for her too. A pretty cage of her own choosing. One she wanted me to be content with as my lot in life.

They wanted me to accept being a wife and mother as the peak of my potential. It's not. Even if I was their daughter, it shouldn't have meant that was all I'd ever be. I'm angry at both of them for that. So angry it's like ice in my veins, moving through me in a freezing wave and leaving guilt in its wake. Guilt that I can't grieve them the way I should. They were my parents, and knowing they're dead just leaves me numb.

It's all so pointless. I put the cap on the perfume and set it aside to bring with us. The sort of memento I should want to carry with me along with their ghosts. My cousins must have taken all the good jewelry after Mom died; there's no trace of it here. The blank walls make it clear the family photo wasn't the only one my father burned or otherwise disposed of. That's fine. There's nothing else I want from them.

Bert finds me shoving everything into trash bags, a growing pile of them, crammed full of my parents' personal effects, scattered all around me.

"You've been busy," he observes, leaning into the doorway.

"What do you mean?" I stop stuffing the bag in my hands to look up at him. Self-conscious under his scrutiny, I swipe away sweat from my brow. I've amassed quite the heap of clothing. That must be what he means. We can probably drop the lot of it from the window instead of carrying each bag down the stairs.

Bert shrugs. "I just mean you've made quite the dent in this. Are we donating any of it?"

It's my turn to shrug. I don't even know where we'd go to take things here. "Most of it probably isn't in good enough condition." The dampness from the walls downstairs didn't spare the bedrooms. Everything in here has the faint reek of mildew. Or it only seems faint because I've been breathing it in all day. I shiver, and Bert comes over to me, lays a warm hand on my shoulder.

"You're freezing again. Come warm up by the fire." He slips his arm around me to guide me away from my Sisyphean task and down the stairs without waiting for a reply. "They fixed the car. Good as new."

"That's good."

"It is." He nods decisively. "Now that you've seen sense about selling, we can leave as soon as we finish cleaning out all this trash."

"Right," I agree, letting him take charge. When did ceding choices to him become a habit? I shake off the thought. We're equals. That's always been the deal between us. Partners.

It's the house getting to me. This cursed house and the memories that won't leave me alone.

We fix a simple dinner of canned soup reheated on the woodstove. The food and Bert—acting more like himself as we share it with two spoons and one can—thaw the chill inside me.

We go back to bagging up the contents of my parents' room after dinner. The memories are still thick as the layer of dust in here, but talking about our friends in the city takes my focus away from what we're doing. I don't have time to dwell on the silky slither of black fabric over my fingers when I pull out the dress Mom wore to Levi's funeral. Or think about the matching outfit that probably still lurks in my old closet.

I don't contribute much to the conversation, but Bert seems to understand. The job goes faster with two people. We're nearly finished in my parents' room when it gets too dark to see.

We won't make any more progress tonight, but I check on the fire again to be sure it will burn until morning and keep the chill at bay. Then Bert cajoles me into bed, and I take comfort in his arms.

"WHAT'S GOING ON here?" Bert is standing over the bed. I blink up at him.

"What do you mean?"

"Is this some kind of joke? Your idea of a prank?" he demands, not explaining himself in the least.

I sit up and rub the sleep from my eyes. My breath fogs the air. It's colder than ever this morning. I've got a sneaking suspicion I'll find the woodstove still full of long-dead ash and the remains of the family photo. The walls are closing in, and Bert finally seems to notice something is wrong.

"I'm not sure what you're talking about, Bert," I say cautiously. Rising to join him, I cast a longing glance at the robe he's wearing over his warmest outfit, then grab mine from the hook on the wall. He doesn't appear to be in a sharing mood.

"You put everything back." His voice is flat. "Why? If you're not ready to let it go, we can just leave it to rot until you are. Why go through all the trouble of cleaning just to dump everything back out again?"

I laugh. "You think *I* put everything back?"

"Well, who else could have done it?"

"I don't know. But it wasn't me."

"You think it's the house?" Bert scoffs. "It what? Reset itself, like some sort of horrific video game?"

"I don't know what it is. And I've already cleaned the downstairs twice. You know how I feel about scrubbing dirt. Why, in all that is holy, would I arrange to have to clean the mess a third time? Besides, use your head, even if I wanted to, how would I have undusted every surface?"

My logic gives him pause. There's a reason we pay for a cleaning service to come to our condo. And there's no way I could have perfectly recreated the years of grime I've scrubbed away twice now.

"I think if neither of us put everything back, we should leave. Now."

"It won't let me." I grind the words out through gritted teeth.

"That's nonsense. I had no trouble coming and going."

"Except when I was in the car with you."

Bert considers, then he lifts our suitcase onto the rumpled bed and starts throwing everything we brought with us inside. "We'll just have to try again. Get whatever you want to keep and we'll arrange for a service to handle the mess once we're home."

With a sigh, I join him in repacking. There isn't much of sentimental value here. I duck out to grab Mom's perfume, the only untouched item in my parents' reset ensuite bathroom.

"You ready?" Bert asks as I tuck the bottle into our bag. "We should leave. Get as far away as we can."

"It's worth another try." I shrug my agreement since I don't have any better ideas. Bert finishes packing.

I follow him down the stairs. It reminds me of a terrible parody of Christmas mornings long past. The anticipation that something magical happened while I slept. Levi used to hold my hand, and the two of us would creep down the stairs to see if Santa came.

When I close my eyes, I can hear Levi's laughter, high and childlike as Mom sings a carol and Dad interjects with the wrong lyrics. He got rid of all our Christmas decorations after Levi died. They reminded him too much of my brother.

When I survey the house from the bottom stair, it is

magical all right, but this magic has nothing to do with sugarplums, home cooking, and heartfelt gifts. The downstairs is just as it was when Bert and I first arrived. Only the bags of groceries and cleaning supplies we left in the kitchen show we were even here.

I shiver and wrap my robe tighter around me. It's wholly inadequate against the icy dread taking root in my heart. I was so certain I could escape my past. Leave it behind me where it belongs.

Bert was right; we should have never come here. He gathers up our bags from the kitchen, scowling. "Get what you need, Kev. I'll load up the car."

When I just stare at him, he leaves our things in a heap by the door. He comes over to me, steps into my personal space, and lays a warm hand along my jaw.

"You're freezing." He sounds surprised by that. "I'll start the heat in the Jeep. This will all look better from a distance, you'll see."

I nod woodenly. Bert is probably right. "I need something from the garage. I don't care about the rest of it, but that's where Levi..." If there's anywhere in this house my brother remains, any happy memory, the garage is where I'll find it.

"The sooner you get what you need, the sooner we can leave this wretched place for good." Bert leans in for a kiss. "We'll be fine." He goes to load the car. I turn toward the garage, staring down the last place I want to go.

My feet are as heavy as lead as I approach the only memento I truly want. Not the ruined family photo in its shattered frame. Not the years of other pictures chronicling a lie about a happy family. The piece I take with me isn't a picture full of lies about who we were. It's the old toolset my brother got from our uncle. The one Levi used to teach me how to fix an engine.

The one Dad used to joke about being central to the two of us engaging in brotherly bonding. It's still covered in the grease smears Mom would fuss over. She said all the dirt made us look like a pair of filthy little boys, even though Levi was too old to appreciate being called a child, and she expected me to push back and declare myself a girl under all the grime.

I never did, and I like to think a small part of her knew and saw. It might be a lie I tell myself, but I choose to believe some small part of her saw the real me in those moments of levity. Some part of my dad could appreciate seeing his two sons together. Some part of my brother didn't see me as a pesky little sister, who he had some patriarchal duty to protect, but as his peer. His equal.

Our hours spent toiling away in this garage had nothing to do with my gender and everything to do with us working together to make something broken whole. Levi said the moment we restored a busted car to life was his favorite feeling in the world. Leaving here the first time let me fix the broken parts of myself. It made me whole in a way I never could have been if I stayed. Now, I wonder if he needed to leave as much as I did, if for different reasons. Bert is wrong that there isn't anything still here for me. There is.

It's the chance to let go of the past and take from it only the pieces that don't hurt. The good memories, unsullied by expectations I never wanted.

Bert thinks we can just get in the car and drive away, but I know better. The house won't let me leave. I know it in my bones.

I still get in Bert's car with my brother's toolbox. It won't start. Bert curses and turns the key in the ignition. The engine sputters and grumbles and refuses to turn over.

"I told you it won't let me leave," I say.

"Nonsense! They must have done something at that cut-rate auto shop."

"It's not the car." I get out.

Bert scowls at me. "What are you doing?"

"Proving my point. Try it now."

He does. The engine purrs to life. "There, you see? It was just a weird hiccup. Get in, and we'll take it somewhere else to be sure it's nothing serious before we get on the highway."

"It won't work," I say, but I get back in.

The lights on the dash blink on as the engine gutters. Splutters. Dies.

"This is madness." Bert thumps the steering wheel.

"Maybe. Or maybe it's ghosts. Or whatever power is resetting the house. Something here doesn't want me to leave again. They don't want me to be happy."

I was right. This place will never let me leave. I want to curl up in a ball and howl at the unfairness of it all.

This house will never let me go. Unless it's gone. I scramble upright, knowing with perfect clarity what I have to do. Now, before Bert tries to force the issue with his cool conviction that he always knows best. Sometimes he doesn't. Sometimes I'm the one who knows what needs to be done. And sometimes, I'm the only one who can do it.

"Look, just get in and drive onto the road. I'll figure something out to join you once you're off the property," I tell him.

Bert scowls. He looks like he wants to take charge, but if I let him, I'll never slip the yoke my parents wanted to saddle me with. I'll never shed the part of me my folks raised to be obedient and polite. Docile.

Bert grumbles something about pigheadedness, but there's a fondness to his tone as he starts the car again. He rolls slowly to the end of the driveway, turns onto the road, and parks on the shoulder. The car idles with its engine purring as though it never had any trouble at all.

I square my shoulders and turn back toward the gaping maw of the house's front door. I'm glad Bert didn't put up a fuss. He doesn't belong here. *I* don't belong here. It's possible some version of me did, once upon a time. No part of the version of me who came home belongs to this place any longer though. And it can't hold any power over me that I don't grant it.

Each step inside weighs on me, heavier than all the furniture and garbage we spent the past few days lugging outside. I try not to think about what I'm doing as I go back to the garage for the last time to find what I need.

I tune out the memories assailing me with every step. No laughter, no songs. No screaming fights or passive-aggressive jibes. It's all so loud I can't make out what they're saying. A constant cacophony, so much noise my head is ready to split open like an overripe melon.

The pulsing ache of the ghosts lends urgency to my actions. They aren't just holding me captive; they'll destroy me if I let them. I don't bother cleaning out all the ashes. I just scoop away enough to get a new fire laid.

This time, I leave the damaged photo frame where it

lies. The kindling catches, tiny flames licking around the larger logs until they find purchase and spread.

I leave the door to the stove flung open wide, and I set the vent to let it take as much air as it requires to spread and grow. The flames dance. I can almost hear the crackling as a living thing giving thanks for the fuel and air. The fire chatters, but I can't quite grasp its meaning. Is it a pleased purr or a greedy demand for more?

No matter, I'll give it what it craves. That's the only way to fight the icy cold clasping me in its iron grip. The house resets whenever the fire dies, so I'll feed the flames until they burn away every speck of the ice holding me captive.

The splattering of the old kerosene from Levi's camping gear falls all around me like fat drops of rain just before a storm. It reminds me of spring showers giving way to a flood. The way those first little flecks of moisture presage roaring sheets of rain. A deluge drumming on the roof and the ground and declaring nature's wrath in a mighty torrent that obscures all other sounds.

So much rain that it scours the world and leaves it smelling of green growing things. The sort of storm that crackles in the air, and when you walk outside after, everything is scrubbed raw and ready for a clean start. That's how the roaring in my ears seems to scream as I walk through the spreading fire. Every crackle of hungry flames devours the half-heard whispers of the dead still echoing in my head. Not for much longer. I am banishing them. Drowning them out. Burning them to ash.

Bert will notice what I'm doing soon. I wonder if he'll come to get me or wait? That's why I had to use the kerosene. I need to be sure the fire burns hot enough to melt the icy barrier around the property before he can do anything to stop it. Hot enough to leave me free to make a life with him far from here. Loud enough to drown out the voices that used to fill every silence.

I don't look behind me. Just like the woodstove's comforting wall of heat on wintry nights long past, the flames at my back warm me to the depths of my being one last time. There's no room for cold in this conflagration.

Ash and sparks drift to the ground. The heat makes the air shimmer until I can almost imagine Levi by my side, watching over me one last time. The vaguest impression of his shape flickers in my periphery. And the hungry roaring fills my ears.

Sure enough, the gravel at the end of the driveway, just where it meets the road, crunches under my feet. I shed my robe there. The fire singed the edges, leaving smoldering patches along the hem. And I'm not cold anymore. I pick my way along the uneven shoulder to where Bert leans against the car, gaping slack-jawed at my handiwork.

"What did you do?" he asks. All traces of his earlier patronizing tone are gone for the moment.

"What I had to do; we can call the fire department when we get to an area with a cell signal."

Bert shuts his mouth and looks between me and the burning house.

"Are you coming?" I ask as I pass him. I don't hesitate or look back. There's nothing left there for me.

I get in the driver's seat. Bert scrambles into the passenger seat like he's afraid I might leave him by the side of the road. He buckles up beside me without a word. And the ghosts? They're not even a ringing in my ears anymore.

I put the car in gear, roll the windows down, and drive. We get far enough from the flames for their devouring roars to fade away. Peaceful silence shrouds the road, a natural stillness punctuated by the trill of birdsong and the steady hum of the Jeep's engine taking us home.

# Acknowledgements

Thank you to Isaiah for helping me to figure out the ending. Kevin wouldn't be half the badass he is without your input.

# ABOUT THE AUTHOR

Alex Silver (he/them) grew up on a farm in Northern Maine and is currently living in Canada with a husband, two kids, and a lovebird. Alex is a trans guy who started writing fiction as a child and never stopped.

### Email
asilverauthor@gmail.com

### Facebook
www.facebook.com/groups/alexsalcove

### Website
www.alexsilverauthor.wordpress.com

### BookBub
www.bookbub.com/profile/alex-silver

### TikTok
www.tiktok.com/@alexsilver42

CONNECT WITH NINESTAR PRESS

WWW.NINESTARPRESS.COM

WWW.FACEBOOK.COM/NINESTARPRESS

WWW.FACEBOOK.COM/GROUPS/NINESTARNICHE

WWW.TWITTER.COM/NINESTARPRESS

WWW.INSTAGRAM.COM/NINESTARPRESS

Printed in Great Britain
by Amazon

19911020R20196